LAST CHANCE

EMMA LAST SERIES: BOOK FOUR

MARY STONE

MARY STONE
PUBLISHING

Copyright © 2023 by Mary Stone Publishing

All rights reserved.

No part of this book may be reproduced in any form or by any electronic or mechanical means, including information storage and retrieval systems, without written permission from the author, except for the use of brief quotations in a book review.

❦ Created with Vellum

For my dad, the first hero of my life. In every word, in every story, you live on.

DESCRIPTION

Some memories detonate on impact.

Fresh from the adrenaline rush of her latest case, FBI Special Agent Emma Last dropped a bombshell on her friend and coworker Mia Logan—she can communicate with ghosts. Worse, one spectral figure is Mia's brother.

And he insists he was murdered.

But there's little time to grapple with the supernatural when the Violent Crimes team is thrust into the heart of Randall County, West Virginia where a local diner is reduced to rubble in a powerful explosion. Although the owner and his daughter live above the restaurant, no human remains are found in the rubble. Did they have the motive, or the skill, to make a bomb?

Or are they the victims of a more disturbing vendetta?

The stakes heighten when another local diner faces the same

fate, its owner and his daughter also conspicuously missing. The pattern is undeniable. As a winter storm encroaches, Emma and her team are in a race against time to find the victims before a third explosion blows Randall County apart.

Last Chance, the fourth book in the captivating new FBI series by bestselling author Mary Stone, drives home a haunting reality: you don't need enemies to become a target.

1

Cross-legged and bleary-eyed, Laura Williams stared down at the bills spilling over her lap as she sat on her childhood bed. The dim light from the single overhead bulb spotlighted the red *Overdue* message stamped across them all.

What am I going to do?

Lifting her head, she forced her attention away from the bills. Her gaze was distant, weighed down by more than just lack of sleep.

A mural of rainbows and unicorns gazed down at her, possibly cheering her on, but they did nothing to improve her mood. Once upon a time, she'd begged her parents for those fantastical creatures, and her parents had obliged for her fifth birthday. Now their pastel-colored horns and rainbow-prancing hooves appeared as faded and jaded as she felt.

Because at twenty-eight, she might as well have been fifty-eight. *Hell, eighty-eight.*

Many of the bills, medical in nature, showed the same overdue charges from her mother's failed battle with breast cancer. Her mom's fight had ended six months ago, but the bills hadn't died with her. They only collected interest and garnered more calls from collections agents. Added to them were utility bills, threatening service disruptions soon...and if that happened, they could say goodbye to Morty's, her dad's burger joint, as well as their three-bedroom apartment above the restaurant.

Laura clenched her eyes shut, refusing to cry another tear over the inevitable loss of her parents' dream. She'd moved home to help the family business stay afloat, giving up her nursing career while her mother lay dying in a hospital bed. It wasn't just ironic, but it was also foolish. If she'd still had a nurse's income, she might've been able to help with the bills...even if they did amount to more than she'd make in a lifetime. Instead, she'd come home to discover her father's health was failing as well, and now he was looking at bankruptcy.

Eklund was a slow-dying town in the mountains of West Virginia, and Morty's decay served as a symptom of that demise. The population dwindled with each passing year, and interstates had redirected traffic straight past their sleepy little borough. The diner, much as she cringed to admit it, just wasn't savable.

"But who's gonna tell Dad?"

Only silence met her question as she gathered the bills back into a messy pile and plopped them onto her nightstand. Her dad said she shouldn't have them so close to her bed, where she was meant to relax, but what was the difference? She could've shredded the damn things, thrown them into a fire...

But the money would still be owed, and the collectors would still be calling every few weeks.

Quitting the hospital was the dumbest thing I've ever done. I'll start job hunting tomorrow. No matter what Dad says. We need some kind of income when the restaurant goes belly-up.

Her childhood bed was too small, but she'd sold her old furniture in the city and not thought about that beforehand. Snuggling beneath the warmth of the blankets and curling her legs to keep her feet from hanging over the edge of the mattress, she missed her mother more than ever. That woman had single-handedly kept their family from falling apart. Even while undergoing chemo.

The six months without her had felt like a lifetime already.

Tension was just fleeing her shoulders, the bed finally warming up from her body heat, when the apartment door creaked open and clicked shut. Her eyelids lifted as she sighed.

"Seriously, Dad? Now?"

He'd been sneaking out to smoke cigarettes lately—no matter how vehemently she protested. It was the last thing a fifty-four-year-old man should be doing with his spare breaths and pennies—and in the middle of the night. He'd probably waited for her to turn her light off, thinking she wouldn't notice. Groaning, she swung her legs from beneath the blankets and shoved her feet into her slippers. Maybe she could catch him before he lit up.

Laura slipped out of her room and into the hallway, only to glimpse the shadow of a figure beelining toward her.

"Dad?"

The figure had something pointed at her. Something like…

Her gut sank as she froze in place. The unfamiliar figure was holding a gun. "What are you—"

"Quiet!" The harsh command broke the silence in the hallway more fiercely than the creaking door had. Then, out of the darkness, a strange woman's face with crazy, panic-stricken eyes emerged to hover in front of Laura.

Only the gun was between them.

"I'm going to need you to do exactly what I say. If you don't, I'm going to shoot you and your daddy. I know you don't want that."

Laura's every instinct screamed at her to flee, but there was nowhere to go. The only doors behind her led to her room, her father's room, and a windowless bathroom. And the windows in the second-floor bedrooms overlooked an asphalt alleyway that would break her legs or even her neck if she attempted to jump. Maybe she could have found a knife for self-defense in the kitchen, but that would've meant getting past the intruder.

And her gun.

There was no doubt in Laura's mind that the gun aimed at her chest was real. The weapon was just as genuine as the off-her-rocker woman with her finger on the trigger.

Laura swallowed the scream fighting to come up her throat, just holding herself back from glancing toward her father's bedroom. "Okay, lady, okay. Let's just talk about what you want."

The blond in front of her steadied her gun, sneering. "What I want? Nobody in this universe ever cared about what I want."

Laura wasted no time. "I care. I'm a nurse. My whole life is about caring. Let me help you, please. Maybe just put the—"

"Shut up!" The woman stuck the gun out straight, aimed right at Laura's face.

She's totally out of her mind. I've got to warn Dad. Save him, somehow, from whatever this is.

The gun gestured back down the hallway, toward her father's room. "No more chatting. It's time to wake up your daddy."

With the cold of the hallway seeping through the thin

fabric of her pajamas, Laura put a steadying hand against the wall, willing herself not to move suddenly, not to show she was following the woman's command or disobeying it. Buying time for…something? If nothing else, maybe her dad would wake up and call 911 from his bedroom before she and this madwoman reached his doorway.

"Ma'am, we don't have anything. No money, not even enough to pay our bills. I swear." Laura licked her lips, hoping the woman would hear the truth in her words.

"Ha, you'd like me to think that." The gun jerked in the woman's hand as she shook her head, her eyes wild even in the dim light of the hall. "You're wrong. You and your daddy have *everything*. Now, you do as I say, or you'll regret it."

The intruder rushed forward.

Laura couldn't hold in a shriek as the gun barrel pressed against her forehead, cold and unyielding.

If this had been an action movie and she'd been Angelina Jolie or Scarlett Johansson, Laura would've swept her hand up, stolen the gun, and turned it on the woman in a heartbeat. But this wasn't Hollywood, and Laura wasn't bulletproof.

"Okay, okay." The whisper trailed out of her throat, then she raised her voice to do as she'd been ordered. "Dad! Dad, I need you to wake up and come out here."

A grumble sounded out from the man's bedroom, and the gun pressed harder into Laura's forehead. Her breath caught in her throat at the bruising cold of the metal, but the tears in her eyes came from the thought of what she and her dad were about to face.

I should've told her he wasn't home. But now she's heard him too. It's too late.

"Dad, I'm in the hallway. Please wake up and come here!"

Tears leaked from Laura's eyes. There was no way this

stranger had a personal vendetta against her father, and she certainly didn't have one against Laura herself, but that didn't change the fact she was trapped in a deadly encounter, clueless and weaponless.

"Against the wall, back to me!"

The woman's hiss lingered in the air as Laura turned her face to the wall. The muzzle trailing against her short blond hair, following her movement, was like a living animal, tracking the best spot through which to find her brain as it *tick-tack*ed against her head. Her breathing picked up speed.

In the next room, the shuffling of clothing and footsteps signaled her dad was out of bed and putting on his robe. Her father's door opened. "What in the world is it, Laura—"

The gun-toting stranger snarled, poking the weapon harder against Laura's skull.

"D-dad, don't—"

"Why…?" His expression had transformed from confused to frantic. "Who are you? What do you want?"

"Mister, your daughter's life depends on your cooperation. You understand?"

Morty Williams froze in his bedroom door, one hand on the doorframe. Faint light filtered into the hallway from his nightstand lamp behind him.

He'd never looked so feeble, with gray hair fuzzed out from his head and his old flannel pajamas hanging on him more than Laura had ever noticed before. Her father had lost too much weight since his wife died, always worried about cooking the very best for every patron at Morty's and never remembering to care for himself.

In the dim light, his gaze raked over Laura and settled on the gun.

"Don't hurt her. I understand what you're saying, but don't you hurt her. Please. You'd be killing us both." He held his hands up high, signaling defeat. "Tell us what you want, but please, don't use that gun."

Laura closed her eyes, the defeat in her dad's voice echoing her own feelings. A gentler man had never existed, and she would've bet money that if anyone had ever tried to rob Morty's, he'd have made sure to give them a hot meal along with the cash in the register.

That was who he was. Gentle and forgiving and always convinced things would somehow work out. He probably figured the gun wouldn't go off as long as they did what was instructed. As if following the rules always got you somewhere.

The thought nearly made Laura laugh out loud, because that definitely wasn't how life worked, as her shifts in the city ER had shown her, but she bit the impulse back and focused on what she feared might be her last few minutes alive with her dad.

Knowing he'd do what the woman asked—though Laura couldn't imagine what that would be—she tried to draw a morsel of comfort from that thought.

The woman pulled Laura against her, into her chest, and moved backward into their little living room. They stopped at the side of the sofa, which had been reupholstered nearly to death and was practically as old as Laura.

I wish I could lie down and hide my head in those cushions like I did when I was little. And just wait to wake up from this nightmare.

Her dear father's steps faltered as he followed them, gestured forward by the gun.

"Now, we're all going to go outside together." The woman's voice sounded steadier now, on track with whatever her plan was. The sheer desperation in it added a deeper chill to the air, rattling through Laura's veins as she listened. "Morty, you're going to lead the way down these stairs. My station wagon's parked in the alley beside the restaurant, and that's where we're going. All quiet, no raising any alarm, or your daughter gets dead. You understand me?"

The man went straighter at the threat, narrowing his eyes at her. "I understand." He focused back on Laura for a second. "Laura-bean, you be strong, and we'll get through this, okay?"

Laura forced herself to nod, even as tears leaked out at the sound of her dad's nickname for her.

He hasn't called me that since Mom died.

Worn down as her dad was, he sounded strong, and she could be strong for him.

The gun jerked against Laura's chest, anger pouring into the woman's next command. *"Get moving. Now."*

Laura's father turned back to the door they'd passed in the hallway and opened it, leaving it gaping for Laura and her captor to follow behind him and down the stairs. Freezing-cold flurries swept and swirled into the building. The crazy bitch with the gun shoved Laura through the exit and outside behind her father.

At the foot of the stairwell, he went left toward the alley instead of into the restaurant.

A decades-old midnight blue station wagon sat taking up most of the alleyway, leaving just enough space around it for the doors to open. The thing looked brand-new, well taken care of, even though it was probably made when unleaded gas was still optional. No matter how old it was, the car sat totally at odds with the frazzled woman waving the gun around.

She should be driving a junker. Peeling paint and bald tires to match her crazy ass.

Laura silenced her thoughts as the woman gave her a jab with the gun.

"Trunk's open, Dad, and your little girl's life is at stake. Get in. You behave, and I'll let your daughter go."

Morty grimaced as he turned away to walk through the narrow space between the vehicle and the alley wall, coming to a stop between their old, dented dumpster and the back of the wagon. He gripped the tailgate's handle and pulled it open.

But there was some fight left in Morty yet. Before Laura could react, he spun on the woman, trying to shove Laura aside.

The gun exploded into the night. Laura's ears rang with the blast, and acrid gunpowder filled her nose.

When Laura opened her eyes, her father was on the ground. He groaned, but she didn't see blood. "Oh god." The words escaped her mouth, but she could barely hear her own voice. "Daddy? Dad, are you okay?"

"It's okay, baby. I wasn't hit. Twisted my damn ankle, though."

"He's fine, but you won't be if he tries anything like that again. Get in, and remember, this gun is pointed at your daughter's head."

"Why're you doing this? Just let us go, lady, please."

There was no negotiating with her, though. The woman's wild energy vibrated at Laura's back as she shifted her weight.

"You need to get in the car, sir."

Morty hesitated before climbing inside the station wagon, hopping on one foot to protect his injured ankle. The sight of him doing so brought a rough sob up from Laura's chest.

A sharp stab of the gun between her shoulder blades pushed her forward. "Tie him up." A roll of duct tape appeared in Laura's hand. "Hands, feet, and mouth."

She leaned in. "Sorry, Dad."

"It's okay, Laura-bean. It's gonna be okay."

"I'm sorry. I love you."

"Love you—"

"*Shut up!*" The woman cut him off, and Laura jerked in response, sobbing openly now. Her dad just nodded, squinting behind her at the woman and her gun as Laura forced herself to keep going.

She started to wrap her dad's wrists.

"No! Not like that. In a figure eight. Loop it."

Laura jumped at the woman's harsh tone but did as she was told. When she got to his ankles, she winced at how swollen one was. He was really hurt.

Blinking against guilty tears, Laura looped duct tape around his ankles in the same figure eight style as before, the gun pressing harder into her back until the woman was satisfied with her efforts. Her father grunted but was otherwise quiet now. She did her best to wrap the tape like a bandage to help prevent the bones from moving, in case he'd fractured something.

"Now his mouth. Then do your own ankles."

Laura haltingly pulled off a strip of the tape and held it up in front of her dad's face. He met her eyes and nodded for her to go ahead. She paused until the woman behind her shoved the muzzle of her gun even harder into Laura's ribs.

"Do it. Now."

In a quick motion, Laura put the tape over her dad's mouth. She bent down and wrapped another strip of duct tape around her own ankles, thinking to leave it loose enough that she might wiggle free somehow. The woman kicked at her feet. "Tighter. And weave it in between, like your dad's! Then put your hands behind your back."

Laura finished taping her ankles before setting the roll down on the ground and holding her hands at the small of her back. The woman kicked the tape to the side, out of her peripheral view. A ripping squeal followed before a loop of the sticky adhesive encircled Laura's wrists and was wound between them, just as she'd done to her dad.

She tried to separate her hands slightly as the woman wrapped the tape. If she could force a little distance between her wrists, that might give her enough room to—

Laura's head was yanked back, and tape slapped across her mouth.

"Nice try, but that was stupid, and it could have cost your daddy his life. Now get in the car."

For a split second, Laura realized their kidnapper must've put the gun down. But the moment was over before she could react, and the muzzle pressed into the back of her head again.

Laura awkwardly joined her father in the back of the vehicle, shifting like an earthworm. He couldn't say anything with his mouth covered, but his gaze was reassuring all the same.

The windows of the cargo area had been covered over with fabric, but the back of the vehicle was otherwise open.

I can't believe this is happening. I can't fucking believe this is happening.

She's going to kill us. She's really going to kill us.

A whimper, trapped in Laura's throat because of the duct tape over her mouth, came out as a high-pitched moan. Her disobedience wouldn't be the reason her father got a bullet in the head. It would *not*.

Laura wriggled her wrists against her bonds and was gratified to realize that her circulation hadn't been cut off. She wouldn't be able to get free—not soon anyway—but she still had blood flow. She desperately tried to remember how the YouTube gurus all spouted how easy it was to free themselves from duct tape. But she didn't have the space to yank her arms down like they taught, and her feet were bare, so no shoestrings to help there either.

"I don't know if I should leave you face up or not. What happens next will be hard for you to see. But all things considered, I'd say it's important for you to understand that no one can be happy forever. *No one.*"

For a moment, Laura feared the words meant the woman was about to shoot her father, but their captor only slammed the door shut, limiting her view to the long back window.

Her chest loosened now that the gun no longer pointed at either her or her father.

The front door of the station wagon popped open, and the woman climbed inside. When the old wagon rumbled to life, she pulled out into the street but stopped across from the restaurant, up against the curb.

Snow continued to drift down from the sky, too wet and light to stick to the roads or buildings, and Laura let herself get lost in the calm drift of the flakes falling past the window. Her breath slowed, her pulse following, and she could hear her father's doing the same. She could almost forget about the gun-wielding madwoman in the front seat.

The sign over the door, proclaiming *Morty's* in fancy cursive script, glowed warm and orange with old-school Edison bulbs. Laura had always loved it. Whenever she'd walked home from school, the sign lit her way as soon as she turned onto the street.

Twenty years ago, her father had an artist redesign it in her mother's handwriting. It was home.

And then, before her eyes, the sign and restaurant and their home above it blew apart, shattered into a million shards of glass, brick, wood, and metal.

A flash and a thunderous wave of heat arced through the night. Her skin burned even in the protection of the car.

The business that had been in her family for three generations exploded.

Morty's Diner, gone in a blink.

Her father squealed in horror behind his tape, and Laura's chest clenched.

She squirmed around, lifting her torso up to turn her head and face forward. In the rearview mirror, she glimpsed their driver's smiling eyes as the station wagon pulled away.

2

Normally, the warm wood finishes and gray-marbled countertops of her kitchen stole the tension from Special Agent Emma Last's life, especially on a Sunday evening when the Violent Crimes Unit case files had been out of mind. Even if she didn't cook much in the space, the clean, modern style suited her, and she enjoyed calling the kitchen her own.

Little about this evening was *normal*, though. Not the conversation or the bubbling tension between her and one of her few close friends in this world.

One step at a time. One conversation at a time. One cup of tea at a time. All of this will get fixed.

Pouring steaming water into two porcelain mugs, Emma didn't feel anywhere near so relaxed as the action might have suggested. That was just the plain truth of the matter. Behind her, her friend and fellow agent, Mia Logan, practically radiated nerves. Despite how long the two of them had known each other, they were in brand-new territory now.

Talking about ghosts—ghosts Emma could see and talk to —had that effect.

But the ghost of Ned Logan, Mia's brother, had made the conversation necessary. During their team's last case, Ned's ghost had followed Emma, insisting his death hadn't been a car accident and that he needed Emma and Mia to investigate it.

Emma had only had a moment to explain to Mia that she could see Ned's ghost.

That had been nearly five days ago.

Though they'd both been stunned by the admission—Emma because she'd actually confessed her secret, and Mia for obvious reasons—they'd been forced to wrap up the case, taking their suspect into custody at close to one in the morning. The next day, Mia was called to assist on a case that took her out of D.C., and Emma had been smothered under post-investigation reviews and the reams of paperwork that inevitably followed.

Now, at the first real moment of downtime they'd had in nearly a week, Mia was in Emma's apartment, insisting on learning every detail.

Breaking the news that Ned's death hadn't been accidental put an awkward spin on the evening that no amount of "stress-relief" tea could ever alleviate.

Emma had spoken of the ghosts and the Other with Marigold, a psychic who understood the enigmas in the world more than most. Telling someone like that about her situation felt like a small relief. For a while now, Emma had been keeping her ability to see and speak to ghosts a secret. A weight had lifted off her shoulders the night she'd confided in Marigold.

However, admitting her abilities to a friend and colleague was very different from talking to a friggin' psychic.

Emma's explanation of Ned's news about his own death had been hard for her friend to grasp. So Mia demanded she go back over the whole thing once more. Again. *Slowly.*

Emma yo-yoed the lemon ginger tea bags up and down in the mugs before she found the will to continue, despite Mia's gaze needling her on. "Can I just tell you I'm shocked at how fast you accepted all this? I wasn't prepared for that."

"It was the *'bedtime is secret telling'* that did it." Mia seemed to be hypnotized by Emma raising and lowering the tea bags, or maybe it was her way of avoiding eye contact. "There was no way for you to know that."

While at the crime scene that night, with adrenaline still pumping through their veins, Ned visited Emma and insisted on talking to his sister. Then he told Emma, *"Bedtime is secret telling,"* a phrase that would only mean something to Mia. Ned apparently eavesdropped during sleepovers when the siblings were little because bedtime was when everyone whispered their secrets.

"I don't even know why I picked that minute to tell you, when I stop to think about it. And then you said you believed me…"

"What did he say again? Exactly?"

Emma didn't even need to think about it. Every word Ned had told her was written in her brain. "He said, 'Accident not accident. Murder is secret. Bedtime is for secret telling.' Ghosts normally aren't very helpful or forthcoming. But this seems straightforward for one of them. He's saying his death wasn't an accident."

Mia accepted a mug of tea as Emma directed them to the oversize island. She clasped it as if the beverage were a lifeline. Her elfin face was pinched, her brown eyes squinting in a way that made her look closer to her age of thirty-one than the early twenties coed she often appeared to be. Especially with her short hair pulled tightly back instead of down, she was almost unrecognizable from the carefree friend Emma normally spent her time with.

With tea in hand, Mia leaned back in her stool and eyed

Emma as if she expected her to turn into a ghost herself. Her lips jittered open and closed twice before she spoke. "I still can't believe it. But thank you, Emma. I do believe it. I believe you."

Emma's chest lightened a touch with Mia's smile. This secret wouldn't come between them after all. Not for long anyway. "I wanted to tell you all of this after we caught Renata Flint, but then you were called away."

"Good timing, Bureau powers that be."

"Right? I've been anxious ever since that night. And then yesterday, I spoke with my new psychic friend I told you about. Marigold. She told me I needed to share the full truth with you as soon as possible. I almost called you, and I'm so glad you got back to town this morning."

"What did Marigold say that made it so urgent?"

Emma dunked her tea bag again before taking a sip. "To quote Marigold, 'The dead speak for a reason, and we must respect this even if we do not understand it.'"

Mia's eyes widened a touch. "Well, that's suitably dark. Did your psychic step out of an old gothic movie? A haunted house, maybe?"

"Try a nice town house in the most normal neighborhood you've ever seen." Emma chuckled, picturing the woman's pedestrian town house. Everything about Marigold was plain and straitlaced, not what she'd expected.

"I just can't believe Ned didn't say more. Especially if there's a reason for telling me, like Marigold said." Squeezing her tea bag as if it could give her more detailed information with enough pressure, Mia peered back at Emma over her mug.

Though Mia had told Emma she wanted nothing more than to speak with her brother again, he'd gone silent and disappeared when Emma had failed to share his full message with Mia in the early morning hours of last Wednesday. And if Emma couldn't see Ned, she couldn't help Mia communicate with him.

Ned's reasons for speaking up weren't hard to understand, after all. He wanted his sister—and maybe Emma—to avenge his death.

Maybe coming clean about everything while at a crime scene hadn't been the best idea. Not with police lights and crime scene techs in clear sight. But Emma hadn't felt as if she'd had much choice. Working up the courage to talk about seeing ghosts—to anyone—hadn't been easy. They were alone, and Ned was there, pressing her…and, well, she gave in.

And if not then, who knows when I would've broken down and done it?

Mia fiddled with the discarded tea bag, her eyes hazy. "And Ned didn't say anything about who killed him? Or why? What he was involved in? Did he have any guesses?"

"When they speak, they don't talk like normal people. It's off, somehow. Like they can only talk around things. It's almost impossible to get a complete sentence out of them."

Sipping her tea, Emma shook her head. She'd told her friend everything now.

Mia couldn't quite hide her disappointment. "Oh."

Emma felt terrible. "I wish I could say he had more information. I'd give anything to say I could answer your questions. But without him here…and even if he was here…"

"You think he'll be back?"

"I do." Emma sighed, gazing around her currently Nedless kitchen, hoping. "But we just have to wait on him. It's a different world in the Other."

A world of ghosts that, apparently, I'm not supposed to see into, let alone enter. How can I explain it to Mia if I don't even understand it?

"I don't know much about the place, but I know that it's…

different. Marigold made that clear to me, more than anything. Priorities aren't necessarily a *thing*…until they are. I'll tell you when Ned comes back, though. I promise."

"You just don't have a clue when that will be." Mia gazed into her tea as if for enlightenment. "And we can't cause him to come back somehow? Maybe with Marigold's help?"

"I don't think so." Emma licked her lips, thinking back to Marigold skirting that very question. "I have no idea what triggers ghosts to appear, to speak, to interact…sometimes, they're practically surrounding me, stalking me wherever I go. Other times, I don't see any at all for days. But it's never in my control. I only know that the deceased people who I thought would be most likely to come find me, my mom and dad, haven't appeared even once."

Mia's face jerked up, her lips parting in a little *o* of surprise. "Oh, Emma. I hadn't even thought to ask. That must be so hard."

Just like Mia. Forgetting herself to think of me as soon as she's got the slightest reason.

Wondering if Ned Logan had been just as caring a human being, Emma forced a smile and used her tea as an excuse not to answer right away. Mia wasn't wrong…and somehow, saying it out loud, that her parents hadn't sought her out, made the fact sting all the stronger.

Emma pushed herself back from the island, shaking off the nostalgic wish making its way up her throat, and moved toward the cabinet. "I think I'm getting a sweet tooth. You want some—"

A solid knock at the door cut off her sentence.

Mia raised an eyebrow. "Expecting anyone?"

"Nobody but you." Emma stepped toward the door. "Who is it?"

"It's Oren. Are you free?"

Oh.

Emma's stomach did a little flip. She hadn't planned on her personal life colliding with her professional life tonight... or anytime soon. "Uh, coming!"

Mia's dimples showed for the first time that evening. "The guy from last night? Mr. Handsome Yogi?"

Already walking toward the door, Emma answered with a quick, "Yes," because, sure, she had told Mia she'd gone on a date with a wonderfully charming yoga instructor the night before...but only that.

Still, the date had been amazing.

They'd gone to a Jamaican restaurant and shared a great curry dish. Then Oren insisted on a round of indoor mini-golf to "work dinner off." Little had Oren known that Emma was practically a professional mini-golfer. She'd kicked his ass. He'd taken his loss well.

The possibility of him showing up during Mia's visit hadn't even crossed her mind.

Opening the door, Emma tried to invite him in with some semblance of grace, but she lost her words upon seeing the gorgeous bouquet in his hands. Shoots of pink, yellow, and lavender petals spiraled upward in a display of spring too early for February.

Emma girl, you are so in over your head.

"I would've picked them myself on the hike I took today, but it's not exactly the season for wildflowers." Oren's blue eyes radiated the same charm that had repeatedly stolen her breath away the night before. "Do you like them? You don't seem like the traditional red-roses type."

Emma's tongue worked to unstick itself from the roof of her mouth as Mia came up beside them, *ooh*ing as she did. "Of course Emma likes them!"

Oren's eyes widened a touch. "Oh, I didn't think about you having company. I'm sorry, Emma—"

"I'm Mia Logan, one of her close friends. And you have

absolutely earned yourself an invite to tea and cookies. Come on in. Right, Emma?"

"No, it's fine." Emma breathed in the heady scent of the lavender, along with the other flowers she didn't recognize. "Please. We were just having some tea. And the flowers are gorgeous, Oren. Thank you."

Oren grinned and slipped into the apartment, easing open his fashionable designer coat once he'd handed over the bouquet. The man moved like a cat, all lanky muscle and quiet steps. Only his easy grin betrayed how casual and down-to-earth he was. "I hope you don't mind. I passed a little florist on my drive back into the city and couldn't resist stopping in."

"I'm so glad you did." Emma led the way over to the kitchen, struggling to remember if she even owned a vase, let alone where she would've kept such a thing. "I have to admit, I only recognize the lavender. What are these other flowers?"

"Those white ones are anemones." Mia lifted an empty ceramic pitcher out from a cabinet. "And the pink ones are camellias."

Oren slid onto a stool, nodding when Emma held up the box of tea in offering. "Your friend's right. The florist called it her winter bouquet, and I couldn't resist. And…Mia, you said? What do you do?"

"I'm on the same team as Emma with the Bureau's VCU." She chuckled when Oren barked a laugh. "What, surprised?"

"I shouldn't be, no. Just…thinking I may be wading in over my weight class. Considering the view." He aimed his blue eyes over toward Emma, holding her gaze until her cheeks warmed.

Yeah, you're not the only one.

Emma busied herself making another round of tea, letting Mia chatter on behind her. The other woman was far more comfortable in an unexpected social situation like this than Emma could ever be. Which was terrific, because it gave her some time to process the gorgeous flowers and the sweet gesture, as well as the turn the night had taken.

Over and over, Oren kept surprising her. Even after their one date, Emma couldn't help thinking the man was a godsend.

Sure, he didn't know she spoke to or saw ghosts, but she almost suspected that if she did admit it, he'd take it in stride. If...or *when*? Was that possible, now that she'd told Mia, who hadn't taken off running or insisted she belonged in a psychiatric hospital?

She glanced over at him just as he swept some of his unruly brown hair away from his brow. He was talking about some trail or another.

Now she knew how he kept that tan glowing in the winter. He hiked. Because of course he did. And she'd been saying she needed someone who'd encourage her to be more physical...

By the time Emma had a mug of tea ready for Oren and a second round for herself and Mia, as well as some cookies set out for snacking, Oren had settled into talking about his afternoon spent leading friends on a hike around Great Falls Park.

As he spoke of the ice frozen into pools, the slick path, the forest, and the call of the river, his love of nature took over the warm kitchen as if the falls were encroaching on Emma's urban apartment. Another person would've made the nearby attraction sound mundane, or else over-romanticized the location to the point of absurdity. Oren and his deep voice, though...

"You two should've seen the melting snow and ice," Oren continued. His blue eyes left Emma's only often enough to make sure Mia felt included—a fact that Emma didn't miss—and Emma couldn't help blushing each time he looked back at her. "The way the icicles dripped down from the stone was magnificent. People say they don't like hiking in the cold, but it's a whole different world."

Different world or not, I could listen to this man talk about paint drying. No, cement drying. No wonder he's such a popular yoga instructor.

"Truly, there's no need to go so far as the Amazon or Antarctica to appreciate nature." A chuckle rumbled from Oren's throat, and he reached out to place one large, warm hand on Emma's knee, gentle and suggestive. "As long as you're with a guide who knows the area, the falls are gorgeous—"

The buzzing of Emma's and Mia's phones interrupted him, and Emma offered a quick apology for the distraction.

Both of their phones going off at the same time meant only one thing. Work.

Mia read her text out loud. "Bring go bags in the morning. New case. Confirm receipt."

Emma sighed, shooting Oren an apologetic shrug even as she reached for her own phone to confirm that she'd gotten the message. "Looks like I'll need a rain check for tomorrow night's date. I'm sorry, Oren."

"I'm sorry to hear it as well, but I'll be here when you get back." His easy grin hinted at more than casual flirtation, and Emma's cheeks blushed hot. The man knew how to get to her. There was no question. "You two have to go save the world. I understand. Just promise you'll call when you get back?"

Nodding, Emma worked on finding her voice, which had disappeared somewhere down into her belly.

Mia stood up with a sigh. "Actually, if you two don't mind, I need to get home and do some laundry if we're heading out of town tomorrow. Oren, it's been an absolute pleasure to meet you." She shook his hand, giggling when he accompanied it with a little half bow. "Emma, walk me to the door?"

Emma trailed a hand along Oren's bicep as she passed him. "Be right back. You'll stay for a while?"

He gripped her hand and kissed it, sending a tremor of nervous thrills through her blood before she stepped away. His lips were so gentle on her skin...

Swallowing down the instinct to purr like a kitten, Emma took a deep breath and followed Mia to the door. When she'd opened it and stepped outside, she even managed to bring herself just a bit down from the clouds. "See you in the morning?"

The other woman's elfin features lit up into a real smile. "Yeah, and you two have fun. He seems really nice."

"He is." Emma shot a glance back at Oren, who'd politely turned away and focused on his tea to give them some privacy. "You'll be okay? I know tonight was a lot."

Mia gave her a quick hug, whispering, "I'll be fine. I'm glad you told me everything, and I guess...I guess there's no hurry. Seriously, you and Oren have fun. Enjoy the night. Hopefully, Ned won't interrupt it. One Logan on your impromptu date is enough."

Emma stifled a laugh. "True enough."

"Tomorrow, though...we have a lot to figure out."

Nodding against her shoulder, Emma didn't bother answering. Mia's comments had just about summed up the story of her life lately.

3

"Eat some more, Leo. You don't want to disappoint your yaya, now, do you?"

Leo grinned as his grandmother winked at him, sliding a second honey-sweetened helping of her famous baklava onto his plate before he could object. The morsel practically begged to be devoured.

When in Iowa...enjoy Iowan treats?

Leo hadn't expected to be in Iowa, but his brother, Aleksy, had called last week, saying their grandmother had taken a fall. Knowing he'd been gone from home too long, Leo seized the stretch of days that opened up after his team's last case. So far, his stomach was pleased with his decision.

He eyed the pastry before taking a bite and humming with satisfaction, enjoying how it made Yaya's cheeks dimple with a smile. The expression lit up her whole kitchen even more than the modern lamps his brothers had installed last summer, a project Leo was supposed to help with before being drawn into dealing with smugglers in Fort Lauderdale. Another time when he'd let down Yaya, leaving his brothers to pick up the slack.

"You should come home more often. I'll fatten you up. You're too concerned with staying trim. You need to enjoy life!" She shuffled over to the country-style worktable in her little kitchen, where she'd spread enough food for their whole family, even though it was just the two of them.

Her dress brought home the point even more. She wore her Sunday best—and had worn such clothes ever since he'd arrived a few days before—because his visit was a special occasion. Her long hand-sewn skirts and embroidered sweaters reminded him of all the times her cheeks had dimpled over his "gentleman dress clothes" for church.

And she hadn't changed much since those days either. Maybe she dyed her hair black and didn't curl it quite so often, and maybe her makeup was added with a bit more discretion...but she was still his one and only Yaya, loving and faithful and endlessly giving.

Especially when it came to food.

The sight of the various Greek delicacies made Leo homesick, even though he sat in the very house where he grew up. He came home so rarely that Yaya treated the short visits as if they were grand occasions. She wanted her family around more, certainly...but it was also a sign that she missed him—the one grandson who'd moved so far away that a trip home meant an expensive flight instead of a fifteen-minute car ride.

"Yaya." Leo sat back, the second baklava half gone. "You've outdone yourself. But don't think I didn't see that little belly Aleksy was carrying around. I'm not just staying fit for vanity, you know? I stay fit so I can help people."

She paused in her fussing over the remaining grape leaves that she hadn't rolled into *dolmathakia*, her smile shrinking just enough to wrench at his gut. "I know, my angel. I know. But who helps you? When are you allowed to help yourself? To live for yourself!" She waved a hand at the calendar on the wall before going back to the leftover ingredients. "Time passes you by. You live your life for everyone else, but when will you settle down and be happy? Come October, you'll be thirty-two. I expected great-grandbabies by now."

She chuckled over what she was doing, and Leo sipped the water in front of him, washing down the pastry. He wished the woman was joking, but she wasn't.

Dang it.

"Leo, Leo, Leo." She waved a loaf of fresh bread at him in admonition, the length of it already wrapped for storage. "You need a family of your own. Everyone does."

Everyone? Maybe. Me...hell if I know. Not now, though.

Not. Now.

"That'll come, Yaya," he turned in his seat, facing her, "but you have to be patient."

She clucked her tongue, shaking her head like every worrying yaya in history. "How will you ever be able to have a family while working such a dangerous job, hmm? You couldn't have been a doctor? A lawyer? A contractor? Like any one of your brothers? Oh no, you had to go off and save the world. FBI."

Yaya muttered something more in Greek as he took another sip of water before breaking down and pouring himself some wine from the carafe in the middle of the table.

In Yaya's house, beer of any kind was considered sacrilege, but he made do.

She noticed the wine and grinned. "Ah, I'll civilize you yet! And then you'll buy some nice girl a bottle of red wine, bring her home, and bring me great-grandbabies. Everything in order, eh?"

Before he could stop it, a flash of Denae Monroe, his teammate and occasional date, formed in Leo's mind. Her smooth dark skin and bright, cheerful smile shot through his brain like lightning. To his horror, his cheeks began to burn.

When Yaya chuckled, he knew he'd been caught.

The urge to rise and help her clean up tugged at him—just to get out of the conversation—but he pushed it down. She'd only stop cleaning up herself and try to force him to eat more food.

"Yaya, my baby brothers will be giving you great-grandbabies before you know it. You'll have to make so much baklava to keep them happy that you'll regret ever offering me seconds."

To emphasize his point, he shoved another honey-sweetened bite into his mouth and made a chef's kiss in a gesture of perfection.

She laughed, the sound of her joy bubbling out of her just like it had all through his childhood. Always finding the goodness in a situation. Always searching out the silver lining he had such a hard time holding onto.

"And I might get around to giving you great-grandbabies someday too."

Whether he believed the sentiment or not, there was no hurt in offering the consolation. Not with the way it made her smile anyway. Plus, this was as close as they got to seeing eye to eye when it came to his career choices. "But give me time, okay? Thirty-one isn't exactly ancient."

She scoffed as he drank some more water, then she scooted by him to the fridge, patting him on the head as she went, as if he were still a ten-year-old boy. In her mind, he supposed, he probably was.

When his phone buzzed in his pocket, she gave him a pointed look even before he could make excuses. "I know, I know. Go on." She waved him out of the room, and he raised the phone to his ear even as he headed toward the front door and the privacy of his childhood home's front porch.

The chill of the February air hit his face. And the dream, which had been haunting him for weeks, jumped to the forefront of his mind. In it, Leo stood right where he stood now, on the front porch of his grandparents' home. He watched his grandfather, his papu, run toward the house. Behind Papu, the trees came alive with a pack of wolves, loping and panting. As Papu sprinted, the wolves merged together, forming one giant, white-eyed creature with teeth like daggers.

"The path to the wolf is covered in innocent blood."

Leo didn't recognize the voice in his dream. But he remembered it.

His shiver had nothing to do with the icy air.

He shook himself, refocusing on his supervisor's phone call. It had to be something serious for her to interrupt personal time off.

"Jacinda, how's it going?" He eased the front door shut behind him, knowing he'd get a lecture if he let it go and allowed a slam to shake the front hall.

"All right. You enjoying your trip?"

Small talk. Not a good sign when it's Jacinda making it.

Last time she'd asked him how he was doing—back in their Miami days—she'd convinced him to go undercover as a high school English teacher for a few weeks, and he'd made a grand fool of himself. They got their unsub, but not before he walked around with the sign *Bite me* taped to his back for half a day and mixed up Ernest Hemingway with F. Scott Fitzgerald for the whole of a week's lesson.

No, small talk was the sign of a big ask when it came to Jacinda.

"Uh, yeah. Iowa in February's a far cry from the tropics and *cervezas* beachside, but it's good to be home. Great seeing my grandmother these last few days, even if she might've added an inch to my waistline."

"Ha, well, I hope she hasn't slowed you down too much." Jacinda paused, and Leo cringed. *Here comes the punchline.*

"Leo, I'm calling because we've caught a case and we need all hands on deck. In West Virginia this time. I need you to come home a few days early so we can get a jump start on this thing in the morning."

"Figured that was coming." He held in a sigh, but knew Jacinda heard the emotion anyway. "I'll get on a flight as soon as I—"

"We've already got you covered. You're booked out of Iowa City into Chicago tonight. Then take the red-eye from Chicago to Charleston, West Virginia. There'll be a car waiting to get you to the bed-and-breakfast where we'll be staying in Eklund, and where we'll meet up with you tomorrow."

Groaning, Leo leaned back against the house and closed his eyes. Not even one more night of rest, which meant this was worse than he'd thought. It also meant his grandmother's hopes of the two of them settling in for an old movie and neighborhood gossip were done for.

Not to mention the idea of a red-eye set his nerves on edge. His nightmares had let up some over the last few days, but it'd be just his luck to wake up screaming on an airplane, surrounded by civilians.

Still, he took a breath of the cold night air, knowing perfectly well what he had to do. "What time's my flight?"

"Ten. You've got three-and-a-half hours before takeoff. Good enough?"

"It'll have to be, I guess. Don't expect any favors from my grandmother in the near future."

Jacinda laughed. "I'd tell you to give her my apologies, but I know it wouldn't matter. I am sorry, though. I wouldn't ask if this wasn't a serious situation."

Nodding into the phone, Leo said what he had to—that he understood, which he did—and closed out the call. Details for his flights would come to him any minute via text, but for now, he needed to get to packing.

And talking to Yaya. Maybe he'd even ask her to give him some of that homemade bread for a late-night snack. TSA would let an FBI agent slide on carrying his grandmother's bread through the security gate, right? No hurt in trying.

With a quick glance out at the old neighborhood, he tucked his phone away and turned back to the door. Work had beckoned him.

But explaining the premature departure date to his grandmother?

Hell, that would be a job in and of itself.

4

Monday morning, Emma parked just an aisle over from where two Bureau Expeditions sat awaiting their team, proof that wherever they were going was considered driving distance from D.C. Since Jacinda's text hadn't offered anything beyond the most basic information, she'd wondered if they'd have to catch a flight. Now, with a winter storm coming, Emma was glad to see the SUVs had been decked out with snow tires.

The week was supposed to get messy fast, and Emma just hoped that sentiment applied only to the roads.

Climbing out with her go bag in tow, she glimpsed a leggy woman heading out of the Bureau's front entrance, Jacinda walking alongside her. The vaguely familiar woman wasn't part of their team.

Pale skin, close-set eyes, and a walk that spoke of centuries of confidence. *Is she descended from royalty?* Emma was lost in wonder. The woman's strawberry-blond hair swung out in a sudden gust of wind.

Mia let out a choked curse as she stepped up beside Emma.

That was when Emma remembered that Special Agent Sloan Grant had recently transferred from Richmond to the D.C. Counterterrorism Division. And, not quite so recently, she was the reason for Ned Logan's broken heart...just before his so-called accident.

Talk about a shitty way to start a case.

Mia's petite frame was a tense ball of potential energy beside her. Emma knew Mia had placed part of the blame for her brother's death on Sloan. Before Ned had climbed into his car and taken his fatal drive, he'd proposed marriage to Sloan. The elegant agent had rejected him. So when Ned drove off into the night, he was emotionally wrecked long before he crashed.

If *he crashed.*

In spite of the new information about Ned's death, Mia appeared to still harbor feelings of resentment and blame—if Emma was judging her tight expression correctly.

If Sloan felt the intensity of Mia's dislike, she wasn't showing it.

Emma slid a step closer to Mia as they walked in step toward the Expeditions. "You okay?"

"Fine." Mia's clipped answer came in time with her stride speeding up, and Emma kept pace. The sooner they got this greeting over with, the better. Maybe the women would be able to reconcile or maybe they wouldn't, but the case would have to come first. It wasn't as if Emma and Mia could spend the morning introducing Sloan to the idea of the Other and updating her on Ned's recent claim that he'd been murdered.

Still, the stranger to the team did an admirable job of appearing carefree and friendly as she greeted them. That was something, right?

Sloan shook Emma's hand as they reintroduced themselves, and then exchanged fast nods with Mia. With a smile pasted firmly onto her face, Mia gave her dead brother's ex-girlfriend the stiffest "hello" Emma had ever heard.

Emma glanced at Jacinda. For her part, the SSA showed no sign of recognizing the melodrama tinging the air. Her red hair hung loose in its normal Hollywood waves, and her makeup didn't give the slightest sign that she'd had an early morning. If anything, her perfectly tailored coat suggested the opposite.

And while their SSA had briefly been distracted on seeing Vance and Denae coming from the Bureau's side entrance, the fact that they were meeting in the parking lot spoke volumes. But at least they were all ready to go, if dressed for extra-cold weather.

Pulled down tight, Vance's stocking cap gave him the look of an overgrown member of a boy band, the way he was bundled into an oversize coat and sidling up to Mia. Beside him, Denae's tied-back curls and stoic expression suggested she just might be the adult chaperone for their little group.

"All right, let's gather around," Jacinda gestured them over to the hood of the first Expedition, "and I'll conference Leo in. He's meeting us at our destination."

Emma exchanged a raised eyebrow with Denae, who mouthed, *Red-eye*.

Well, shit. There goes this being a normal case. No way would Jacinda call him back from vacation and *bring in an extra body if we didn't need a lot of help.*

Jacinda set her phone on the hood of the SUV, allowing Leo to give a quick greeting from the small screen before jumping in. "Okay, team. Our destination is Eklund, West Virginia. In the early hours of yesterday morning, a small restaurant was blown to pieces. Remnants of what appear to be a homemade bomb have been found."

Vance huffed out a breath, standing a step closer to Mia

than was strictly professional. "Enter Counterterrorism Agent Sloan Grant, I presume."

Sloan gave a thin-lipped smile before Jacinda nodded.

"Exactly. The establishment's owner," Jacinda consulted notes on her iPad, "is fifty-four-year-old Mortimer 'Morty' Williams. He and his daughter, twenty-eight-year-old Laura Williams, were presumed to be sleeping in their family's apartment home above the restaurant when the explosion occurred. However, local County Sheriff Dudley Gruntle hasn't been able to find any human remains in the rubble. He's to call immediately if that changes."

"Do we believe they would have found them in the ruins?" Denae asked. "Or is there a chance we're on a needless hunt for the already dead?"

Emma kept herself from cringing. Hunting the dead wasn't exactly what she'd hoped for this morning. Of course, that might be slightly better than them hunting her.

Jacinda frowned. "Sheriff Gruntle is responsible for the entirety of Randall County, West Virginia, and has three officers total, all green newbies, to spread out over the seven small towns in his jurisdiction. He's understaffed, but my impression is that it's hard to believe he would've missed human remains in this case. Sloan?"

The Counterterrorism agent pushed her long hair behind her ears, glancing around the team. "I saw pictures of what remains of the bomb. Even with the gas line blowing, I don't think it would've made for a hot enough explosion to obscure adult-sized human remains."

"You see why she's coming along." Jacinda offered a tight smile, sliding away her iPad. "Sheriff Gruntle can't afford to put his entire force on this case, and even if he could, they wouldn't have the same resources we do. A thorough investigation needs to happen posthaste, especially considering we have missing persons."

Vance pulled his stocking cap lower, squinting against the wind. "So he's requested assistance from the Bureau, hoping the case might be a quick fix for federally trained experts."

"Special Agent Grant has expertise with explosive devices that the rest of us simply can't match." Jacinda glanced around the group as if for argument—which made sense, considering she'd only joined their team a month earlier—but nobody responded. "And we don't have time to take a crash course right now. The type of bomb that was used may tell us more about the unsub, but we'll go over that on the drive, which should take loosely four hours. We'll find lunch on the way, so gear up your stomachs for fast food. Everyone ready?"

Emma glanced from Denae to Vance, hoping to entice one of them with her expression to ride with her and Mia, safely separating her from Sloan. Though Jacinda seemed unconcerned, the tension between the two was palpable. Which might make for an interesting trip, to say the least. And how much more interesting would it be if Sloan knew her dead ex-boyfriend had been making appearances as of late, or that his accident hadn't been an accident at all?

She hitched a boot toward the go bag at her feet. "Ready as we'll ever be. Anyone mind if I drive?"

Leo barked a laugh from the phone that Emma pointedly chose to ignore as Jacinda handed her a set of keys. One side of her lips quirked up. "We might hit weather. Need I tell you to exercise caution?"

Emma grinned as she shouldered her bag, mostly because of the smile their SSA's comment had brought to Mia's face. "Me? Never."

Because the faster we get there, the faster we find those missing people, and the less time Mia has to spend walking a tightrope with Sloan.

5

The tabletop was nice and smooth beneath my fingers. Not sticky with residue from its earlier wipe down, nor tacky from previous patrons or leftover crumbs.

Despite having promised myself I wouldn't finish the whole whopping helping set before me, I dipped my last crinkle fry into the barbecue sauce. Fries that delicious should never be wasted.

Savoring the salt with the sweet sauce, I gazed around the Gold Moon Diner. Stained glass lamps hung over each table —dated, yet just the sort of thing that made the space feel timeless—and most of the place's patrons were old-timers well into their retirement.

The menus were simple laminated trifolds with all the usual suspects being advertised, right down to the place's famous peach cobbler and apple pie for dessert. I imagined they were just as delicious as advertised, but I preferred to judge a place by their fries. Hence the crinkle fries for breakfast, along with a burger.

Dad had taught me that. Fries that lacked seasoning signaled an unseasoned chef, or maybe a chef who just didn't care about their customers. Oversize fries? Lazy management and necessarily under-seasoned potatoes that might not even be cooked all the way through. Undersized? Well, that meant the diner was just aiming to be a rip-off of every other popular fast-food drive-through.

Nah, fries of the right size and seasoning pointed to a place that didn't just have longevity, but also good people behind it. And if I was going to give my money to a place, I wanted to know who ran it, for better or worse.

Plus...sometimes a gal just needed a decent basket of french fries to help ease her troubles.

Either way, I'd gotten little enough sleep that it might as well have been anything but breakfast time, and I appreciated a little diner acknowledging that not everyone worked the same nine-to-five schedule as white-collar types. I also gave the server credit for not arguing with me. Some did, and they did not get a twenty percent tip.

Truly excellent fries. A well-seasoned burger patty that's just thick enough to feel like a real treat. Nice atmosphere. Accommodating service and plenty of space. A booth open for single diners like me...

I like this place.

And better yet, the Gold Moon Diner of Phillipsie, West Virginia, had only one lone server attending its customers. Luckily, there weren't many.

I could handle one person. Just not two.

Watching the lone server, who looked like a frazzled college student during exam week, I forced the remains of my burger down my throat and worked to ignore the shiver trying to ruin my meal as I sat there wondering where my appetite had just gone.

Well, no. I knew the answer...and just didn't want to acknowledge it.

I still can't believe I did what I did. And I don't know how to make it better.

How the hell did I lose my cool like that? Enough to build a bomb and destroy a building? And kidnap people?

Who the hell am I?

The scramble after the explosion was a blur in my mind. I remembered driving down a dark road, listening to my hostages try and suck in air through their noses. The headlights illuminated my way through the West Virginia trees toward home. I'd parked the car next to the root cellar.

Somehow, the father and daughter had half hopped, half rolled down the cement stairs. They landed at the bottom, bent and crooked like earthworms after a rainstorm.

I helped them across the floor, to the deepest part of the cellar, and took the tape off their mouths. I couldn't leave them like that, even though I knew they'd yell at me the minute they could use their voices again.

And they had. Oh, how they had yelled.

Questions, demands. Angry words and accusations.

Insults.

All of it deserved. All of it earned by yours truly.

I couldn't blame them, but they wouldn't stop until I waved the gun at them again.

Not wanting them to freeze and not knowing what else to do, I threw blankets down. Put in a pair of space heaters that I hooked up to my generator. Then locked them in.

Once everything was secured, I sat on the ground outside the cellar door, listening to their futile attempts to scream for help. Eventually, their voices died down.

Maybe I sat there for hours?

Then I was hungry. Starved.

Now here I sat. I swallowed some water and licked my lips. Tried to block out the sight of that building blowing sky-high. In the moment, it'd felt so good. So damn good to blow that little piece of happiness into smithereens.

But now…? Now I couldn't for the life of me remember how I'd gotten up the gall to do it. My anger at the Williamses had dissipated nearly as soon as I'd gotten them tied up and into my dad's old wagon. Which had been easy as pie too.

Since then, I'd mostly felt confusion. Frustration.

This was not supposed to be my life.

Well, no, of course it's not. I stared into my coffee, tapping a jagged, bitten nail against the rim of the cup. *Life hasn't been what it was supposed to be since Dad died.*

The server filled a coffee cup and giggled at an old man's joke. He looked lonely, and it had probably been a bad dad joke, which made me like her more. She was working for her money, on her own and alone in the world, just like me.

My fingers played along the smooth tabletop again, trying to block out my memories even as they kept fighting for attention.

There's no way to make it better. You can't blow things up and then make them "better."

I licked my lips and sipped down some coffee. I deserved acrid, lukewarm, bitter coffee, but the damn stuff was delicious.

Playing the scene back, I thought, not for the first time, that it had been like someone had taken over my body on Sunday morning. Well, Saturday night when I'd started the ball rolling. I would never hurt anyone otherwise. I'd grown up getting hurt…so, yeah, I always thought, *I'd never hurt anyone.*

Except…I had.

The server appeared at the side of my table, friendly and unobtrusive—just like a good server should be—and held up a full carafe of coffee in her hand. "Refill?"

A slight layer of sweat gleamed on the woman's forehead, proof of her work ethic. Her name tag read *Cassidy* and had a tinge suggesting the young woman had worked there for months, if not years.

"Please." I held up my coffee cup for her, taking care to keep it steady. "Been a long morning so far?"

"Ha. I can't even feel my feet anymore, but who needs 'em, right?"

I enjoyed a deep sniff of my refreshed coffee and gestured to the seat across from me. "Why don't you take a load off now that all your customers have their refills? Just for a second?"

The server hesitated for only a moment before plopping down across from me, introducing herself as Cassidy Freese. "I'd shake your hand, but I'm probably sticky, so you just enjoy your coffee."

I hadn't thought about us introducing ourselves. *Shoot.* I hid behind a sip of coffee, my brain flying a mile a minute. Finally, I thought of my favorite book growing up—about an orphan who found a home. *Anne of Green Gables.* "I'm Anne. Nice to meet you."

"Nice to meet you, too, Anne." Cassidy's gaze roved over the little diner, clearly making sure that nobody else needed her for the moment. "This is what I love about this job. Meeting nice people. It's what keeps me going and makes me feel like, hell, even if I'm just pouring a cup of coffee or flipping a pancake, I'm helping people. People gotta eat, right? Can't go out and make the world a better place on an empty stomach."

Nodding along from behind my coffee cup, I grinned at the young woman as she kept up her friendly ramble.

It was just plain nice to meet such a sweet and innocent human being.

Just like me, really.

Because I was. I was a good, sweet human being. Deserving of love. Happiness.

Much as anyone was anyway.

I am good. I am deserving. I absolutely am.

Whoever did those horrible things, that person is gone now. Plain ole gone. And I will not let her come back.

Not for the life of me, I won't.

6

Emma eased up her lead foot, trying not to tailgate the Bureau SUV ahead of her. No need to invite Jacinda's irritation on the way to Nowhere Town, West Virginia.

"You'd think Leo was driving." Emma frowned at the surrounding traffic, one thumb tapping the wheel.

"Ha." The single syllable response was all Mia offered. Instead, she went back to staring out the passenger-side window at the traffic, appearing content to remain in silence.

In the back seat, Sloan Grant did the same. And while Emma had no idea why Jacinda had assigned things so that the three of them ended up riding together, cloud of awkwardness included, there was no way she could abide four hours of silence. Tension be damned.

"So Sloan, how are you finding D.C.?" Emma glanced into the rearview mirror, the other woman meeting her gaze with an easy, pink-lipped smile. Understated makeup set off Sloan's frighteningly perfect cheekbones, but her big hazel eyes were astute. The woman recognized the need for idle chatting.

Small favors granted, considering how long we're stuck together. Now let's see if we can thaw out Mia.

Sloan shrugged. "I spent enough time up here while in Richmond, so it's not totally foreign, but I wouldn't say I'm quite settled. Still stumbling around for favorite restaurants and the best shopping hours to beat the crowds. You know how it is, coming to a new place."

Emma glanced sideways at Mia, wondering if she'd jump in, but the other agent remained entranced by the traffic. "And how'd you get started in the FBI? Counterterrorism's a pretty specific unit to end up in if you're not gunning for it for a while, but if you'll forgive me for saying so, you're young to have been on that path."

"Ha." Sloan grinned, her white teeth shining in the dim interior of the vehicle. "No, I wasn't gunning for it. I was in the Army in Afghanistan. Explosive Ordnance Disposal. When I followed up my service years by joining the FBI, this was a perfect fit. Wouldn't exactly make sense to put someone whose specialty is defusing bombs on kidnapping cases, after all."

"Or in the Violent Crimes Unit normally," Mia shifted in her seat, speaking under her breath, "but it looks like we're lucky to have you."

The words had sounded natural—though Emma could still read the tension in her friend's shoulders. Maybe something of a truce could be formed, however, because anything less would just be unfortunate.

Sloan seemed like a down-to-earth agent, and for her to have dropped whatever she'd been doing to join this team with no apparent complaint, she was either a kind person or a very good agent.

Either way, I should stay the hell out of it. More drama's one thing I don't need.

Before Emma could consider how to keep their conversation going, Mia's phone buzzed, and she held the device up to signal for attention. "Looks like we're ready for the rest of the briefing."

Once Jacinda confirmed everyone could hear her, Leo took over. "Someone in each group pull out an iPad, and I'll send some files through. Tell me when you're ready."

Sloan kept Mia's phone in hand for their viewing while Mia angled her iPad for the other agent. "We're ready when you are, Ambrose."

"Like Mia said..." Vance sounded off with a yawn. "You wanna be in charge, get on with it."

Emma smiled at the wry tone. Now this was feeling like a normal briefing all of a sudden.

"Sorry if I'm putting you to sleep, Jessup." Leo's voice trailed off as he consulted with someone in his location. "Meanwhile, I'm already in Eklund, and I passed some more photos to Jacinda that she's sending to everyone's iPads. Morty and Laura Williams are still missing. Their vehicle is here, damaged by the blast, so they're officially considered missing persons. With the state of the restaurant and apartment, there's no telling if they were killed and then taken or taken alive, but we haven't seen evidence of violence so far."

"Other than the bomb," Denae cut in, voice ripe with sarcasm, "right?"

"Yeah, yeah, you know what I mean." Leo sighed. "Gimme a break, guys. Going on about four hours' sleep here, most of it on a plane."

"And we appreciate it, Leo, truly." Jacinda spoke up over anyone else who might've thought to. "What else have you got?"

"Not much right now." Leo paged through notes, looking away from the screen. "Morty's burger joint was a longtime staple of the community. He's run the business for the last twenty-seven years, and his father ran it before that. Seems like he was well-liked. Family hit a string of bad luck in the last few years when his wife got a cancer diagnosis. She passed a few months back. Sounds like they were struggling with debt and folks round here were wondering if they'd be able to keep the diner going."

Vance *ahem*ed to get the team's attention. "No enemies? No loan sharks looking to cash in on a bad loan?"

Leo frowned and glanced around the open area where he stood, which looked like a quiet street near the center of town. "Once you see this place, I doubt you'll wonder about that. It's a small community, and folks seem to legitimately like the Williamses. Everyone I've talked to has praised Laura for moving home to help her parents. It's a dying town because interstate changes took traffic away from the downtown businesses, but it's the small town you see in Hallmark movies, if more run-down."

Emma forced herself to ease up on the gas again before glancing over at the phone. "Small towns still have their secrets. Maybe there was a long-standing feud between families? If the Williamses ran the diner for a few generations, that could be plenty of time for grudges to build up and turn violent."

Jacinda sighed, but the expression signaled agreement. "Emma's right. Leo, could you get on that? Maybe the sheriff can help you dig into domestic disputes or other issues that might indicate a family feud is relevant here. I doubt his newbies will be familiar enough with cases that go back more than a year or two."

Leo affirmed but said nothing more.

"There's a lot to nail down in this case." Mia leaned sideways, away from her iPad's photos and toward the phone. "We're talking about a small, insular community, but it would still mean interviewing every member and cross-referencing to cases the sheriff can recall or bring up from his records."

Now Emma pressed on the accelerator. "That's assuming the sheriff doesn't recall disputes that are clearly relevant. Maybe a competitor is behind it. When the economy is on the downturn, money gets scarce and business gets more cutthroat."

"But," Mia added, "there must be dozens of small-town diners scattered around the county. Competition could be a reason, but to blow up a whole building? I hate to say it, but it feels random to me. Like a prank gone wrong, or—"

"Sorry, Mia," Sloan cut in, "but I have to disagree with you. You don't blow something up randomly. Shoot someone, or stab them or run them over, sure. Maybe even kidnap someone. But making a bomb and planting it is a different beast entirely. A bombing takes planning. Materials have to be obtained and devices have to be built, all of which happens off-site and with something of a plan in place beforehand. This restaurant or this father-and-daughter team or both…this isn't random to someone."

Though Mia appeared unflustered, Emma tried to take the sting out of Sloan's disagreement. "I agree…but the attack could also just be a statement of sorts. As in, the bomb itself wasn't random, but the target was. A means to an end instead of a direct attack on the Williamses."

Sloan frowned. "Statements are made on purpose. If the unsub acted with that goal in mind, then our crime just became even less random. If the business itself meant nothing to the unsub, then the town of Eklund does."

"So…" Vance cut in, his voice raised high enough that Emma wondered if he'd felt the ever-mounting tension in their SUV coming over the phone, "maybe we're dealing with a pissed-off local who's got some bone to chew with the tiny municipality. On top of talking to the sheriff, we should consider any legal squabbles in the town. Those might be worth looking into."

Denae took up the train of thought. "I still like the competition angle Emma mentioned. If business is tight, we should look at other diners. Even if nobody had a bone to pick with the Williamses, one less diner competing for limited business in a small town, where the belt keeps getting tighter…that could mean real profit for other businesses. Diner culture attracts regulars and passers-through, so one place going boom means the others all just got a bigger clientele."

"Denae, you haven't seen…" Leo yawned, long and loud, "this town. Sorry. Tired, like I said. But seriously…this is a small town. Gaining five more customers, or the equivalent, doesn't seem like a fair trade-off for the risk."

Emma cut sideways in traffic, taking advantage of a break in the fast lane as her team kept postulating. Vance's and Denae's determined entrance into the conversation had quieted her own SUV just a tad, which wasn't a bad thing. And Mia didn't seem to have been put off by Sloan shooting down her "random" hypothesis either.

Thank goodness.

The fact was, Emma liked that any interest Sloan might have in fitting in with the team wasn't holding her back from voicing her opinion. There was no point in having the woman along if she'd serve mostly as deadweight, piping up only when asked specifically about bombs and IEDs. If she was willing to make waves and think outside the proverbial box, all the better.

As long as the waves had nothing to do with dead loved ones anyway. They needed Mia's head on straight as well.

7

Gripping the overhead grab bar as conjecture continued between her colleagues, Mia flinched as Emma took advantage of a sliver of an opening in the middle lane and flashed the Expedition sideways.

Once again, Mia wondered how on earth she always forgot about Emma's daredevil driving until she was strapped in next to her. She might just have to have the reminder tattooed onto her hand at this rate.

But unlike her driving, Emma's attitude showed definite restraint. If Denae or Vance had been in the vehicle, Mia doubted they'd have been able to refrain from saying anything about the tension between her and Sloan. Or their history. Did the other agents even know about it?

Vance did, but Mia wasn't sure about the others.

Of all the dumb luck, for the one agent in the Bureau who Mia was on bad terms with to be on loan to their team…

A lump rose in her throat as her mind shifted and thought of the conversation Emma had had with Ned. For a while now, Mia had held Sloan culpable in Ned's accident. She remembered that day well. He'd called her and told her to expect a new sister-in-law. Mia remembered being distracted by a case. She couldn't even recall what that case had been.

The next thing she knew, bad news seemed to come from all sides. Sloan had told Ned she didn't want to marry him.

And then Ned was dead.

Separating the two events—Sloan's rejection and Ned's accident—felt impossible to Mia. The cause and effect seemed so clear. Sloan hurt Ned. Ned, unfocused and in emotional pain, had driven off the road. Ned died. Ergo, Sloan caused Ned's death.

To now learn that Ned had been killed, and to also learn that Sloan's rejection had nothing to do with it, was almost dizzying. Mia felt like handcuffs had been locked around her heart and lungs. Her feelings were muddled and confused.

Maybe Sloan's priorities had been in the wrong place that day. Maybe she refused to get engaged because of her laser-sharp focus on her job with the Bureau. Mia could understand that.

But she should've been better to him. He deserved better. For what time he had on this damn third rock from the sun, he really, really did.

And that is on her.

Even if Ned hadn't been killed in that accident because he'd been so off-balance after Sloan Grant had broken up with him, he easily could have. And Sloan had allowed him to drive off, after all.

And who said a ghost knew for sure what killed them anyway?

I'm going crazy.

With the angels on her shoulders bickering back and forth, Mia forced herself to think, for a moment, what would've happened if Ned was right. If someone had killed him. Hell…if the woman sitting behind her right now had said yes, based on what Ned now claimed, maybe they'd have both ended up dead in that accident.

The idea of the two of them dying on that date sent a steel-toed boot of shame straight into Mia's gut, stealing her wind, but even that physical rush of self-awareness couldn't shake off three-plus years of resentment. Logic and reasoning didn't measure up to all that built-up rage and frustration.

Especially when Mia still didn't have any real answers as to who'd stolen her brother from her life.

Because, so what if Sloan wasn't *technically* responsible? She'd hurt Mia's brother deeply. And that had been the last real thing that had happened in his life, which was in itself pretty damn unforgivable. Maybe if he hadn't been emotionally wobbly, he'd have recognized something was wrong that night and been able to save himself.

Which meant, in the end, his death was Sloan's fault, one way or another.

Emma coughed loudly—*too loudly* for the sound to be casual—swinging Mia's attention back to the conversation at hand. Right, they were on a case...and she'd been daydreaming. Distracted, because of Sloan...just like her brother.

Shit.

Mia rejoined the conversation, thinking out loud. "What if they're not missing persons? What if Morty and Laura were in on the bombings to begin with? Did it themselves for insurance money to take care of all those medical bills? It would be awarded to their surviving family members, true, but they could benefit if they were in on it. Maybe they just wanted to disappear with a big fat paycheck?"

"Then they'll show up pretty fast, right?" Emma overtook a slow Volvo. "They can't stay missing if they want to collect."

Sloan traded Mia's phone for the iPad. As soon as it was in her hands, she scrolled through the photos. "I need to get my eyes on the explosive used. That should tell us whether it was professional or amateur. I don't imagine either of the Williamses knew a lot about bombs."

Jacinda's face filled the phone's screen as she spoke up once more. "We'll need a full investigation of the entire Williams family, including any members out of town. There's an adult son, David, who the sheriff has already notified and who's coming in from Los Angeles as soon as possible. We need to know whether Laura or Morty had the skill to do this, or a motive or bad blood. Or, if they're truly just the victims they appear to be, we need to make sure there are no enemies who'd wish them this level of harm."

Emma nodded. "Definitely can't depend on the local sheriff and deputies, they're spread so thin."

Ned's face flashed in Mia's mind, with his easy smile and shining eyes. "Everybody's got enemies if you dig deep enough, I guess...even if they aren't always aware of them. The Williamses might not even have seen the danger coming."

Leo agreed, but as he began going through a list of the local business owners who might've been considered competition, Mia's mind had already begun to drift again.

Her brother couldn't have seen his own killer coming or known there was that level of ill will bent in his direction.

Right? If he had been aware of something like that, wouldn't she have known? Not to mention Sloan? Ned hadn't been a dumb man. He wouldn't have kept that quiet to protect them, not when they were FBI...

At least, she didn't think so.

Maybe Emma could ask him at some point, if he came back. For now, though, he seemed to have disappeared on them.

Again.

8

Eklund, West Virginia appeared just about exactly as Emma had imagined it. An old off-highway town that had once been held up by mining and manufacturing jobs, but now held on only by the toothless gums of bygone industry and determination. Big, boxy buildings with easy-to-read signs and sidewalk placards lined the area, with little side streets leading directly over to what counted for suburban homes in areas like these.

The streets were potholed but passable, and Emma counted only two traffic lights in the area as she followed the GPS to their destination. No pedestrians lingered around out of curiosity, which seemed a little odd, but maybe they'd missed the crowd.

And besides that, there was the sky.

Bleak, white…the kind of sky that promised bad winter weather to come. Buried among the clouds was the outline of rolling hills. Emma imagined that Eklund was encircled by green for miles in the summer months. But on a day like today…anyone smart would be tucked up by a fire if they had no reason to be out waiting for the storm.

Or unless they're building bombs, Emma girl.

Emma shook off the thought just as a pothole bounced her toward the ceiling. She sent a fast apology to the women with her. "Sorry. Almost there."

Mia waved out the window toward an old-timey barbershop. "Look at that. A pole with red and blue swirls just like in the old movies. Not sure I've ever seen one in person." Through the glass, an elderly Black man waved back at her, nodding. Yet the man's frown suggested he knew why they'd come.

Though the main street's businesses weren't shuttered, just like the cars lining the street, they hadn't seen new paint or updates in years, if not decades.

Emma focused forward, finding their destination even before the GPS alerted her. The site of the explosion couldn't be missed, and when Emma approached, even the state police techs combing the building stopped to look up. The Bureau's SUV stood out like a sore thumb.

She parked across the street from the blown-out remains of Morty Williams's restaurant.

Even without knowing what Morty's had looked like before the blast, she noted the clear devastation. Once upon a time there'd been a two-story building. Now a shell of blackened brick filled with charred rubble dominated the street. The back of the building still stood, more or less, so Emma could get a sense of the original structure.

Main Street was dominated by other two-story brick buildings, which seemed to belong more to the early twentieth century than the early twenty-first. Emma imagined Morty's storefront had looked similar. The skeleton of windows and charred studs looked nothing like the nearby businesses now.

"Oh my." To say the place was demolished felt like an understatement.

When she pulled on her coat and stepped out of the SUV, Emma decided it couldn't be more than twenty degrees. The wind blew down through these mountain towns like Mother Nature had a bone to pick with any human who wanted to eke out a living outdoors. A smoky, burnt odor floated in the chilly atmosphere.

The combination of the scent and temperature was strange. It confused her senses, smelling something so hot in such cold air.

Leo waved from across the street where he, Jacinda, Denae, and Vance were waiting, all holding the Tyvek suits they'd be putting on before entering the crime scene proper. "Over here!"

While Mia and Sloan went ahead, with a few arm lengths between them, Emma noted, she grabbed three Tyvek suits from the back of the SUV. She caught up to the other agents and handed Mia her suit first, then passed one to Sloan as a man in a sheriff's coat approached.

Emma stuck her gloved hand out to greet him. "Sheriff Gruntle?"

He squinted his brown eyes at her and nodded. "At your disposal, Sheriff Dudley Gruntle. Name's my own personal unfortunate event." He offered an easy smile, suggesting he'd added that tag a zillion times in his short lifetime. "And this here's Chief K.B. Stace from the fire department. Nice to meet y'all. You three FBI as well, I presume?"

The potbellied fire chief remained quiet but shook hands all around. He was older than the sheriff by about three decades, and despite his belonging to the small town, Emma got an impression of competence coming off him just from the way he held his own among the introductions while remaining half focused on the tablet he'd been reading prior to their arrival.

Mia stuck out her hand. "Special Agent Mia Logan. With Special Agents Emma Last and Sloan Grant."

The sheriff shook each of their hands in turn. "ATF is supposed to be sending somebody as well, but their closest team is dealing with an issue in the Monongahela. Some kind of international arms deal involving park rangers. I don't pretend to know." He then spit to the side, and Emma half expected the fluid to freeze in the air. "So thanks for coming. You can see there we've got a makeshift command point."

Echoing Gruntle's assertion, Leo gestured off to the side toward where a small canopy covered some folding tables, chairs, and laptops. "Wind's getting more frigid by the minute, but it'll block the snow when it comes."

"Where's the explosive device?" Sloan asked.

"Remains of what we think is the device are sitting in evidence at the station." Sheriff Gruntle waved toward the ruins of Morty's. "But I wanted you to see the results of the blast before taking you down there. 'Specially since we've got weather coming in tonight, if not sooner, and that'll be sure to change the scene. State police have sent over help to comb through the crime scene and are hard at work in what's left of the restaurant."

The team suited up, and every one of them but Sloan reluctantly removed their thicker gloves to replace them with nitrile ones. As the sheriff led them toward the bombed-out building, Emma wished for a share of whatever kept Sloan immune to the chill.

Maybe it was her focus. Since they'd reached the scene, the D.C. agent had grown more intense in her movements, almost hyperaware of her surroundings.

She's probably seen this kind of thing before, and it was probably a lot worse than a single building.

With that in mind, Emma reevaluated her earlier thoughts. Sloan's focus might well be born of remembered trauma, and this crime scene couldn't be helping her deal with that.

As she examined the charcoal-colored, skeletal remains of Morty's, Emma couldn't help thinking that the father and daughter couldn't have done this. Blasting apart a family legacy, destroying three generations of work, seemed such a waste. And nobody could be foolish enough to think they'd get away with collecting insurance money when they'd be the primary, and probably the only, arson suspect.

Morty's had been reduced to a giant pile of rubble and ash between two other similar brick buildings. Each building had chunks falling from the sides, so the neighbors didn't go completely unscathed.

Denae gestured to the curtain fluttering out from a shattered window surrounded by soot-covered brick. "Anybody hurt from these other businesses?"

The sheriff shook his head. "Nah, the Williamses are the only ones who live above their business on this stretch, and Main Street had shut down for the night long before the explosion kicked off. These two other buildings sustained damage, obviously, but they're repairable. Have to hope insurance comes through."

Emma stepped in beside Sloan and Mia to the very edge of the blasted restaurant and peered upward to a few blackened rafters still hanging across the open sky.

"Based on the radius of the rubble, looks like the main blast came from near the kitchen." Sloan stepped over the detritus, already taking over the scene.

Vance tapped a hand against the sheriff's upper arm as Sloan probed deeper into the mess. "Did the gas shut off automatically? I'd think it had to with the limited fire damage to the neighboring buildings."

"Yeah. This building's old enough they didn't have an updated valve installed, but some of the others did. We shut everything down, though. It'll be a couple cold days for the folks on this block. Might even close down until the line's repaired."

Heavy flakes of snow began to fall as if on cue, their whiteness emphasizing the blackened remains of Morty's, which boasted charred metal chairs, dented booths and appliances, and various lengths of splintered wood. Across what must've once been the bar top, half of a sagging mattress still smoldered, presumably having fallen from the upstairs apartment…which no longer existed in any form to speak of.

Emma reached down and picked up a twisted square of metal. "'Formworks Appliances.' Guess this was a toaster oven door." Dropping the ruined metal back onto the sidewalk, she stepped aside as a tech maneuvered his way back out the front window of the old diner and shrugged at the sheriff as he moved toward the canopy.

"We're sorting through everything. To be straight with you, we spent most of our time digging and searching for Morty and his girl. It seemed more important to save lives than protect the scene."

The telltale signs of digging and shifting were clear to Emma. Burn-scarred rafters, which once held the second floor, were stacked in neat piles along the perimeter. Rescue teams must've gone looking under the beams for human remains. "You found no trace of them?"

"We're still looking for remains, just in case, but it's mostly a fire investigation at this point."

Denae turned to face the sheriff. "What about a vehicle?"

"We have personal items from the second floor, as you can see. Their car is still parked behind the building. Took some damage from the blast." The sheriff called over to Sloan, who had made her way to the center of the ruined building.

"I'm guessing you found about as much as we did? The center is pretty much cleaned and mapped at this point."

Sloan addressed them over her shoulder as she kept looking around, seemingly at home in the cold. She wore gloves and a heavy coat like the rest of them but didn't shiver or hold her arms around her torso.

"The gas line was definitely tampered with. And what's going on with this spot? Looks like an outlet might've been there?" Sloan swirled a finger around the mess, her eyes taking in every single detail. She lifted a piece of melted plastic, looked at it thoughtfully, and handed it to the nearest tech. "Bag this. Mark it here on the map."

Sloan continued her survey of what Emma assumed must be the blast's origin. The way the D.C. agent peered at the ground and traced lines with a pointed finger made it clear that Sloan had identified a critical area at least.

"Hard to tell yet whether the device was meant to destroy the upper residence or the diner most of all, or if the apartment above was more of a side effect of the main damage. Could be the unsub just wanted the whole thing gone. This type of damage, though, we're looking at a device that was more about getting rid of the building. I wouldn't rule out the owners deliberately setting this."

The fire chief scoffed. "Lady, all due respect, you don't know Morty. He'd cut off his own leg before harming one brick of this building. His daughter grew up here. No way they'd do this."

Emma expected Jacinda to correct the man, but she stayed silent, instead looking to Sloan for a reply. When she gave none, Vance put up a hand. "As much as we respect your familiarity with the Williamses…"

Sloan noticed Jacinda watching her and picked up the thread. "He's right. We can't rule—"

"You can rule it out." For Fire Chief Stace, the possibility of the family committing arson was closed.

Sloan had the grace to flush, and Emma liked her all the more for it.

"In terms of finding who did this, knowing the goal of the bombing will help us focus." Emma nodded, trying to support Sloan without alienating the local authorities. "If the unsub had wanted to punish Eklund at large, they could've gone way bigger. Agents Jessup and Grant are just pointing out the restaurant itself seems to be the target…not the neighborhood."

Sloan pressed her lips together, most likely pulling back from accusing the Williamses, Emma assumed. "Right. The point is, a few different charges could've been used. The gas line's been tampered with. My initial look indicates the building was flooded with gas and then something ignited it. Could be someone set a candle on a table, opened the gas line, and walked out. Or a delayed ignition device was used. Could've been made with objects as simple as fireworks or gunpowder. But the gas did most of the work."

"Agreed." Chief Stace gestured over to some yellow flags fluttering within the building, which Emma guessed marked a gas line.

Sloan turned toward the sheriff. "Sir, we need to get over to the station ASAP and see what kinds of materials you've recovered. That'll help me determine whether we're dealing with a novice, a pro, or a pro who wants us to think they're a novice. For now, every possibility remains open."

SSA Jacinda Hollingsworth, who had stood at the periphery of the blast zone, stepped forward, at last inserting herself into the discussion. "That sounds like a great plan. Sloan, head over to the station and get a look at what the sheriff's team has uncovered. But then come straight back here to take over the on-site investigation to make sure no extra pieces are missing."

Emma winced. She didn't envy Sloan the time in the cold.

The fire chief offered to drive Sloan, and the two headed off to a nearby waiting pickup with the county's logo on the side.

"We've had a lot of illegal sales going on this past year." Sheriff Gruntle studied the remains of the diner and spoke so quietly that Emma almost didn't hear him. "Fireworks and firearms both, you wanna know the truth. My guys and I have done our best...but it's been hard to keep track of all that on top of the local pop-up meth lab. Seems we get a new one sprouting every time we think we've shut it down. Taken most of my manpower to deal with the drugs, and 'til now, I considered it my number one priority."

Triage in small-town West Virginia. Drugs, weapons, and bombs, oh my.

In the grand scheme of things, a meth lab usually would've ranked higher than fireworks. And those were also prone to exploding.

Emma forced what she hoped was a sympathetic smile. "Sheriff, have you considered...I know the Williamses were respected members of the community, but like Agent Grant said, we have to keep every possibility in play until firmly ruled out."

His eyes narrowed. "What're you getting at?"

"You mentioned meth labs popping up around town. Those blow up sometimes. We know that wasn't the case with Morty's, but what if they'd gotten in with the wrong people, as a way of paying off their debts? Could competition between dealers have led someone to target Morty's for some reason?"

Jacinda stood back, her approval radiating off her as she let Emma take the lead on the conversation.

Sheriff Gruntle, on the other hand, eyed Emma with a stern glare and shook his head. "I see what you're sayin', and I appreciate you needing to cover every base. But I'll just say what Chief Stace said earlier. You can rule that right out."

A snowflake landed directly on Emma's nose, heavier and flakier than the ones before it, and she brushed it away on her sleeve. The stuff was already starting to accumulate on her Tyvek suit, and everyone else's, making the entire team look like creepy snow people with green hands.

Sloan's examination of the scene would provide more details, more direction for their investigation. Emma could wait until then and would pursue whatever other leads she could for now.

"You mentioned illegal sales of fireworks and firearms in the area. What can you tell us about that?"

Sheriff Gruntle smirked and gave her a nod, as if to congratulate her on choosing the right path to take. Emma would let him believe whatever he felt like, so long as it gave her a worthwhile lead to follow.

"We got one fireworks dealer, a local, who's pretty shady. I ain't been able to pin anything illegal on her," the sheriff dusted up some snow with his boot, kicking at it in clear frustration, "but I wouldn't trust her so far as I can throw her...and that ain't far. I don't think she'd do something like this, but she might've sold something to someone who would."

Jacinda waved Leo back over to the group, and, once the team reconvened and got out of their Tyveks and put some real gloves on their hands, she pointed toward one of the Expeditions. "Leo and Emma, you two go check out Ms. Shady Fireworks. Sheriff, you'll get them the information?" He nodded, immediately pulling out a notepad to begin writing. "Mia and I will head over to the Randall County Police

Station after Sloan and go over evidence, as well as set up a game plan."

"Where do you want us, Boss?" Denae placed her gloved hands on her hips, nodding her chin at Vance as she did.

Jacinda pointed back to the charred remains of the diner, still crawling with techs and firefighters. "You two stay here until Sloan gets back and keep an eye on our crime scene. Let us know if anything else comes up to change the picture or the plan."

Emma caught Vance's scowl, but Denae only chuckled and tugged him toward the side alley to continue exploring. Their steps left tracks in the snow.

A game plan wouldn't do their team much good if this storm turned into the next snow-pocalypse, but at least the white stuff might put a damper on any further explosions.

Assuming they were dealing with a bomb-happy unsub and not rival meth gangs at war over distribution turf.

9

Taking his foot off the brake, Leo steered into a slide and brought the SUV out of it without a hitch.

Beside him, Emma released a breath. "Nice job."

"I'm good for some things." He forced himself to give an easy grin, never taking his eyes from the messy road. Over the years, he'd spent hours learning to drive in all kinds of weather. After his parents' deaths on icy, snowy roads, Leo was determined to never lose anyone in a car accident again. Driving in snow was old hat to him, but he hated it and the memories that came with it.

At least Emma hadn't fought him too hard, bowing to his experience in navigating these conditions. If he had to deal with her driving on these roads, he might have a panic attack. But she'd accepted the passenger side without complaint.

Maybe she wasn't as stubborn as he'd thought.

That didn't speed up the trip, though. As they traveled five to ten miles an hour down a narrow mountain highway, the drive to Janice Bobson's house was a long one. Leo squinted into the nearly whiteout conditions of heavy snow.

The windshield wipers did their best to keep up...but it wasn't enough. Beside him, Emma peered at her phone and sighed.

"This weather's only going to get worse. We'll be sleeping in the Expedition if we don't make this a quick trip and get back to town." She leaned in toward the GPS, eyeing the road ahead for any sign of a turnoff. "Bobson's road should be coming up."

Leo slowed the SUV, thankful they were the only ones dumb enough to be out in these conditions. So little sunlight was getting through the heavy flakes, especially this late in the afternoon. Even with the lights on low beam, he was still catching enough glare that safe movement amounted to little more than a crawl.

He found himself muttering under his breath, counting down the feet to go with the GPS.

A little turnoff ahead finally signaled their destination, and Leo crunched their vehicle onto the gravel and then uphill. The narrow lane left no room for a turnaround, so he only hoped nobody would come barreling down the mountain toward the highway. They'd all regret this trip if that happened.

The sheriff had told them that Janice Bobson's house would be the second turnoff on the right up the mountain lane, and Leo thanked the stars for their GPS. Somehow, the unit knew where they were going even though they'd seen no road signs and were dependent only on the address the man had given them. When the driveway came up, Leo took it without bothering to look for any landmarks. This area was the definition of the boonies.

Emma pulled the hood on her coat up, staring at the sprawling, run-down mountain home before them. "This wasn't exactly what I pictured when Sheriff Gruntle talked about a country house."

"Not exactly croquet sets and rocking chairs, huh?" Leo brought the Expedition to a halt in the driveway back toward the road since a little metal gate cut anyone off from getting within fifty feet of the house itself.

Stacked firewood filled one side of the front porch, but that stockpile was neater than anything else about the property, aside from the expensive new pickup sitting in the drive. The house was badly in need of paint, and patches on the roof betrayed need there, as well. The long porch that stretched across the front of the house was full too.

On the side that didn't house wood, a beat-up sofa and two ancient recliners stood out among smaller heaps of junk, all of it turning white beneath the snow drifting in on the wind. Indeterminate lumps around the property's yard suggested all manner of junk, which had already been buried in the winter storm.

As Leo put the vehicle in park, Emma pulled on her gloves. "Race you to the front door?"

"In this storm? Not a bad idea."

Emma was out the door before Leo had pocketed the key fob. He stumbled from the driver's side door, slammed it shut, and sprinted through the wet snow with a barking laugh as Emma reached the porch and shook herself off like an oversize Labrador. Even at a run, she'd accumulated snow on her shoulders and hood.

"Man alive, it's coming down," Leo bolted onto the porch beside her, rubbing his ungloved hands together. "And by the way, Agent Last, you cheated. Talk about an unfair advantage—"

Whatever he might've said next died in the wind, as the front door swung open to show a middle-aged woman brandishing a rifle. Their fleeting moment of silliness was over. Both agents drew their weapons as if they were Old West gunfighters.

"Who the hell are you, and whatchu want? Talk fast!" The woman all but snarled, swinging the rifle back and forth between them.

"Whoa, whoa, whoa, ma'am." Leo kept his finger off the trigger, doing his best not to escalate the situation. "I need you to lower your weapon. We're federal agents. I'm going to retrieve my identification now." He slowly reached for his wallet while maintaining his attention on the woman with the rifle.

With his ID in hand, he flipped it open. "I'm Special Agent Leo Ambrose, and this is my partner, Special Agent Emma Last. Sheriff Dudley Gruntle sent us up here. We're hoping you can answer a few questions we have about a situation in downtown Eklund."

"Lemme see that ID. From you too," the woman snapped at Emma. Thankfully, Leo noted, the rifle was no longer pointed directly at either of them. But she didn't put it down either. Instead, her eyes narrowed, and her lip curled until Emma lifted her own ID up and flipped it open, revealing her badge.

"Lower your weapon, ma'am. Place it on the ground."

Janice Bobson wasn't a complete fool. She lowered the rifle slowly to her feet and allowed Emma to pick it up.

With the woman disarmed, Leo holstered his gun and held out his ID so she could fully examine it. Emma did the same, keeping a grip on Janice's gun.

She bent forward over the IDs, her frizzy hair brushing Leo's fingers. Just when he thought she might bite his knuckles, she straightened.

With the woman calmer, Leo proceeded. "We just have a few questions regarding an explosion that occurred in downtown Eklund this weekend."

"So that busybody ole Gruntle reckons he's just gonna pin that on the local fireworks lady? Dudley couldn't even stand up to me hisself either. Ha. Man ain't half the sheriff his daddy was, and his daddy weren't much."

"Ms. Bobson, whatever issues you have with the sheriff—"

"I got 'em with you, too, you better believe it!" The woman pointed a long, arthritic finger at him. "I'm out here sellin' sparkly explosives, so now all ya'll reckon I'm some kinda expert who knows how to make a dadgum bomb? Y'all Feds are dumber'n I thought."

Leo's pride bristled, but Emma's hard voice spoke first. "Okay, but do you know how to make a bomb?"

The woman scoffed. "That ain't the point. I ain't no low-life bomber. I got better things to do with my time. Not to mention a business to tend to, which you two busybodies are interruptin'."

"Ma'am." Leo willed his smile to give off its usual charm even in the face of this curmudgeonly old bat. "I do apologize. I know what it looks like, us being here, but we're starting from scratch and are hoping you can tell us if you've noted any suspicious buyers of late."

"Son, turn your dang head!" The woman snarled—it might've been meant as a laugh—gesturing out at the snow. "It's February here in West Virginia, and ain't a soul with a lick o' sense gonna be buyin' fireworks this time o' year. I ain't had no buyers of late. Not since New Year's Eve, which is pretty fuckin' normal for January and February round these parts. Now, I got shit to do, inventory to order up and send out, and unless ya'll got a warrant, the two of you can give me back my gun and be on your happy way."

Emma glanced at Leo to see whether he had any ideas, but Janice was smart enough to read what the gesture meant.

No warrant.

The woman nodded, her lips pursed in satisfaction. "Like I thought and like I said. I'll be takin' my rifle back."

Emma kept a firm grip, shaking her head. "Sorry, Ms.

Bobson. You can pick up your property at the Eklund Sheriff's Office."

"You *bi—*"

"*Federal agent.* You're lucky we're not charging you with brandishing a deadly weapon."

"Well, Missy Federal Officer. The fact remains...no warrant, so y'all can get gone. Now."

The door slammed in their faces, and Leo blew out a breath that sent snowflakes whirling as he turned back toward the Expedition. Covered in white, the hulking shape loomed in wait with only the relatively warm hood showing black through the snow it was melting on contact. "I hope there's a scraper in that vehicle, or we're gonna get soaked trying to clear it off."

Emma opened her mouth to reply, but the door behind them jerked open.

Leo already had his hand on his weapon, ready to shoot back if the woman had a sawed-off shotgun or anything else with a barrel.

Instead, a scraper landed hard on the porch between them before the next slam of the door rattled the whole house.

Leo tightened his hood and picked up the scraper, not bothering to wave a *thank-you*. As he stepped down, there was a muffled yell from the window.

"I'll be damned if I take in two federal agents during a snowstorm! Y'all clean off that vehicle and get gone before you learn firsthand just how treacherous the winters are in these parts. And leave my damn scraper on the porch when you're done, or you'd better believe I'll be sendin' a bill!"

Emma snorted laughter as they hurried back to the vehicle. She put Janice Bobson's gun in the cargo space. Then she began using her scarf to sweep snow from the top of the vehicle as Leo worked on the windows, getting rid of the snow and the bare starts of ice.

When he dropped the scraper back onto Janice Bobson's porch and hightailed it back to the Expedition, his phone was just starting to buzz.

Emma already had the engine running, and he handed her his phone to answer so they could get going before the snow had more time to accost the SUV.

"You've got me and Leo, Jacinda," Emma held up the phone for her to see them, "but Leo's driving. We're leaving the Bobson place now. No joy to speak of here."

No joy in more than one way. Talk about a firecracker.

"Drive safe, Leo." Jacinda sighed, frustration showing on the small screen as she pulled at her messed-up red hair. "I'm calling to let you know the National Weather Service has upgraded our afternoon snowstorm to a blizzard, if you haven't already guessed. Get to the B and B as soon as you can. Safe to say, there won't be anyone out setting off bombs tonight."

"Will do, Boss. We have to make a brief stop at the sheriff's office to deal with a small property issue." As Emma gave another snort of laughter, Leo smiled while he pulled carefully out onto the gravel lane, heading back down the mountain. "But it'll be awhile. Our lodgings are the opposite side of the station from where we're at now."

Emma groaned, apparently not having connected that particular set of dots, but Jacinda only nodded and signed off.

"Settle in." Leo upped the power on the windshield wipers a notch before loosening his coat. "This isn't gonna be a fast drive."

"No kidding." Emma stared out into the roadway, untensing only slightly when they reached the narrow highway and were able to turn onto brine-treated roads, back toward

Eklund. "We're lucky this didn't happen earlier, and that the sheriff had a chance to survey the site and collect any evidence at all before this hit. Most of the scene will be completely contaminated by the time this weather clears up."

Leo squinted into the whiteout, too focused to reply for a minute. "You know, where I grew up, blizzards were a yearly event during the winter months, and no one batted an eyelash. Just drive safe and slow if you have to go out, and you're just fine."

Although, after living in Miami the last three years, this didn't exactly feel familiar. He wouldn't tell Emma that, though.

She scoffed, leaning over to fiddle with the radio. "Leo Ambrose, you sound like an old man. You need me to find you some old-timey rock and roll to go with that old-timer wisdom?"

He grinned. "Sure. And thanks for the compliment."

10

A couple hours after their run-in with Janice Bobson, Emma sat at a table at the Littleby-Littleby B and B. She ladled up a second helping of the rich beef stew, spilling it over her second pile of mashed potatoes. After only a second of hesitation, she grabbed a third roll on the side.

Vance raised an eyebrow at her second full plate of food, and Emma pointedly forked up a heavy bite of perfect potatoes smothered in the stew's gravy as a response.

Especially compared to a lunch composed of a wilted fast-food salad and overcooked chicken fingers, the food was delicious. As an added bonus, the meal was finally warming her up after their standoff on Janice Bobson's front porch and the snowy drive away from the woman's house.

This dining room was a far cry from Janice Bobson's brand of Appalachian hospitality.

Deep-cushioned chairs and flowery wallpaper gave the space an old-fashioned comfort. Although Emma and her colleagues still wore formal attire from the workday, bombings and kidnappings seemed a million miles away. Just for now, Emma allowed herself to enjoy her meal and set aside the danger looming beyond it.

Between the blizzard outside, the intense cold icing the windowpanes, and the otherworldly howling wind, Emma was almost ready to think the Other was making an appearance. She half expected a ghost to rise through the middle of the table.

She and Leo had pulled up to the Littleby-Littleby B and B after a painful, hour-long drive that shouldn't have taken more than twenty minutes on a clear day. Within minutes of entering the daffodil-yellow Victorian—with its hand-painted sign portraying fat bumblebees—they'd been ushered into the dining room. The warm setting had been a welcome sight for eyes made sore by the whiteout.

Emma had taken a bit more time to thaw toward the place than the others. Something about the antique wooden furniture and compartmentalized rooms left her waiting for a ghost to come calling, white-eyed and wanting.

But it's warm, Emma girl. If there were ghosts spying on you through hidey-holes in the walls, you'd feel it in the air.

Right? Right. So enjoy your damn dinner.

Ignoring Leo's observant side-eyeing, Emma did her best to do just that.

The house was gorgeous, inside and out, so that wasn't really the issue. It was just that between the historic architecture, the middle-of-nowhere location, and the man shoveling snow outside, the place gave off some serious *The Shining* vibes.

At least this old house has that huge wraparound porch. I don't remember anything like that from the movie.

Not to mention that deck out back. Talk about a standout attraction.

The wraparound porch bled into a sturdy deck at the back of the house, overlooking what could only be considered wilderness. The house itself had been built at the top of a slope that stretched down as far as the eye could see into a thick pine forest.

Emma had gazed out across the space only briefly earlier but found it easy to imagine bears lurking beneath the structure or appearing along the edge of the woods, all seen from the high-up safety of the deck.

But tonight wasn't the night for such things. Not with that howling wind and the cold sky spitting snow as if to bury them all for the foreseeable future.

Emma's eye caught on a shadow in the corner, and Leo squinted at her from across the table, but she shook her head and gave an abbreviated answer once she'd swallowed the food in her mouth. "A little snow-blind still."

He grinned in acknowledgment and went back to his stew.

The truth was, Emma did remain a bit snow-blind, but this Victorian mansion was ripe for ghost sightings. Maybe she hadn't seen one yet on this West Virginia venture, but she was certainly on the lookout. The Other had never felt so close, outside of actual visitations.

Their two servers brought out another few carafes of water, more hot rolls, and steaming potatoes. Denae helped herself to a second plate, towering higher than Emma's. The weather and the environment had turned all of them into hungry monsters.

One of the servers paused at the exit to the kitchen. "Beer or wine?"

"Maybe later, thank you." Jacinda waved the man off with a polite smile, having answered before giving anyone else the chance. But they all understood why. Even if they were snowed in, they might as well have been in a briefing room, despite appearances.

Jacinda peered around the table to make sure everyone

was settled in and past the point of starvation, with plenty of food on the table to keep plates full if need be. Then, as soon as the servers left again, the big doors swinging shut behind them, she cleared her throat to gain the team's full attention.

"Our hosts have been gracious enough to give us this private dining room, considering the reason we're here, so I think we should make use of this time. Sloan, can you fill everyone in on your conclusions?"

The woman wiped her lips with a napkin and nodded. "Sheriff Gruntle's guys did a good job of finding the bomb's remains, which is very impressive considering the device was made from items you can find anywhere. I still haven't sorted out exactly what role each piece played in the bomb makeup, but I have an idea. What I can say is, whoever did this relied on gas supplied to the building to cause the most damage. The perpetrator disconnected supply lines to the water heater and ovens in the restaurant."

Emma coughed. "And the city's supply didn't shut off why again?"

"No EFVs were in place. Excessive flow valves. They'll trigger in the event of a line break, whether that's caused by earthquake damage or tampering. But the law only requires them on new construction or renovation. Morty's was in an old building, like the sheriff said."

"What kind of materials are you finding?" Their SSA leaned forward, pushing her plate of half-eaten food out in front of her.

"There's glass and filament, which indicates a bulb of some kind. The only reason this sticks out as odd is the entire building was recently reset with LEDs to save energy."

Vance scoffed. "But no EFVs. Seems like another tick in the 'they did it for the insurance money' column."

"Not really." Sloan shook her head. "EFVs would be installed if alterations were made to the physical structure.

Light fixtures amount to superficial alteration. Back to the bomb…a random light bulb seems strange in a building full of LED fixtures. There's also some kind of residue, which might be gunpowder. Lab work will take time to determine if it came from fireworks or ammunition and may not return anything definitive. The best I can say is that the perpetrator used something that would spark and set off the gas. And there's a plastic piece, which melted, and I can't quite figure out yet."

"Janice Bobson gave us nothing. So we can't help you on the fireworks front at the moment." Leo set down his water, grabbing another roll as the bowl passed him by. "But we got the impression she hasn't sold anything this month or last."

"Gunpowder keeps pretty well. A sales timeline might not help us anyway." Sloan frowned, her eyes glazed, as if she was thinking back to what she'd seen that afternoon. "At the same time, there's no doubt that the person who made the incendiary bomb was far from an expert. The materials seem simple. A light bulb filament can give off some intense heat, over thirty-five hundred degrees Fahrenheit, easy. If someone knew how to turn that into an ignition source…"

Processing the details, Emma sipped her water. Sloan's presence was already paying off in spades, it seemed, yet leading them nowhere fast.

"You know, even if gunpowder was used, I don't know about Bobson." Emma reached for the butter. "She's either the world's greatest actor or she had nothing to do with the explosion. The only thing connecting her to our case is that she sells things that go boom. Sure, she waved a gun in our faces, but that could've been because of a host of other illegal activities that we don't have time or concern to worry about."

"Or," Leo twirled an empty fork around, "out of pure spite for law enforcement. I wouldn't put it past her. And I didn't get the impression she'd be the sort to hide her know-how. If that woman puts together a bomb someday, I bet she'd want to show off just how well she can do it. No amateur hour."

"Sassy, huh?" Mia pursed her lips, nibbling on a dinner roll. "Well, I didn't really get the impression the sheriff thought she was behind it. Still, having a good suspect off the bat would've been nice."

The wind howled, shaking the window frame, and flickering the lights. Emma's gaze shot toward the window, but the glass panes held steady. Still, her nerves spiked, tension raising her shoulders and tapping her foot against the lush carpet even before she could remind herself that the air remained warm and comfortable.

With no sign of the Other to be seen or felt. Not yet.

Jacinda frowned at the storm, gesturing for everyone to refocus on their food. "Let's finish up before we lose electricity for good. Let our hosts clean up. Tomorrow, we'll start talking to more local businesses and see if we can find anything from local surveillance videos."

Attempting to ignore the howling wind, Emma had just cleaned her second plate when their hostess knocked on the door and stepped inside.

"Just wanted to check on y'all. Everything to your likin'?" She peered around the table, gaining a smattering of yeses and thank-yous and appreciative murmurs from those with their mouths full. The white-haired woman's eyes eventually rested on Jacinda. "Am I interruptin'?"

Jacinda shook her head, patting her lips with a cloth napkin. "No, I think we're about done. This has been lovely, thank you."

Without asking, the woman called for the servers to bring in dessert and after-dinner refreshments. A moment later, the two college-aged guys cleared their dishes and replaced them with little cake plates. Trays of wineglasses and bottled lagers followed. Emma's mouth watered at the sight of the buttercream pound cake and raspberry glaze set down in front of her. She tried not to gawk at the pecan pies placed at each side of the table.

She might just gain ten pounds if this case didn't clear up fast.

"You must be Special Agent Emma Last, my dear," the woman scuttled around the table to shake Emma's hand, smiling, "since I met everyone else earlier. Leo got his pick of rooms first thing this mornin'. I'm Ms. Wanda P. Littleby, not to be confused with my dear deceased mother-in-law, Ms. Wanda D. Littleby. You just let me know if you need anythin' at all."

Mia giggled behind her napkin, suggesting that each one of them had gotten some form of this same speech over the course of the evening.

Ignoring Mia, their hostess gave Leo a shake of her head as she put a piece of pound cake directly on his plate. "Now, you ask me, your friend Leo got the worst of the rooms, he did. Chose the rose-wallpapered one decorated by the prior matriarch of the family, my dear mother-in-law. Bless his heart. A sure sign of him not getting enough pamperin', not knowin' the difference between my decorating and hers."

Leo choked on his beer, but Emma returned the woman's smile and thanked her as Jacinda let out a quiet laugh. And with that, the woman began walking around the table and pouring glasses of wine for everyone who hadn't picked up a beer from one of the trays. The wind seemed to howl louder, as if demanding its own sweet treat.

As Leo gave a satisfied sigh after taking a long pull from his beer bottle, he gestured outside. "Sounds like that storm's trying to break your windows."

"Oh, wouldn't be the first time." Ms. Littleby poured herself a small glass of wine, asked Jacinda if she could join them, then took a seat with a happy groan when given the go-ahead. "It's that mountain wind that curses the Appalachians. Ungodly, unforgivin'. I should tell you…" She shook her head.

"Tell us what?" Sloan prodded.

Sloan seemed to expect something related to the case, but Emma had already pegged the woman for being more focused on gossip and legend. From the twinkle in Ms. Littleby's eyes when she sipped her wine and grinned at Sloan, Emma suspected her colleague had just taken the bait for an old wives' tale.

"Well, since you ask." Ms. Littleby settled deeper into her chair, and Emma could've sworn the storm moaned against the Victorian's siding, just to appease her wants. "There's an old local legend about a man who shot his wife, Constance. They had three children. And when that heathenish wife of his began runnin' around on him, flirtin' up a storm at the local tavern…"

"Scandalous," Leo murmured.

Ms. Littleby smiled and waved a hand in front of her face. "Heaven tell me where she got the time, raisin' three little 'uns…well, if you so please, he shot her and left her for dead in the mountains. She moaned and screamed somethin' awful, but nobody found her in time. Or maybe nobody cared to, the way she'd been behavin'."

Mia's eyebrows were at her hairline. "That's terrible."

Their host simply shrugged. "Blood loss and the cold took her, slow-like. Next day, people around these parts said they'd thought they'd heard some wounded bear left for dead by hunters and being torn apart by wolves, or maybe a mother bear mournin' some dead cubs. Maybe that was Constance and people wanted to tell themselves otherwise, havin' ignored her pain all through the dark winter night. But say what you will, it was too late for Constance."

Ms. Wanda Littleby gazed around the table, sipping on

her wine and nodding as if she'd told the story a hundred times. Emma imagined she had.

"When was this?" she asked.

"Dear Constance died near on a hundred years ago now. And her children all moved away, but her husband lived to his old, old age, and nobody ever did pin her death on him. Even though he was a right scoundrel, and she a ne'er-do-well slip of a girl who shouldn't 'a never married an old goat like him. Want to know what people say?"

Leo leaned forward. "Of course."

She gave him a little wink. "People say…and I'd believe them if I were you…that when the wind gets this intense, it's because Constance is wailin' at the locals to avenge her. She did it to her own self if you believe the tales of how she acted, but still, she caterwauls up a storm now and again."

The room went silent, only the wind outside and the ticking grandfather clock making sounds as the agents absorbed the old ghost story. A second later, the wind seemed to wail all the louder, as if on cue, cutting across the Victorian's shutters in a way that shook the wall and rattled the chandelier above.

As high-pitched as the angry weather was, their host giggled in a way that made her lose a few decades for just a moment, and the storm seemed to lose its intensity.

"Well, maybe she's wailin' for you. FBI agents in our little town of Eklund. Never thought I'd live to see the day. Maybe Constance didn't, either, and now she wants your help after givin' up on all us locals. Just be careful she don't trap you in those hills out of her own spite for people doin' right by each other!"

Emma forced a laugh that mirrored the polite chuckles and responses of her colleagues, but the raspberry topping on her dessert suddenly tasted too sweet on her tongue. The room had gone cold, the air heavy, and she'd glanced around to find exactly what she'd been fearing ever since driving up to this old place.

Leaning against the dining room wall in a tattered prairie dress, a white-eyed woman shook her head in disgust at the old ghost story. A gunshot wound, still round and bleeding, left a wide, red mark across her chest. Her hands clenched and unclenched at her sides, blood trickling from the open wound.

"Useless. He's just useless." The ghost's iris-less white eyes seemed to rove the room before coming back to Emma, who'd frozen in her seat. "Useless as the wind."

Emma's stomach turned over the stew she'd so enjoyed, fighting off the cold that none of her colleagues felt in the face of the ghost's glare.

"Everything's useless." The ghost scowled, trailing one ghostly hand along the window, as if to embrace the wind outside, before turning her ghastly form and facing Emma directly. "Always happier without me. When I wasn't there. I shouldn't have been there. Like you shouldn't be here."

Emma shook herself, picking up the conversation around her as Ms. Littleby continued telling her ghost story. "Her husband's been dead for well over a century now." Their host helped herself to some more wine. "But his wife may still be wailin' yet, the way this storm sounds."

Constance, assuming that was her name, nodded at Emma from the side of the room, hands still in fists against her skirt as blood dripped down her dress and onto the floor.

The ghost lifted one hand and gestured toward the table, her gaze focused on Emma. "You shouldn't be here."

Dipping her fork into the pound cake on her plate, ignoring the spreading raspberry sauce, Emma did her best to refocus on her colleagues and pretend she hadn't just met Constance the Wailing Wind, but the dessert didn't have the same flavor or attraction it had before.

From down the table, Mia laughed a touch too loudly, and Emma realized she wasn't the only one faking lighthearted merriment. Mia's giggles and remarks had been pronounced and dramatic all night—and Emma had just now recognized it. Sloan's presence having an effect on her, Emma guessed.

And Vance had a pull to his mouth that suggested he'd realized the same thing, but the newest member of their team and Denae were laughing as if they didn't have a care in the world. As it turned out, Sloan had acclimated quite well to their caravan and done so quickly.

Just as Emma considered whether they were far enough into the night for her to make a graceful exit, Jacinda stood and made her own excuses. Breathing an inward sigh of relief, Emma pushed herself up from her chair to follow suit.

If Constance made another appearance, Emma wanted to be alone. For starters, this ghost talked in complete sentences. Maybe she could hold an actual conversation with a resident from the Other for once.

But if Constance didn't grace Emma with her presence again…well, that'd be fine too. Sleep sounded damn delightful right about now.

11

The Gold Moon Diner had served me a perfect burger and fries for breakfast, so I'd come right on back for dinner. The storm decided to get serious on me just as my food arrived, prompting me to stick around and go over my photographs.

I could still taste the food, though, and it did wonders for my mood. This time, I'd ordered a milkshake along with my cheesesteak and fries, and nothing about the meal disappointed. Cassidy was working a double, and true to her grace from when I'd ordered lunch for breakfast, she'd said nothing about me ordering a giant milkshake while snow poured down outside.

When I sucked down my last luxurious sip of vanilla and enjoyed the final greasy bite of dinner, my hand stilled upon reaching for my wallet. The sidewalk was invisible, and my car was nothing more than a white-wrapped lump against the curb. I didn't even have a windshield scraper.

And yet, there were people waiting on me, things I needed to be doing. The milkshake might have been a nice distraction from reality, but I did have a reality to get back to. Soon.

I'd half stood from my table when Cassidy's sneakers skidded to a stop by the entrance. I turned to see her ushering an over-bundled man out the door and yanking it closed again after him.

"He drives the local plow...see it there? Or I'd tell him to stay too." The server gestured to the few other patrons in the place, all of whom were lingering over their meals or sipping coffee. "You're staying, right?"

I opened my mouth to disagree, to make some excuses that were absolutely not the truth or anything close to it, but she pursed her lips and narrowed her eyes. She began wagging her finger at me like a woman three times her age. "After you've eaten two meals with us today, you'd just better sit right where you are. You can't go out in that weather 'til the snow's let up. Don't you dare, Anne."

Wow, it's been a long time since anyone worried over me. Over my safety.

For a moment, I thought my eyes might tear up. When the moment passed, though, Cassidy was already backing away.

"No choice, Anne. In fact, I'm going to bring you some more of those fries you love and a second milkshake to make sure you stay put. How's that for service?"

Instead of disagreeing, I realized I might as well put off my own reality a bit longer. The girl was right, no doubt. It wasn't as if I'd do anyone any good if I went driving in a blizzard and crashed into the side of a mountain.

At least I'd brought my bag in, thinking I might dig into it over coffee. Instead, I picked at the fries as I opened my portfolio, careful to keep one hand clean. I'd stored my father's old, crumbling negatives in the back. There wasn't much I could do about the delicate strips breaking apart. Most of them were powder by now.

Turned out, humanity's means to capture memories were just as fragile as the memories themselves.

And that very fragility allows me to prove to others how fragile their lives really are. All it takes is a little heat and the film dust...

Shutting down those thoughts, I focused on my own, more recent photos. There were some contests coming up fast, and I needed to parse out which images I'd be sending.

I definitely don't need to be thinking about blowing things up. That's not me. That's not what I do. I save memories, preserve them. To remind people of what's been lost.

As I lingered over five different close-ups of a rusted-out old bridge, thinking about the urban decay submission call coming up, Cassidy appeared at my shoulder again. I'd flipped to pictures of closed-down diners, and she leaned in close with a little murmur of appreciation.

"You said you were a photographer, but gosh, Anne. These are something. I can't believe the detail. Look at all these places. I can even read this one's menu..."

A little bubble of pride warmed my heart. Being able to pay the mortgage with my photographs was more than a lot of artists could lay claim to, but good, old-fashioned praise was unbeatable. Especially when it came honest, and this girl was nothing if not wide-eyed and sweet. Too sweet to lie well, definitely.

"Thanks. That means a lot. Which do you like?"

She pointed to one of the two shots I'd been torn between, her finger lingering over the cracked *Closed* sign hung across a little café advertising fresh croissants before she went off to help another customer.

The shot was a good one. I'd gotten candids of the owner on the day he'd had to close down, as well, but his tears made me so sad that I hadn't put those in my portfolio. I preferred my photos of places to people anyway. Places didn't let people down, even if neglect had taken its toll. A place always kept something of itself alive, a charm or a sense of what it used to be. Those were the ones I took special care in photographing.

One decision made, I kept paging through my portfolio as the blizzard raged, with Cassidy stopping by every so often to *ooh* over my work or offer an opinion when asked. I finished off my second helping of fries and milkshake and ordered some coffee to keep the night going. I'd have to leave at some point, but Cassidy was right that the roads weren't safe just yet.

Another patron had pulled out a book, and two others sounded like they were doing crosswords together on a phone.

If I had to guess, the storm had been upgraded to a full-on blizzard. As if on cue, one of the patrons doing a crossword got everybody's attention, phone in hand. "They're saying blizzard conditions now."

That could mean I'll be stuck here for days. Blizzards aren't fickle things, but they can be unpredictable.

I tried not to think about the people who needed me. They had food and water and warmth. They would be fine, even if I didn't get back to them for a day or two.

But longer than that...

I comforted myself knowing that if I was going to be stuck somewhere all night, away from home, I could have done worse than the Gold Moon Diner. The booths were comfortable enough to serve as emergency beds. And Cassidy would no doubt keep us warm with coffee and hot food. At least, assuming the power didn't cut out.

That might happen, and just like that, I couldn't help being antsy to get moving. Just as I was closing my portfolio, the crossworder couple hollered out another update, saying road closures were in effect.

Damn wind. I've done what I came here to do. To see Dad's grave. And now I'm stuck for more reasons than one.

Oregon might as well have been a continent away from West Virginia, given this weather. It didn't much matter that my time here *felt* over and that I needed to get back to focusing on my career. Not to mention distancing myself from what I'd done when I wasn't me.

Or, as I'd rather view it, what some awful, alien version of myself had done.

Unfortunately, this storm had its own ideas.

Outside, a man clomped to a stop on a horse of all things, and the woman who'd been reading bundled herself up and hightailed it outside to swing up behind him.

Cassidy appeared beside me again, shaking her head. "Horses are safer than cars in this weather."

I peered down the road after the riders. "Isn't it too cold?"

Cassidy shrugged. "Naw, that's the Miltons. They only live a few blocks back, and that mare Galilee could get them there without sight or bridle to guide her, she's been making the trek home for so many years."

I smiled at the thought. Having a horse who knew the way home was unimaginable to me when I could sometimes barely find my own way home. Life had gotten to be so complicated.

Cassidy tapped my shoulder, grabbing my attention. "Listen, those two over there are gonna get picked up by the man who drives the plow, the one who left a little while ago. He's their son, and he'll be back for 'em any minute. That just leaves you for us to figure out, and I'd like you to stay the night here. I live right upstairs, and it's no trouble."

My teeth knit along my bottom lip, near to drawing blood. I

didn't relish the idea of driving in this blizzard, but staying with Cassidy? That would delay my getting back for hours. Not that I wanted to head back. Unpleasant chores waited for me there.

In my mind's eye, I saw Morty and Laura and imagined their frightened faces staring up at me. My chest hurt, anxiety building up against my ribs like heartburn, and I brushed away the thought. They could wait.

I smiled, actually feeling a spear of relief with the realization that tonight I wouldn't have to venture back onto the highway or face my own personal nightmares back home. "You know, I think I'll take you up on that. I bet I couldn't even find my car in this. It's probably just a mound of snow!"

Cassidy grinned, clapping her hands together. "Great! It'll be a good old-fashioned sleepover. I'll close up in just a little while at nine, then we can go upstairs. You can meet my ridiculously cheesy dad, and I'll get you all settled in on the couch with a stack of blankets. It's one of those big fluffy numbers that's even more comfortable than a bed."

The girl was already turning away, but my blood had gone as cold as my milkshakes. "Your dad…lives with you?"

"Huh?" Cassidy turned back, eyes squinting a bit as if I'd surprised her. "Oh, of course. But don't worry. He won't mind. He'd insist. But, yeah, this is his business. I just manage it most days, but really, we run it together. He does most of the cooking, and I'm front of house."

She gave a little curtsy and a laugh before twirling off to see to the other customers who were now zipping and buttoning themselves up in their winter coats and hats.

I stared after the young server as pain welled in my chest and spread through my veins fast enough to make me dizzy.

The lights felt too bright, the people too loud. The images of closed-down diners in my portfolio suddenly seemed friendlier than this space, which had been open too long and gotten more than its fair share of love. Far more than its fair share.

Those diners in my pictures had deserved better, just like me. What made this place so special, with its fancy milkshakes and perfect fries and laughter and friendship and smiles?

Seconds ago, Cassidy felt like a new best friend. Someone I could trust with my personal well-being overnight and whose opinion I cared about, at least as much as I cared for any fan of my work. I'd adored her, in fact. She'd seemed so sweet.

But now?

She was just another *other* whose happiness mocked my past. Just like this place mocked my memories and everything I sought to honor through my photos.

Cassidy was the antithesis of everything I lived for. And getting more than her fair share of love in the bargain.

No, she was nothing like I'd thought, and this couldn't be allowed.

I wouldn't allow this.

Cassidy glanced back over at my table, her knowing little smile transforming into an unbearable smugness that raked its sharpened teeth over my heart, enough to catch my breath and dash every well-wish I'd had for this little diner over the course of the day.

That smile was filled with puffed-up, self-satisfied happiness. With just barely concealed evil, as well. The young woman's eyes bored into mine like jackhammers, pounding away at my very being.

Clenching my fists, I worked to calm down before packing up my portfolio. I'd accidentally tear it to pieces if I wasn't careful, feeling the way I did just now.

Cassidy's ugly voice chimed from across the room. "Anne, are you okay?"

I swallowed, bitter bile threatening to rise. Somehow, though, I found my smile. "I'm fine, Cassidy, just fine."

Closing my portfolio ever so gently, I picked up my coat as the plow truck pulled up outside for the last of the diner's other customers.

"And I can't wait to meet your dad."

12

Cassidy rarely slept a whole night through anymore. Not since her dad had started having heart problems. Now the clock blinked two forty-five from her bedside table, flashing red across her abandoned water glass.

Her room was silent, but beyond the table, the window ran white with the blizzard going strong outside, snow spinning down shifting the light from the building next door. The sight reminded her how easy and welcoming her dad had been when she'd brought Anne upstairs earlier. She was so lucky to have him.

Upon meeting Anne, he'd grinned at her as if she were his own kin and smoothed down his thinning hair as he introduced himself.

No question of whether they had the resources to take care of a stranger, or whether Cassidy ought to be inviting a new customer in from the cold. Just his same old friendly smile and a welcoming hand. Despite being slowed down by heart disease, the man was still a charmer who cared about everyone, every day and every night.

Whatever woke me, I'll feel better if I check on Dad and make sure he's not the reason I woke up. Can't hurt, he sleeps so deep.

Giving herself one more moment beneath the heavy comforter she so loved, she steeled herself for the chilly floor. They'd been trying to keep their electric bill lower than last winter, which meant every night was a touch too cold. The sacrifice had made for a better Christmas, though, and might even mean they could take a weekend off later in the spring. They'd see.

She swiveled out from under her covers, the iciness of the tile flooring seeping through her socks on first contact. Maybe she'd also check on Anne while she was up, make sure their stranded guest was warm enough and didn't need another pillow or blanket.

Not bothering to turn on a light, she pulled her robe on and moved toward the narrow hallway but had to smack a hand over her mouth to hold back a scream before she even left her room. A figure loomed in the darkness near the couch, moving stealthily as if to stay hidden in the shadows. The figure took another step, which allowed some light to seep in over their shoulders, and Cassidy's breath escaped her with a deep-chested grunt of relief.

"*What the...*Anne, you scared me."

Their guest was right there by her doorway, between her room and her dad's, as though she'd been standing there... staring into Cassidy's room and watching her sleep. Had she been sleepwalking?

Adrenaline pounded through her veins, and Cassidy found her breath hitching. What the hell was this woman doing?

Anne smiled, tucking some of her blond hair back behind her ears. Dimly, Cassidy noticed how neat it was, as if she hadn't been lying down to sleep at all. In fact, Anne's appearance didn't reveal a single wrinkle in her clothing, no strands of hair out of place. Nothing. She appeared awake, alert, and ready for the day to start.

At almost three in the morning.

"I'm sorry to scare you, hon." Anne patted her arm, her hand lingering as if for comfort, though Cassidy felt no real relief from the touch. "I just lost track of which door belonged to the bathroom."

She couldn't remember it was the closest door to the living area? I know I left the door open for her.

Little butterflies of discomfort fluttered in Cassidy's belly.

Forcing a smile, Cassidy gestured to the next door down, diagonal from where they stood. In the gaping darkness, she could tell the door sat open and that Anne must've passed it to get to the closed bedroom doors. "It's right there."

The woman smiled, murmuring a little thank-you, and Cassidy stared at her for another moment.

"I'm just…I'm just going to check on my dad and go back to sleep. Unless you need anything?"

Anne gestured her on, and Cassidy turned away, but then she heard…

"I just need you to be a little less happy."

Cassidy froze mid-step, her body going colder than the surrounding air as she processed her guest's words. When she had, she whirled around to confront the odd wish, only to come face-to-face with a gun.

Anne's other hand reached into the bathroom and switched on the light, casting a glare over the weapon's barrel.

Cassidy stumbled a step backward. "Anne, what—"

"Shut up." Anne put a finger to her lips as if for emphasis and narrowed her eyes so that lines appeared in her brow, adding a decade to the age Cassidy had guessed earlier. "I need you to be quiet and do exactly as I say."

Mouth dry, Cassidy nodded, fumbling with the tie on her robe, tightening it around her waist so she wouldn't trip on the fabric when she did move. Because what this woman was actually thinking could be seen in the tense way she held herself, and in those knowing eyes...

If she wanted to live, Cassidy must absolutely not do what this woman instructed. Following her orders would be suicide.

Anne grinned, gesturing with the gun for her to turn. "Now, you're going to wake up—"

Without giving herself time to second-guess the instinct, Cassidy grabbed a painting off the wall and hurled it as hard as she could. Anne fell sideways to avoid the hit as Cassidy whirled back toward her father's room, just six steps down the hallway.

Her hand was out and reaching for the knob. She'd get inside, push his dresser in front of the door, and...and they'd jump from the window, that was what. Or call 911 and hope Anne didn't shoot her way into the room before the cops arrived.

Gripping and turning the knob, Cassidy flung the door open and got one step inside. "Dad, we need—"

The deafening roar of the gun silenced her, and her legs gave way, surrendering to an intense, searing ache. Her howl of pain drowned out anything Anne might be saying, the stabbing burn of her left knee and the blood pooling out from her body stealing all her focus.

On her side, she stared at her leg, bent sideways in the wrong direction beneath her robe. "Oh no, you didn't. Oh no, you didn't..." Her voice trailed into sobs as the hollow pain spread through her leg, up and down, burning so hot that she felt she'd melt into the cold flooring.

Nearly stumbling to his knees as he pulled himself from bed, her father moaned her name and clutched the bedside table for support. "Cassidy, what...? Anne—"

"It's your fault I did that!" Anne shrieked at Cassidy. "Your fault! Stay still, you stupid brat!"

The crazy, armed photographer loomed in the doorway, waving her gun so wildly that she hit the doorframe and knocked another painting to the floor, glass breaking when it hit the hardwood. Still at the bedside, her father flinched backward before Anne's next scream sent him to his knees.

"Cassidy, oh, Cassidy..." His repetition of her name was a low chant in the background, and Cassidy didn't recognize the wails coming from her own throat as she tried to drag herself toward him.

Her knee felt as if it would tear off in the effort, burning with even worse pain than when she'd broken her wrist. Dimly, she sensed her dad reaching for her, and she was grateful when his hands landed on her shoulders, anchoring her to something more than the pain, finally.

Anne aimed the gun, sighting it above Cassidy's head and toward her father. "Stop. *Stop.* The two of you are going to do exactly as I say now. Do not make me kill you. I am not a killer."

As Cassidy's dad's curses echoed in the background, she would have laughed if she could. Despite the grim situation, a bitter chuckle threatened to escape her, and she clamped her lips shut.

With trembling fingers, she reached out, touching the hot blood flowing from her injured knee. Sticky and wet, the blood covered her hand and glowed crimson as Anne turned on the overhead light.

In an instant, the nightmare surged into vivid life, painted in stark, relentless color. Though Cassidy's instinct was to close her eyes and deny what was happening, the truth was undeniable, leaving her trapped in its harsh, unforgiving reality.

13

A growl sounded out in the darkness, demanding Emma's attention even before she'd come fully aware. She bolted up, nearly tumbling from the side of the B and B's overly soft mattress. The cold of the room had numbed her limbs, driving the breath from her lungs.

Blinking into the near pitch-black corner, she focused on the source, pinpointing the hulking shadow of a wolf.

A wolf. In my fucking hotel room.

Emma inched her hand sideways, fumbling for the light switch on the nightstand lamp. When she found it, though, she wished she hadn't.

The massive black animal sat on its haunches in the southeast corner of her room, a picture frame dangling from its maw. The wolf's fur gleamed black, making its huge teeth look stark white. Twice the size of any dog she'd ever seen, the creature growled and focused its ghostly white eyes on her, intent. The picture frame in its mouth shined silver in the night. It was the one from Emma's nightstand back in D.C.

Of her and her mom, taken just before her mother's death when Emma had been only two. From back when her mom had looked so similar to Emma's own image, with her same sky-blue eyes, longer hair, and an easier smile.

On instinct, Emma glanced at her bed stand, where she'd left her gun for the night, but before she could pull the weapon from the drawer, the wolf bit down with a crunch, *glass sprinkling to the ground as the picture cracked from the pressure of the beast's bite.*

Emma pinched her tongue between her teeth, hard, willing herself to wake up, but the wolf's empty white eyes stared back at her as that growl grew louder. Fiercer and angrier, until the creature vibrated with the threatening sound. Then it spit the shattered picture frame to the floor.

In one smooth motion, the wolf rose and snarled. As its front paws moved, pacing forward, Emma was already going for her gun. When it leapt at her—calculating a wide-jawed attack on her neck—she dove sideways from the bed, a strangled scream escaping her as she fell to the floor and nearly hit her head on the nightstand.

She jolted upright beside the bed, the comforter tangled around her legs and torso. The room was black and silent—most definitely no growling—but her heart threatened to pound out of her chest, as if she'd just run the last breakneck stretch of a marathon.

Fumbling, she reached up and found the light switch, then her gun, even before she began untangling herself from the bedclothes. Scanning the room all the while, she saw and heard nothing. Outside, the blizzard had weakened, but snow continued to swirl in flurries. No other movement broke the cool static of her room.

No creature from the Other or anywhere else.

No oversize wolf threatening to tear out her jugular.

No broken glass or mangled picture of her and her mother either.

Just an empty room, which had been the setting for a very vivid nightmare.

"And Mom's picture is at home in my apartment." Emma breathed out, aiming to center herself with the sound of her own voice, short of other options. "Granted, it's probably face down since it keeps on vibrating and falling no matter what I do, but it's there, back in D.C., right beside my very own bed. Not in West Virginia."

Right?

Emma snorted at the fact that the question had even occurred to her, her tailbone twinging a complaint as she pulled herself back up to sit on the side of the bed and catch her breath. Racing heart aside, she was none the worse for wear...but she still wouldn't be getting back to sleep. Not after that dream.

Instead of trying, she touched her phone to check the time. *Four in the morning. Awesome.*

"I'll find the coffee maker downstairs. That's what I'll do. Nothing wrong with getting an early start."

That was a lie, but an early start beat sleeping in the realm of that wolf any day of the week.

She threw on a sweatshirt and her running shoes, not bothering with socks. She'd get ready for work later...for now, she just wanted out of the room. And maybe her striped pajama pants didn't exactly shout *federal agent*, but anyone who wanted to judge her at four in the morning could judge to their heart's content as far as she was concerned.

Padding out into the hallway, Emma had just reached the top of the staircase when Jacinda barreled out of her room, nearly running Emma into the wall. "Emma, I was coming to wake you. To wake everyone. Help me out by taking the third-floor bedrooms because we need to get going." Jacinda paused for breath, straightening her long-sleeved shirt with a grimace. "Sheriff Gruntle just called. There's been another explosion."

"Blizzard or not, huh?" Emma sighed, meeting Jacinda's

thin-lipped frown. "You take that side of the hallway, and I'll get this one?"

Fifteen minutes later, Emma was clearing snow off one of the Expeditions as the last of her colleagues hurried out the front door of the Victorian B and B. Denae and Vance didn't hesitate to join the rest of them in scraping away snow from the warming vehicles, all of them working in silence. The blizzard had finally dizzied itself to an end, but everything had been covered over in a thick layer of powder.

Lumps of white clung to the trees and the shrubs and the lawn, everything glistening beneath the night's stars. The porch and sidewalk lights made the whole area glow like a sort of wonderland.

"It would be gorgeous if it weren't so cold." Mia angled the scraper at one rearview mirror, working at the ice crystals. "Sometimes, I forget how much more pleasant this job can be in the summer."

"You're forgetting the sweat and humidity," Vance drawled with a sigh.

With the Expeditions cleared of snow, Emma climbed into a back seat behind Leo—who'd become quite insistent on taking the driver's seat in the lousy weather. Denae took the passenger side. Leo got them going as Jacinda brought the other SUV up behind them.

Their mini-caravan made the half-hour drive northwest with little incident beyond Emma wishing she were at the wheel. Even with the snowfall, she couldn't see any reason to drive as slowly as Leo did. Thankfully, they didn't have far to go.

"Jacinda said Phillipsie, West Virginia is even smaller than Eklund. At least it's close." Emma peered through the windshield, gauging the speed of the other SUV ahead of them. "Leo, at this rate, we might make it in time for the building's remodeling."

"Better safe than sorry, Mario Andretti."

Denae gave him a swat on the shoulder, laughing. "You could pick it up another mile or two per hour, grandpa."

Emma forced a smile as her colleagues continued with the light banter, willing herself to focus on the moment. That was part of why she'd spoken up, after all. The woods along this narrow highway seemed to loom darker and deeper with every minute, appearing to be the perfect hiding spot for wolves.

Big black wolves with dead eyes and picture frames in their mouths.

A sign announcing Phillipsie caught Emma's attention, and she shook the haunting images from her mind.

"The Gold Moon Diner is on Main Street." Denae pointed ahead, but the gesture was unnecessary.

The diner was still burning as Leo pulled up across the street from the sheriff's truck. But it looked like the streams of water shooting out of fire hoses and the falling snow were going to make fairly short work of the blaze. Steam drifted upward with the smoke. Crystals of ice fell with swirling snowflakes.

At this point, it was clear all efforts were meant to save neighboring businesses and not the diner itself. Tucked between other buildings, just like the last targeted diner, this one had been taken down to the studs by its blast, having been a building of wood and siding rather than brick and mortar.

"Nobody survived this." Emma surveyed the smoking ruins, wondering if the wet snow had done anything at all to cushion the damage. If nothing else, it must've stopped the neighboring buildings from burning down, which was something. Climbing from the SUV, she stomped her feet into the ice to gain traction before even attempting a step.

Pieces of siding and half of a booth, blown out across the

sidewalk and into the thoroughfare, rested against another building. Wood and siding and other detritus decorated the streets everywhere within the vicinity. Emma toed a charred pillow before she headed toward the sheriff with Leo and Denae.

She squinted in the night as Vance waved them forward, a self-satisfied grin lighting his face. "They screwed up this time, you better believe."

Scanning the broken glass of nearby buildings and the ruined diner, Emma considered for a moment whether the man had lost his mind entirely…but then he pointed across the street, beyond their Expedition.

"You see Dale's Hardware Store right there? I was in there yesterday, checking purchases of the items Sloan found at the first scene, since Eklund doesn't have a hardware store."

"Tell me you got a description of the customer."

Vance shook his head but kept smiling. "Even better. They just updated their surveillance cameras. Up and running at all hours. We're gonna catch this pyro bastard."

14

Leo lingered in front of Dale's Hardware Store, stomping from one foot to the other, fighting against the urge to shiver right out of his boots. Finally, the store's owner showed up with a key.

"Sorry to keep you waiting out here in the chill. I wasn't planning on opening up until later with the storm we just had. Most folks needing anything'll be shoveling and plowing for a few hours before they can get here."

Following the man inside, Leo looked for the position of security cameras, noting their locations and gauging in his mind how well they might have captured the events of last night.

The sooner I make it through this footage, the sooner we get our break.

A short while later, he shifted in the creaky chair he occupied, waiting for Dale's aging laptop to boot up. The office set into the hardware store's warehouse space wasn't much—mostly cream-colored drywall and endless invoices posted to a corkboard—but at least it was warm.

More than he could say for most other spaces in this

town.

The past day had been playing minor havoc with his anxiety levels, especially on the road. His parents had died in a car accident in weather like this. Having no desire to follow in their footsteps, he'd stolen every opportunity from High-Octane Emma to get behind the steering wheel.

Leo figured there had to be something on the video footage. If Dale's computer would reach its full operational potential, the team might get a clear image of their unsub for the first time. With that, and what evidence they could gather from the scene, they could have a real break in the case.

In general, there'd been far more evidence left behind at this scene than their last demolished diner. The snowfall and ice had kept the unsub's fire at this location from burning the diner to total ashes. True, the structure had been taken down to the foundation in plenty of spots, but what hadn't been wood was more damaged than erased.

Here's hoping Sloan finds more of our unsub's materials. If we can figure out what they are and where they're being purchased, that'll give us even more chance of catching them.

He'd hoped Dale's camera upgrades would include interior ones as well, but really, the hardware store's exterior was of more importance.

The outer cameras were set to capture activity along the fence that bordered Dale's lumber yard, to the right of his storefront. One camera also caught the street and sidewalk facing the Gold Moon Diner's entrance.

"Had a lot of theft from the lumberyard last season. Prices going up makes people desperate."

Emma knocked the door open with her boot and sidled in carrying two disposable coffee cups, one of which she handed to Leo. "As ordered. Find anything yet?"

What I wouldn't give for Yaya's gourmet brew and some of her baklava right now.

He grimaced at the taste of the coffee, his eyes never having left the screen. "I should have had you bring a cup for Dale's computer too. The old clunker is finally awake."

Leo clicked open the file containing last night's footage and sped through to the hour of the explosion.

Easing down into the chair beside him, Emma pulled the plastic lid from her cup and sipped her gas station brew. "We're going to catch our unsub this time." She leaned forward, positioning her elbows on the cluttered counter beside Leo's as they watched the film go by at three times the normal speed, showing nothing but snow whirling down from the sky. "They left too much behind."

"This unsub's need to destroy, despite the uncooperative weather circumstances, is going to be their undoing. I can feel it."

Emma huffed what might've been a laugh. "Vance said something similar outside, and I told him it was the cold he's feeling. You sure you don't have the warm office and caffeine talking in here?"

Leo grinned, but the words on the tip of his tongue disappeared in the face of an early morning change in the video. "There!"

He pointed, drawing Emma's eye to the alley beside the restaurant where a figure appeared moving awkwardly through the snow. The person had emerged from behind a lump that had to be a vehicle.

Leo noted the time and information on a notepad Dale had provided him. "Looks like around three eighteen a.m., we have a figure approaching a snow-covered vehicle in the alley."

Emma leaned in close to the screen. "Hard to see what's happening with all the snow."

They watched as the figure began slicing a hand down the

windshield furiously, wiping snow away. The person did the same to the driver's side window, then opened the door and climbed in.

A few moments later, the vehicle finally began moving, sluggishly, and emerged from the alley to nose across the camera view. It stopped in front of the hardware store, with the driver's side facing Dale's cameras.

Leo kept recording their observations. "Why'd he stop?"

"Making a phone call? We could check network data, but if any signals got through in that storm, I'd be surprised."

The car remained idling across from the restaurant.

"So much for getting an eyeful of our unsub. That has to be who we're looking at, but all I can see is a dark blob."

Emma *mm-hmm*ed. "I sure hope the diner's owner and daughter are in the back of that car."

"Still too hot to search for remains, even with these temperatures?"

"I think so. Apparently, Howie and Cassidy Freese lived above the restaurant, but that's not their car. Sheriff Gruntle confirmed they drove a pickup. It was parked behind the building."

"I'm guessing it burned too?"

"Yup."

"So we potentially add Mr. Freese and his daughter to the list of missing persons, like the Williamses."

Emma nodded. "Jacinda and Denae are reaching out to family and friends. Howie Freese is divorced and has family in Chicago, so it's just a matter of them answering a nonlocal number to confirm he and Cassidy aren't there visiting."

Leo nodded, coffee cup to his lips. "From what we heard of the Williamses, I didn't really peg them for the type to destroy the place themselves. Looks like this confirms it. Hey, the car's moving again."

She only grunted, concluding what Leo had just realized.

"We can't see the back of the damn thing. No chance of getting a license number."

Leo leaned in, his coffee all but forgotten. Instead, frustration burned bitter in his throat. "Forget the plates...we can't even tell for sure if there's anyone else in the vehicle besides the driver. We might still find the Freeses out there."

In front of them, snow swirled down, partially obscuring even the parts of the station wagon that had already been cleared. The vehicle parked farther down the street and stopped. Vague motion suggested the swishing of windshield wipers, but nothing else in the scene moved for nearly five more minutes in real time.

Then, without any prior warning, an explosion lit the screen, making Leo blink, even though he'd been expecting the blast. His vision cleared just in time to see the station wagon shifting out of the camera's view, never giving them a look of its back end or plate.

Debris flew out across the sidewalk and into the road, the light of the explosion and roar of fire flooding one whole side of the screen with blinding exposure. A bent barstool rocked in the snow in the middle of the street, light flickering with the flames beyond it as the two of them took in the eerily quiet scene.

Leo stared at the camera feed, waiting for something more to show itself as a clue. "So what, the station wagon waits around for a few minutes...we don't know why...and then our guy sets off the bomb from the car? If he's setting it off remotely, why does he stay so close?"

Pointing to where the alley let out into the street, Emma traced her finger along the circle of debris spread out from the blast. "Yeah. Look how strong the explosion was here. That's got to be when the gas went up. Our guy's lucky his whole car didn't go with it."

"Maybe whatever he's using for a detonator doesn't have

a long range?" Leo wished they'd gotten more from the footage. Maybe with a better technical setup, they'd have some more luck. "We should get this over to the sheriff's station...maybe even upload the video to our techs back in D.C. and see if they can make something out of what's here."

Leo stood, stretching as Emma rewound the footage to rewatch the blast. He ducked his head out from the office door and waved toward the lone figure hunched over the front counter, who'd been politely minding his own business while the agents dug through his security feed. "Dale, we're gonna have to take your laptop and the footage to the station. I'll make sure the sheriff gives you a receipt."

The man raised one arm and gave a lazy thumbs-up. "Do what you gotta. Get that bastard caught before he comes for my place too."

About to reply, Leo was pulled back to the office when Emma yelled. "Leo! Get in here. Look at this."

Emma's excitement did more for his heartbeat than the caffeine had, and he spun on his heel to return to the laptop. The video in front of her showed that same stool in the middle of the street, slowly coming to a standstill, but Emma didn't pause to rewind this time. Instead, she slowed the feed down to half speed and grinned at him.

"Watch."

Leo leaned in, knuckles white on the countertop beside where Emma gripped her coffee tight. He hadn't yet blinked when the same dark station wagon shot past again, going far too fast for the elements. And this time, the back end of the vehicle did face the security camera.

Desperation paid off in our favor. Hallelujah.

He grinned. "He turned around. That gives us a direction of travel and might narrow our search area for a possible location. Now let's see if we can beat the blizzard to get the plate number."

15

Emma gripped Leo's elbow to keep him from rushing out the door. "Hold on. Before we get out of here... small towns don't leave many options. Let's see where this asshole's going."

He exhaled a long breath but did as she asked. "Okay. Quickly."

With a map of Phillipsie pulled up on her phone, she aligned the layout with the angle of the security feed and gestured for Leo to take a peek. "The Gold Moon Diner's on the eastern end of Main Street, and there's only two blocks of town left past that location if we just look at the direction the station wagon's heading."

Leo clapped her on the back in acknowledgment, grinning along. "And at the speed the suspect's going, it's highly unlikely they're planning to turn off into town. They're headed back to the highway."

Emma opened up a new window on the laptop to view a larger image of the region of West Virginia they'd been focused on. There was only one rural highway east of

Phillipsie that angled southeast to Dellington before heading on to Eklund.

A grunt from the doorway drew their attention back to where Dale Fawns had been drawn in by the excitement. He waved one meaty hand at the map on the laptop screen. "I'll save you the trouble of asking. Don't know if you saw it on your drive over in the dark, but the only business on that highway is a single gas station. Ownership's changed hands a bit, but it's open for business."

Sliding her phone into her pocket, Emma thanked the man before refocusing on Leo. "There could be CCTV footage at that station. If the station wagon's on it, we know it passed by. If not, it tells us it turned onto a side road first. That'll narrow our search grid."

Leo folded up the laptop, wrapping the cord around it. "Hell, maybe the driver even stopped for gas in the storm and had their picture taken. Dale?" He glanced up at the older man still lurking in the doorway. "You got the station's name and number?"

Without a word, the man disappeared, only to reappear a minute later and hold up his own phone for Emma to stand and take down a number. "Fast Service Service Station, repetition intended."

Must be a theme around here.

Emma nodded her thanks even as she typed in the number, and listened to the phone ring as Leo tucked away their supplies and sipped his coffee. For her part, she was only interested in the next lead.

"Hello, this is the Fast Service Service Station. Everything's fast here."

The attendant sounded young and rehearsed, and Emma couldn't help crossing her fingers. "Hi, this is Special Agent Emma Last with the FBI. My team and I are in town investigating the explosion in Eklund—"

"And the one in Phillipsie. I heard it on the news." The man's voice rang high with excitement, raising Leo's eyebrow from where he stood nearby.

"That's right, sir. We're hoping you can help." Emma paused for effect, crossing her fingers that the friendly citizen on the other end of the line would be just as eager to hand over security footage as he was to get the call. "Were you open last night, during the storm?"

He cleared his throat, and the excitement drained from his voice, probably from realizing he wasn't about to end up on the news himself. "Nope, closed due to the blizzard. But I can tell you nobody purchased gas in off-hours. We'd have record of it."

"What about early morning customers? Did anyone stop in driving an older model station wagon?"

He *hrrmm*ed again. "No, ma'am. We've had no customers we didn't recognize, and nobody driving a vehicle like you described."

He's as helpful as a brass bucket of hot oil on a summer's day.

"Do you have security cameras that might have captured footage of the stretch of highway outside your business?"

"We sure do have security footage. You're welcome to it, if you think it might help. We make sure those cameras stay working at all hours, just to scare anybody off from causing trouble. Local drug heads and whatnot."

Emma flashed Leo a thumbs-up. "My colleague and I will be there as soon as we can. Thank you."

The man muttered, "You're welcome" even as Emma hung up.

Bundling into her coat, Emma led the way back out into the heart of the cluttered hardware store, where Dale was filling in a woman about the recent goings-on, waving his hands for emphasis as he did so. The woman smiled and nodded and patted him on the shoulder as he kept up his storytelling. She pushed by him to meet Leo and Emma mid-aisle.

Patient wife if I ever saw one.

The middle-aged woman held out a small cardboard box to Emma, smiling past her at Leo. "You two need to eat. Here are some doughnuts." She nodded backward to the counter by the entrance, where a tray sat with two steaming to-go cups. "Fresh coffee from the diner next door too. Don't worry. We've got your friends outside taken care of also."

Emma blinked, but Leo was already turning on the charm and offering a grateful smile in return. It made the woman blush like a schoolgirl. God bless him. And her. This was the closest thing to breakfast they were going to get.

As Dale Fawns kept on filling his wife in, proving that he'd been listening in to every word spoken between Emma and Leo in his office, they shifted their bags to help themselves to the provisions. Outside, Denae, Mia, Vance, and Sloan were huddled around their own box with Jacinda standing a few feet away on the phone. Emma waved in the direction of Dellington as she and Leo hurried out the door to climb into the Bureau's second vehicle. "Following a lead!"

Leo thumbed the ignition. "I'll drive. You update Jacinda."

Emma bit down on one end of a cinnamon doughnut, warm and fresh, as she pulled out her phone, putting their SSA on speaker to share the lead. "Any footsteps or tracks were obscured by the end of the blizzard and the plows coming through before we arrived," Emma finished, holding herself back from stuffing another bite of doughnut in her mouth, "but Dale's camera footage may have at least given us the unsub's path. If we can catch the same vehicle on the CCTV at the gas station, we might get a clearer view of the plate or confirm where they headed from here. Or both."

"Finally," Jacinda sighed out, "something worth celebrating. Definitely head over there and check it out. I was about to call the others to fill them in, but I'll tell you now. We're seeing much the same as we did in Eklund. Tampered gas line used to provide fuel for the explosion. Sloan doesn't have a sure bet on how things happened, but the working theory is that our unsub is setting up an initial small explosion leading to an almost immediate gas explosion. Identical to what was done at Morty's."

Emma glanced at Leo, smirking when she saw the chocolate mustache he sported. "That would explain why our unsub waited around. They wanted to give the gas a chance to spread into the space."

Jacinda hummed agreement. "That's what I'm thinking. The burn pattern led Sloan to an ignition source, an outlet near the gas line. The same materials as before, glass, a melted clump of plastic she now thinks is part of a wireless outlet, and that same powder. We've collected more samples to be analyzed and will continue looking into where the items might have been purchased once we're able to identify them. Here's hoping lightning strikes twice for us today."

"Fingers crossed for all of us and the people around here too."

"Topic change," Leo choked out, wiping crumbs from his coat as he drove. "Based on the video, the progression was fast from ignition to eruption."

"Definitely." Jacinda paused, muttered voices suggesting she might be conferring with Sloan. "The period of time between the severing of the gas line and detonation is still unknown, but we'll keep digging. You two follow that car. I want a full update as soon as you know anything. Don't go off the radar on this one."

Leo promised they wouldn't, already pressing the gas pedal farther down to the floorboard as they turned onto the brine-treated highway.

Emma allowed herself a smile but kept her snarky

comments to herself. Maybe the man had taken some driving hints from her after all.

16

Mia rubbed her hands together while waiting for David Williams—Morty's other child—as she inched closer to the heating vent in the Randall County Police Station's breakroom. At least her ankles might warm up at this rate. If the youngest Williams took his time arriving, that was.

For her part, Denae held a steaming cup of coffee close to her face, remaining near the burbling pot even though she hadn't sipped a drop. The little break room had a window leaking in winter-chilled air, and although it offered some calm not found in the rest of the station, not much could be said for its temperature.

"Coffee not strong enough for you?" Jacinda asked from the doorway.

"Not by half." Denae shifted against the counter, raising one eyebrow at their boss. "David Williams get here yet?"

Jacinda nodded down the hall. "First interview room on the left, soon as you two are ready." On that note, she disappeared again, presumably to keep juggling the various attempts at lead-chasing and their mostly demolished crime scene.

Mia shrugged off her coat and hung it on the overladen coat rack at the edge of the room, wishing they'd had a little more time to defrost after all that time spent outdoors at the crime scene. But David Williams had flown all the way from Los Angeles to Clarksburg and then driven down to Eklund to help find his missing family. He didn't deserve to be kept waiting.

Denae gulped down half her coffee with a muttered curse, following behind Mia. When they reached the interview room, Mia paused to peer through the window and take in the young man sitting alone at the table.

Maybe in another time and place, he would've looked older, but here, he appeared closer to sixteen than twenty-two. Lanky and hunched over the table, hands locked in a prayer position pushed up against his forehead, and with a sharp part to his hair.

Opening the door for herself and Denae, Mia pitched her voice low. "David Williams?"

He jerked straight upright. "That's right. Thank you for taking the time to see me."

"Thank you for taking the time to come." Mia sat down across from him but didn't get a chance to get another word out before he leaned forward, deep-brown eyes on hers.

"Ma'am, I need you to listen to me. There's no way on God's green earth my dad would destroy his own business for the insurance money. I know what it must look like, but—"

"We don't believe he did." Mia allowed her comment to sink in, seeing how her assurance had not just silenced the man before her but deflated him. Just fear tearing at his insides. "We've moved past that theory because of a second explosion that occurred overnight while you must've been in transit. I'm sorry you weren't alerted to it as soon as you came in."

He sighed, sitting back in his chair. "Yeah, uh...I didn't know. Who else got hit?"

"The Gold Moon Diner in Phillipsie," Denae shifted in her seat, the old wooden chair creaking beneath her, "but I'm afraid we can't share any more details than that. With the second explosion taken into account, however, nobody believes your family blew up Morty's for money. I promise."

"My family's still missing, though?"

Mia swallowed hard against the lump suddenly in her throat. "Yes, your family is still missing."

"Look, I know you said you can't give me any more details," David leaned in, focusing his gaze on Denae, "but the sheriff told me there were no bodies found at Morty's, which means my sister and dad are out there somewhere. Were Howie's and Cassidy's bodies not found either? So maybe they're all together, all missing?"

Denae reached out and gripped his hand. "It's possible they're all together. Or it's possible they're in separate locations. We don't know, David. I'm sorry. Do you have any idea who might've wanted to hurt your family?"

The man before them shook his head hard and slumped his chin into his hands, jerking the little metal table between them forward with an ear-piercing squeak. "Everyone loves Dad and Laura. Howie and Cassidy too. But if something horrible's happened to them...to any of them...you need to find out who did this and hold them responsible."

Mia wanted to assure David they'd find his father and sister alive, but she couldn't.

Denae stood, signaling Mia up beside her. "Someone else will be in to ask you a few more questions, but if you'll excuse us?"

David Williams nodded, his lips parted. His eyes were

glazed now that he'd gotten over the initial defense of his family and the surprise of hearing about the Gold Moon Diner. As if his purpose in coming had been in defense of his family's honor and integrity, and now that he'd been set back on his heels, it was all he could do not to fall down.

Mia sympathized. This day wasn't going nearly as planned.

Out in the hallway, Denae charged ahead to the bullpen of the little police station. Jacinda held her phone against her ear and wore a frustrated frown. She ended her call and asked for an update from their interview with David Williams.

"He confirms everything we've been told about the family business and his family's standing in the community. Got defensive at first, of course, but we put him at ease."

"Did he give you anything new? Any old family feuds that might've been kept under wraps, even in a town as close-knit as this one?"

Sheriff Gruntle's head snapped up. "I know you big city folk like to think we're all hicks in the sticks, but these are good, honest people out here. We don't get up to feudin' and fightin' the way the storybooks and Hollywood like to make you believe about us. Wish you'd all figure that out."

"Sheriff," Jacinda paused, staring at the man, "we appreciate your position, and your concern over what may or may not be happening underneath your nose. It's entirely possible you've missed all the signs pointing to a rivalry or feud between your neighbors precisely because you're too accustomed to living with it to see it for what it is."

Gruntle, true to his name, had only an ugly sound to offer in response. He threw the list of names he'd been reading onto his desk. "I'm familiar with the Freese family and the Williams family too. I know these people and, sure, I'm *accustomed* to living with them as neighbors. That just means I'm better able to gauge the likelihood that any one of 'em might've taken it into their heads to blow up their own buildings or anybody else's. This is the work of an outsider. It has to be."

Mia took a hesitant step between the sheriff and the SSA, hands out to ward off any more frustration turning into aggression.

"Sheriff Gruntle, we also have the complication of meth labs being operated in your jurisdiction. Were your people able to determine if Morty's might have been targeted for some reason related to competition between dealers or gangs in the area?"

He sat back and snapped his head from side to side. "Not a chance. The labs we've shut down are always outside of town, far outside. They don't sell around here either. As far as we can tell, the products are shipped your way, closer to D.C. or out to Richmond."

Jacinda reached for the list of names on the sheriff's desk. "This is family and known associates of the missing people, correct?"

"That's right."

"What can you tell us about Blair Freese? Her name is the only one I haven't heard before."

"Howie's ex. She moved away with one of their daughters, Winnie...must have been ten years ago now, after they got a divorce."

"And Cassidy stayed behind?" Jacinda asked, her voice tight.

"Cassidy stayed, yup. She wanted to finish school with her friends here in Randall County. But she followed her mom and Winnie to Chicago right after she got accepted to college. I figured she would've stayed gone. Most kids her age do after they get out of here."

Mia accepted the list from Jacinda, who had pulled her

phone out again and begun tapping numbers. "Sheriff, when did Cassidy come back?"

"Last week, I think. Maybe the week before. She turned up saying she decided to take a gap year instead of going to college right away. Wanted to help her dad run the Gold Moon and save up some money."

Jacinda waved for their attention as she put her phone on speaker. "Blair Freese, this is Supervisory Special Agent—"

"Oh, it's Blair Molina now. Has been for a decade."

The woman sounded out of breath, but casual...not like someone who'd had any idea that a part of her family had been the target of a bombing. Mia fought not to cringe away from the call. The woman was in for a rude awakening.

"Wait, did you say you're an agent?"

"With the FBI, ma'am. Supervisory Special Agent Jacinda Hollingsworth, and I have my team with me."

A nervous laugh tittered through the phone. "Oh, well, I'm sorry I didn't pick up. I was teaching a morning Pilates class, see, and—"

"Mrs. Molina, please, this is important." Jacinda waited only a beat to ensure she had the woman's focus, then carried on. "We'd like you to confirm the whereabouts of your ex-husband and daughter Cassidy. Are they with you in Chicago?"

The silence lasted only a few seconds, but Mia's heartbeat, pounding in her ears, stretched out the wait time as Blair Molina processed what Jacinda had asked her.

"I...no. I mean, Howie and I didn't exactly part on the worst of terms, but I haven't spoken to him in months. Cassidy moved back to be with her father and help him run the diner. She was going to get her business degree, but changed her mind..." Mrs. Molina paused a moment. "Agent, where are you calling from?"

The sheriff slapped a fist against his thigh and cursed

beneath his breath. Beside him, Mia mouthed to Jacinda that she'd alert the others as Blair Molina's voice rose higher, repeating her question.

"Ma'am," Jacinda closed her eyes, resting her back against the desk, "I'm calling from the Randall County Police Station in West Virginia. I need you to—"

The woman's voice began shrieking questions, demanding to know why the FBI was calling and what had happened, overtaking the room and silencing everyone nearby as Jacinda hurried to take the call off speaker and find more privacy in which to deal with the frantic mother on the other end of the line.

Was it a coincidence that they were both father-daughter teams that had been kidnapped? Mia very much doubted it.

17

Emma hadn't even had a chance to introduce herself or Leo before the man with the goatee in the wrinkled button-down reached out his hand from behind the checkout counter of Fast Service Service Station and gripped hers in welcome. Behind her, Leo tugged the door to the station tight to guard against the wind.

"Manager Marino Deluis, at your fast service." The man had the grace to flush with a bit of embarrassment over the pun but didn't take it back. "My guy, Mark, said you were on your way over."

Emma forced a smile and shook his hand. "Special Agent Emma Last, and this is Special Agent Leo Ambrose. We'd like to look at your CCTV footage if we could."

Leading them through a maze of junk food and candy, the man brought them to a back office, where he punched up some buttons before a small monitor. "Mark said you want the early morning?"

"Yes, sir, thank you. And we've got it from here." Emma waited for the man to take the hint, holding his gaze until he rose and backed out of the little room.

Leo shrugged out of his coat and shut the office door.

Emma scrolled forward in the video, moving just past the three thirty a.m. mark before she slowed down. "It never fails to amaze me how many folks think we need instructions to wind through security footage. Like we haven't done it a gazillion times before."

As he sat down next to Emma, Leo grunted in response. They were both already focused on the video in front of them as the minutes ticked by. The camera faced the highway with most of the feed obscured by snow. "Looks like the weather was worse here than in Phillipsie at the time of the explosion."

Speeding the video just a touch, Emma nodded. "The highway winds between mountains, so the worst of the weather probably got funneled into the pass. What d'you think, it's usually a fifteen-minute drive between the Gold Moon Diner and Dellington, and another fifteen to Eklund?"

"And add at least twenty minutes in each stretch for the snow." Leo's hand shot out to the video. "There you go! We've got our vehicle at four ten a.m."

Emma froze the footage and peered at the feed more closely. "Looks like it. And the timing makes sense. No way to get a plate, though." She sat back in her chair, staring, and finally inched the video forward, obtaining nothing better by way of a view.

"Well, at least we know they were still on the road at this point. I don't think it's likely that we'd have two station wagons out in a blizzard at that time of night." Leo tapped his fingers against the desk, dislodging some papers and then bending to pick them up. "What do you want to do? Follow the trail, or regroup with the team?"

Emma grimaced, considering the string of little towns in this part of the state. "There's no telling if Dellington was the destination point or Eklund or somewhere else in the county. Or the state or the country, for that matter. But I think we head to Dellington and check out the town. Especially the main street."

"I agree." Leo stood up and stretched. "Our unsub's hit two restaurants now, both on small-town main streets in Randall County. It can't hurt to at least dig around and see what we find. Maybe we'll come up with some better CCTV footage. Hell, even doorbell cams. Anything."

Emma shut down the monitor, stood, and pushed her chair in. Outside the office, they thanked the manager and the grinning clerk for their time before hightailing it back to the SUV. Emma kept one eye peeled for any white-eyed spirits who might be willing to help but saw no sign of the Other.

No surprise. It didn't matter how hopeful she was about the ghosts, as they were never as helpful as she wished. Plus, in the middle of nowhere on a narrow highway, running across any ghost at all would've been more coincidence than anything.

Less than ten minutes outside Dellington, Emma's phone buzzed.

"Hey, Mia." Emma glanced at Leo.

He slowed the SUV a touch, and she angled the phone so he could hear her. "We've left the gas station and are going to hunt around Dellington. What's going on there?"

"David Williams arrived and gave us the same firm, unwavering opinion that his sister and dad couldn't have blown up Morty's. We've also been in touch with Howie Freese's ex, who confirmed that neither he nor their daughter Cassidy were visiting. It doesn't rule out that they're off somewhere else, but for now, we're looking at a possible four missing persons."

Emma's seat belt seemed suddenly tighter across her chest as the similarity hit her.

"Leo, Mia…if we have two father-daughter pairs who were running restaurants while living upstairs of them, that cements a pattern. These were our unsub's targets."

Mia murmured, "My sentiments exactly."

Leo cursed under his breath, his hands tightening on the wheel. "Patterns are good, but if the unsub's targeting families…"

"Everyone could be in for a lot of heartache." Emma sighed, still preoccupied by the new connection when she focused back on the phone. "Jacinda want us back at the station?"

"No, just giving you the update." Mia paused. "We'll call if we get anything else in the way of info. Still nothing on the device fragments. She's convinced that'll lead us to the unsub, and Jacinda's giving her free rein on that."

Emma knew Mia meant to indicate Sloan but was surprised she couldn't bring herself to speak the woman's name. All these families at risk must have Mia really feeling her brother's absence.

"Let us know what Sloan finds out. We'll call with anything that comes up while we're out here."

Mia waited a moment before replying. "I'll tell her… Sloan…to get in touch. You two do the same. And stay safe. I'll make sure the others get the father-daughter note on our pairs of victims also."

Emma signed off and flicked the vehicle's heater up a notch, willing some warmth back into her bones before they had to venture into the cold mountain air again. Now that they had a clear victim profile, they needed a break in the case before more names got slotted into the missing persons column as proof of their theory.

She just hoped they could find that break without having to wait for another bomb to go off.

18

Cassidy's knee throbbed with heat, the pulse of pain overshadowing even the cold and the fear. In the dank, dark cellar room, with one of the space heaters having died, it was far too easy to imagine they'd been forgotten and left to die.

With every shiver racking her body against the stone wall at her back, her knee screamed. The pain and pressure from the bullet wound were excruciating. Even against the backdrop of a musty room with sharp, uneven stone walls and her wrists and ankles duct-taped together tightly enough that her extremities were numb from lack of circulation and the cold air, the bullet controlled her existence.

Beside her, her father lay bound in the same manner. Passed out, but she could hear him breathing. For now, that was good enough…at least he wasn't aware of his daughter's pain when he was sleeping. Across the small room, Laura and Morty Williams huddled together in a near mirror image of Cassidy and her own father. Bound by duct tape and silenced by the cold.

In the corner, the one working space heater still hummed

with warmth, but Cassidy guessed the room couldn't be warmer than fifty degrees. At least they were dry, though. That meant they wouldn't get hypothermia, no matter how cold they felt…right?

Inspecting the small cellar for the hundredth time, Cassidy searched for anything they might have at their disposal to help but saw nothing of use. Plastic shelving ran along one wall, holding sparse supplies of kitty litter—for snow, she imagined—and folded tarps. Nothing with sharp edges that could cut through duct tape, assuming she could even bring herself to reach it, the way her leg felt. Even breathing bothered her knee, so shifting her body away from the wall sounded akin to torture.

Laura Williams coughed, jolting herself awake. Her eyes were red-rimmed, even in the dim light. She cleared her throat, resituating herself and giving a grim-faced nod in Cassidy's direction.

Cassidy'd been in too much pain to respond to the other woman's questions earlier, only capable of sobbing over her knee before passing out from the pressure of their captor wrapping her ankles too tightly with duct tape for her wound to take the abuse. "You're Laura Williams, right?" Her voice was raspy, but she cleared her throat and tried again. "And that's your dad? Your pictures were on the news."

Laura glanced at her sleeping father. "Yeah, that's us. You and your dad own that diner in Phillipsie, right? The Gold Moon?"

Bile rose in Cassidy's throat at the memory of their beloved diner exploding into smithereens right before their eyes. "We did."

A few seconds passed before Laura flinched at the realization of what they'd both been through. "Right. Sorry."

Cassidy nodded. "You've been down here the whole time you've been gone?"

"Yeah." Laura shifted against the stone, grinding her ankles together in what looked like an attempt to loosen the ever-present duct tape. "Two days, at least. Feels like more. Sitting in our own piss, freezing our asses off. Nothing but water for sustenance."

Cassidy's throat tightened. The urge to pee had left her earlier, but she knew it would come back with a vengeance, not to be outdone by the bullet in her knee.

"That crazy blond bitch who forced you and your dad down here did the same to us. Hasn't fed us once. She took us right out of our home above our diner and blew it into dust." Laura rocked her head back against the wall behind her, biting her lip. "We're gonna die down here."

Beside her, the elder Williams woke up and struggled to a sitting position. Seeing his daughter fighting down tears, he nudged her with his elbow.

Cassidy had to look away, down at her own father. The mirror of the father-daughter relationship was too painful to watch, even with the burning heat in her knee and the cold sending a numbness through her hands. Some distractions were just too torturous.

When Morty coughed, Cassidy finally looked back at the man and addressed him. "Morty Williams." She nodded at her father. "I think you know my dad, Howie Freese. I'm Cassidy."

"Been awhile. Sorry to see you again under these circumstances." The quiet man's voice had a dignity to it, despite the desperate nature of their situation. His strength grounded her in the cold, reminding her of her own dad in better days, before divorce and heart disease had started grinding away at his health.

Cassidy glanced back to the staircase and their one potential escape route. "She told me her name was Anne. I just don't understand what she wants with us."

Morty snorted. "Can't be nothin' good." His face softened a touch. "I see you're injured, but it looks like the bleeding's stopped."

Laura leaned forward. "We could use some of the water to clean out the wound. Maybe ask her for some bandages if she comes down."

Cassidy shook her head. Her knee had stopped bleeding, and even though it still hurt like hell, she would rather not look at it or touch it. She'd ask Anne for some bandages, though, the next time she came back.

If she comes back.

Morty coughed a few times, hacking like a smoker, which Cassidy figured he was.

"Is your dad okay, Laura?"

"As good as can be down here and like this. But at least now he can't sneak outside for a cigarette. What about your dad? Is he good?"

"He's...got a heart condition. He's breathing."

Laura nodded, her gaze returning to the staircase Cassidy and her father had been forced down at gunpoint.

Anne had to come back sometime, right?

"She didn't even free our ankles to get us down those stairs. Told us to make our way down on our butts." Morty paused to spit sideways into a corner, away from his daughter. "Brought us down here and set up those heaters, so the nut must have her reasons. Wouldn't've bothered otherwise."

"I'm glad she took the tape off our mouths anyway." Laura shifted toward her dad, resting her head against his shoulder for a moment. His calm seemed to have bled into her.

Cassidy only wished she could feel some of it herself. Throughout the night—had it been nighttime?—the outside world howled. Wind drifted through the tiny gaps in the cellar door, causing the work light that dangled from the ceiling to sway and spin, creating eerie shadows this way and that. The *Small Space Heater That Could* had chugged along, barely keeping hypothermia at bay.

Laura sighed. "But I don't know. Maybe it just means we're in the middle of nowhere and there's nobody around to hear us scream. Even if the drive didn't seem that long."

When Cassidy laughed out loud, her knee screamed with the jarring, turning her laugh into a whimper. As she caught her breath, she met Laura's eyes again. "You forget where we live? Little county in West Virginia? In these parts, it doesn't take long to be in the middle of nowhere."

The other woman gave a grudging nod, but Cassidy couldn't respond. She was too busy digging her nails into her palms, trying to brace herself against the white-hot pain radiating outward from her knee.

With her luck, the thing was probably infected. She didn't think infections could spread very far after a couple days, but she knew next to nothing about wound care. Her experience was limited to treating the occasional burn or cut—the common hazards at a diner. If pain was any indication, though, Cassidy was in trouble.

Her knee couldn't have hurt worse if Anne had cut her leg off, and maybe that would at least have put her out of her misery.

Don't think like that. Dad needs you.

She bit down hard on her lip, using the little pain to distract herself from the major injury as tears threatened to run down her cold and dirty cheeks yet again. Her dad let out a little snore beside her, and she envied him. Whether he was more catatonic or in shock than asleep, she didn't know, but the sound of his snoring was reminiscent of her old life. A breath from before the disaster.

Because each time she closed her eyes, the image of their diner blowing sky-high painted her retinas with fire.

"Sounds like none of us spotted any houses when we

were brought out here." Morty's voice had gotten softer but remained steady. "She's storing us down here like canned goods in the winter."

"But why?" Cassidy's question had come out as more of a little girl's wail than a grown woman's query, but she couldn't bring herself to care. And nobody had an answer.

The noise of scuffling echoed from the ceiling corner above the stairs, and Cassidy turned her head that way along with the others. Across from her, Morty snorted. "I guess you can ask her yourself. Sounds like she's coming back. But I wouldn't count on any clear answers. That woman has lost her damn mind."

19

Standing at the gaping entrance of the storm cellar, I remained as frozen and still as a statue. The decrepit stairs before me might as well have been a hundred flights down, the way I felt. Sure, I knew I needed to take those poor folks more water. I knew I needed to think about getting them some food probably too. But how?

Not just logistically, but *how*? Facing them seemed beyond me. Looking them in the eye, knowing I'd left them alone in the cold. They'd judge me and stare at me with hate in their hearts. As I moved forward, their hate would haunt me.

"You comin' down or what?"

That first old man's voice echoed up into the snowy wonderland around me, proving I'd not imagined the whole escapade. He was down there along with three others, and all I was doing was letting in cold and prolonging things past… past whatever this moment was. I swallowed down an answer and picked up the supplies I'd set down to open up the locked root cellar.

Time to face the music. At least briefly.

Down the stairs, one step at a time. I could do this because I had to.

Mom's words echoed in my mind, spurring on my steps. *"Always a scared one, aren't you? Always wanting to shirk your duties? Stop being such a frightened brat, Ruthie, or I'll give you a reason to cower!"*

A step groaned beneath my weight, and something skittered off in one corner, but I kept moving. Kept breathing. I could do this.

"I brought you some water and more blankets." I gazed around at my four captives, three of whom were awake and glaring back. Cassidy looked terrified, and her daddy slept beside her. The other two just looked pissed. I steeled myself. "Now, y'all don't fight me. I'm here with water and blankets, okay? You fight, I'll just go right back up those stairs and you'll maybe die of exposure."

I actually sound like I mean it. Good for me.

Morty Williams spat into the corner of the room by way of answer.

I took a deep breath. The old man was all piss and vinegar, but he wasn't dumb. I narrowed my gaze on him. "I'm coming to you first, old man. You fight, I'll shoot your daughter."

Cassidy whimpered behind me, but I kept my gaze on old Mr. Williams. I remembered he'd been in the Army before taking over his daddy's diner, and I wouldn't put a fight past him.

His stare remained so fixated that I thought he might recognize me. The girl I'd been way back before I'd escaped this crap county. The girl with raggedy braids done up by her dad, who never quite knew what to say or where to look.

But finally, he nodded, and I crouched at his side, holding the water bottle to his lips. He sucked down about half of it.

Then I wrapped a fresh blanket around his shoulders. The man didn't thank me, but I didn't expect him to.

You're imagining things. Ten years ago, you were a hundred pounds heavier with glasses and brown hair. As mousy as your mom wanted you to be, Ruth. Not the woman you are now.

I went through the same process for his daughter, worrying about her especially. She was too thin to be down here in this cold, no extra flesh to protect her. Maybe I oughta try to get them a third space heater down here, after all.

Especially because that second one seemed to be kaput.

One more thing to do. By now, the hardware stores I'd been to would know my face and name. I'd chosen ones far away from here, but that meant going to bigger cities, where the stores all had cameras.

Somebody saw me. They had to.

"You're so damn useless. Couldn't get anything right if you tried."

When I moved across the space to Cassidy Freese, I did my best not to look at her knee. I'd meant to shoot her in the thigh rather than explode a major joint.

"You're so damn stupid. You're going to have to kill them. There's no other way."

Mom's voice just wouldn't let up.

Swallowing acid in my throat, I shut the voice down and pushed the water bottle toward Cassidy's mouth. She sipped at it some but didn't take down as much as Mr. Williams. I guessed that was fine since she hadn't had time to become dehydrated. From my pocket, I pulled out a couple of pain relievers and shoved them between her lips, then brought up the water bottle again.

Her brow furrowed, but she drank them down. The least I could do was take away this girl's pain. For now anyway. I'd betrayed her trust horribly. Taking her captive during a snowstorm after she'd invited me into her and her daddy's home to keep me safe from the elements. Such a kind and selfless thing to do for a stranger.

And such a stupid one too.

Cassidy Freese did not deserve a happy life with her father and the little diner of her dreams. Not if me and Dad hadn't been allowed to have ours. But I didn't have to torture her before I introduced her to real tragedy. Because that had to be what was coming, even if I was having a hard time admitting it to myself.

When the girl had the pills down, I shook her dad's shoulder. He jarred awake—eyes wide—downed some water, and wheezed back against the wall, appraising me as I settled blankets tighter around him and his daughter.

"What do you want with us?" Cassidy's whimper bled into muffled tears. The sound tempted me to wipe them away with the blanket, but that wouldn't do her any good. I knew from experience that tears could be endless, and this little girl's sadness wouldn't be no different from mine.

In the center of the room, I turned in a circle to watch the huddled masses of flesh and tried to reckon with my way forward. I didn't have a plan yet. Not beyond apologies anyway. "I'm sorry for the conditions."

The wind howled from above the storm cellar, as if to punctuate my words, and I fought not to flinch even as Morty Williams scoffed at me from under his blanket. "That girl's got a bullet in her leg, and we're near freezing to death. You think your apologies mean much to us?"

"You're useless."

I swallowed down a retort. Mom wasn't talking to me. Not anymore.

But the man wasn't wrong. "Sir, everyone...if I can find a nicer place to keep you until...well, if I can find a nicer place, I will. This'll have to work for now."

Laura scowled. "Until *what?*"

I don't know, dammit.

I licked my chapped lips, wincing at the sting, but I didn't answer the question.

But what came next?

Before this week, I hadn't known I was capable of blowing businesses to kingdom come, let alone kidnapping, but I'd done it. Twice.

I'm not a killer, though. I'm definitely not a killer. That's why I didn't leave these folks to burn in their restaurants.

I saved them.

Watching Morty eye me, I sat cross-legged in the middle of the room, resting my behind on the quilted bag I'd carried supplies down in. I drank down the remaining water and thought about my own parents. What if we'd been in this position?

Dad would've been doing what Howie was doing, sleeping or being complacent. Not fighting back. Not struggling. Just surviving.

My gut clenched at the idea of how he'd bent over to accommodate Mom's whims and ignore her violence. Picturing his old gun, now safe in my camper, I wondered why he never used it on her. His excuse—love—was too pathetic to stomach. Maybe he thought it was easier to roll over for her, after all, or didn't mind the abuse. Unlike me. Perhaps Howie and he could've been cousins once upon a time.

Mom, though? Hell, Mom might've killed me before taking any of my water, or died of dehydration, stubborn as she was.

"If you were on fire, I wouldn't spit on you to put you out, Ruthie."

That was a big no, more than likely. She'd never have been caught off guard in her home. Never have allowed a stranger to intrude on her "happy" home where she made life hell for her daughter and husband.

I wondered if she'd be proud of me now. For torturing these people.

The thought sent a cold slice of dread through my blood. My mom had had no reason at all for her violence. No reason for inflicting pain on others. She'd just been a sadist.

But I had reason. I had *every reason* after what Mom had done to me and Dad. Hurting us, embarrassing us, rubbing her control in our faces over and over again. She'd not allowed us an ounce of happiness, and by the time she was gone, we had so little time left.

So little time to be happy.

These people didn't deserve the time they'd already had. They deserved to know tragedy, just like I had.

I glanced over at Cassidy and her father. The desperate look on the girl's face made me want to laugh and puke at the same time. Bile rose up my throat, and I sprang to my feet and stumbled back toward the stairs.

That was when my breakfast and my lunch came up and painted the wall.

Behind me, Morty cursed, and his daughter started crying. Still, I crouched, heaving in the corner. When my gut stopped clenching, I willed myself to walk back over to the people who were now my responsibility, for better or worse. It was past time to gag 'em again. That would keep them from sharing their love, whatever remained of their happiness, for another minute.

These people didn't know torture. My mom, though…she had. And as a result, me and my dad had suffered.

Like they would. Soon.

Cassidy started praying out loud. I blocked her out as I tugged kitty litter off a shelf and sprinkled it over my mess, soaking up the stink and the liquid. The people behind me wouldn't thank me for it, but I had no desire to be reminded of my weakness for any longer than necessary.

Besides, I had other worries. And a future to plan.

Because that was the crux of things. Destroying happiness was one thing, and I'd mostly already done that, but what now? What was I supposed to do with four adult hostages? *Four?* And what madness had made me bring them here, of all places?

If anyone found out what I'd done, I'd spend the rest of my life in prison. Talk about a list of crimes I'd racked up. Bombing. Breaking and entering. Kidnapping times four. Assault. I'd shot Cassidy in the damn leg, for crying out loud.

I was screwed. And I couldn't sit in a prison cell all day every day. I couldn't even bring myself to stay in one town. My photography called for me to travel, to see beauty in the world. I deserved that...travel and a bit of peace for myself.

Stuck in a cell, I'd go mad.

All I'd do would be to think back to the few good years me and Dad had after Mom died. And I'd spent ten years trying to forget those. I wouldn't let them back in now. That slice of happiness was dead for me, just like it would soon be fully dead and buried for these folks.

I shoved the remaining cat litter back onto the storage shelf, frowning as I turned back to Cassidy, the kidnappee who I felt most guilty for taking, after the way she'd treated me.

"I have to kill you."

The girl's lips began to tremble.

I crouched in front of her, willing both myself and her to accept the fact. It was simple, after all. "I have to kill you."

"No! No, Anne, you don't. You absolutely don't!" Cassidy babbled as Morty cursed behind me and his daughter began to sob louder, but I forced myself to listen to Cassidy, and do her that small favor after everything else. "You can just let us go and disappear. You haven't done anything unforgivable yet. Everyone down here is breathing. We're fine. If you can just get me some bandages and maybe some antibiotic cream? My knee..."

The poor thing held in a sob, and I could tell she was hurting something awful.

What have I done? I'm such a fucking idiot.

I shoved myself to my feet and turned away from her, my gut churning again. The twentysomething sounded like a child, the way she was weeping. I couldn't kill a child.

My eyes practically blurred with the weight of the situation as I climbed back out of the cellar, slamming the heavy door shut behind me, and making sure to lock it even though I knew nobody else would come out here but me. Cassidy's wails echoed up through the door, and I sat down hard on the stairs.

Tears froze to my cheeks, and in the howling of the wind, I imagined I could hear my mother laughing at me. Daring me to do what I couldn't do as the tears came harder and faster with nobody to save me.

Just like always.

20

Emma had already raised her finger, pointing at the speedometer, hoping to urge Leo to pick up the pace, when her phone rang. Their SSA's image popped up, and she lowered the volume on the radio.

"Hey, Jacinda. You have me and Leo here."

"On your way to Dellington?"

Leo slowed the vehicle further still. "Seeing if we can pick up on what might be our next target. Or our unsub. If they stay in this area and stick to the pattern, we figure some general investigation could pay off since we know which direction they headed."

"Makes sense." Paper rustled on Jacinda's end of the conversation. "While you're there, I want you to question a man named Frankie Munn, specifically. He owns a Dellington lumberyard that burned down two years ago."

Emma met Leo's gaze and lifted an eyebrow. "He have some suspects in mind, or…?"

"The opposite. Sheriff Gruntle brought me Munn's name. He was under serious suspicion of arson, allegedly looking for the insurance money he'd get as a result. The fire was declared an accident caused by...get this...faulty gas pipes, but he's not clear of the stink in anybody's view. His court case was suspect as hell, in part because the judge was an old buddy of Frankie's father."

Leo whistled. "Talk about a lack of impartiality."

"Bingo." Jacinda muttered something on her end before continuing. "We don't have anything connecting him to the victims, but he's held a grudge against the Randall County D.A.'s office for 'hauling his ass into a courtroom.' Gruntle's words. Munn maintains he was wrongly accused and is pissed because the county won't reimburse him the lawyer fees, even after his case was dismissed."

"His connection with fire and gas lines is enough for me." Emma considered how much bad blood it would take to measure one's revenge via violence directed at random strangers. "And Gruntle thinks this guy would take his hard feelings out on...random mom-and-pop diners? In his own community?"

"Munn has a mean temper and is incapable of letting a grudge go." Jacinda sighed. "I understand the skepticism, Emma, but lacking a clear list of suspects, bad blood within the community is worth a peek."

Leo glanced at Emma, and she fought down her inner cynic to offer him a nod. Jacinda was right about them lacking any real suspects. Looking into the local sourpuss couldn't hurt, especially if he'd already been in the sheriff's line of sight when it came to a gas fire.

As they neared Dellington proper, Leo slowed the vehicle even further. "I can check Frankie out while Emma canvasses the main street storefronts, assuming anybody's open for business after that storm. Unless you think we need to stick together on this one?"

"Just keep me updated," Jacinda said.

The SSA signed off, and Leo pulled to a stop in front of a

closed antique shop. "Meet back here in thirty, maybe forty-five minutes?"

"Don't go getting kidnapped, Ambrose," Emma grinned at him, unbuckling her belt, "but if you do—"

"You'll be my white knight." He swung up a quick salute as Emma stepped out of the SUV. Wet snow embraced her boots from where a plow had shot it up onto the sidewalk and made it three times deeper than necessary. *Lovely.*

Once she slammed the door, Leo pulled away from the curb and left her to examine what amounted to Dellington's primary thoroughfare.

It could have been a carbon copy of either town she'd visited so far. Dellington boasted the same series of small businesses as Eklund and Phillipsie, minus the bombed-out ruins of local diners. Even with the streets plowed, however, it seemed most store owners had chosen to stay home and warm rather than open shop to the few customers who might chance the weather.

Nevertheless, the storm hadn't stopped their unsub.

Emma moved to the central block of the street and gazed up and down the row, marking the few restaurants that stood out from the pack, among them a pizzeria with a cartoon image of a smiling chef hanging from a flagpole. No traditional diner to speak of, so that might be their best bet.

Heading in the direction of Leonardo's Pies, she pulled her gloves from her pockets, but her hands froze with the leather only halfway onto her fingers.

The Other encroached as if it were its own blizzardy weather system. The air grew thicker, foggier with atmosphere.

Glancing around, Emma spotted the interloper. Leaning against a low brick wall fronting the alley between Leonardo's and the boutique next door, the ghostly figure of an old woman stared at Emma with a sneer on her lips, one middle finger raised in a rude greeting.

Her dirty blue jeans and grease-stained blouse seemed to complement her disposition.

Am I ever going to make it another week without being threatened by a fucking ghost?

Emma gave only half an eye to the shuttered storefronts as she stalked past them toward the ghost. Better to rip the bandage off without delay since they were in private.

"Why the hell are you giving me the finger?"

The woman stepped forward to meet Emma. "You don't follow the rules. You're useless."

Emma made a conscious effort to loosen her body, willing herself to appear unbothered as she examined the woman anew.

The ghost's body offered no hint of identity, nor signs of what caused her death. But the set to her lips made it clear she'd been a predator in real life as well. No ghost conveyed that much malice without having been a living and breathing pain in the ass to begin with. Emma only had to think of Pastor Bud Darl's ghost, and what she knew to be true about the man, to confirm her suspicions.

Ms. Charming here could probably go ten rounds with the good pastor and it'd still be a draw.

"If you want me to back off," Emma stepped forward, coming within a few inches of the figure, "maybe you should just tell me who's behind the bombings in Randall County. Solve both our problems."

"Should burn you, and I wouldn't spit on you to put you out." The ghost spat invisible slobber, making Emma flinch, even though she was pretty sure the woman wasn't talking to her at this point. Her face had twisted into a malevolent rictus, and her empty white eyes aimed over Emma's shoulder.

Dread ran along Emma's spine, freezing her more effectively than the cold ever could. Her ghostly acquaintance wasn't done, though.

"You should leave. We don't want you here. I'd burn you down myself if I could." The woman uncrossed her arms and stepped back through the little brick wall she'd been leaning against.

Emma was left staring at the pizzeria sign, swaying in the winter breeze. The cartoon chef grinned at her in place of the ghost woman's glare, and still Emma remained frozen on the sidewalk.

She tugged her gloves on and stuffed her hands back into her coat pockets for added warmth. The chill found its way into every crease and under every hem.

Was that ghost related to her case? It couldn't have been a victim because neither crime scene had any human remains present. But all the talk of burning put Emma on alert.

This case was all about diners, and the ghost had just retreated into a pizza joint. Close, but not the same thing. Still…

Was this place their unsub's next target?

Emma pulled out her phone, groaned that her gloves wouldn't let her text, pulled them off with her teeth, and typed out the business name, which quickly returned a page of hits. Top of the list was the Leonardo's website with *About Us* and *Our History* links nested underneath.

Sure enough, the pizzeria had once been a diner. R&A's Grill, to be specific. Specializing in plating the biggest and best burgers in West Virginia if you took their slogan to heart. The bomber had targeted existing diners so far, so Leonardo's might escape notice.

Or maybe we'll have to advise Sheriff Gruntle to send a patrol around on the regular.

Emma tapped out a quick text to Jacinda, suggesting just that. The SSA called a second later.

"You think Leonardo's could be a target?"

"I don't know, Jacinda." Emma held her gloves in her cold, bare fingers now. "It was a diner, so it could be our unsub would aim this way. That would assume the bomber knows about Leonardo's history."

"So we'd be looking for local connections, which we're already doing. But this gives us more reason to look close to home. You're alone, right? Our Leonardo is off talking to Frankie Munn?"

Emma laughed. "Yeah, Leo the L-E-O is going to circle back for me in about thirty minutes. I was thinking I'd talk to the pizza shop owners if they're around. The place looks open, but the rest of the street is mostly dark storefronts."

"Okay. Don't take any risks."

When Jacinda ended the call, Emma pocketed her phone, thinking about what she'd say to whoever was inside the pizza shop. As she stepped through the door, the warm aroma of fresh pizza from the oven greeted her. But the dining room was empty, and only one employee seemed to be around.

A man walked back and forth behind the counter with a phone against his ear. He hadn't noticed Emma yet, and bits of his conversation filtered across the unoccupied booths and tables.

"Yeah, not a soul…I made one pie. Gonna close up."

He ended the call and startled when he spied Emma by the door.

"Didn't see you come in. Sorry, no slices left, but if you want a pie, I got an extra here. I was gonna take it home, but you can have it. Fifty percent off if you pay cash."

Emma smiled and approached the counter, lifting her ID

and introducing herself. "We're investigating the bombings in Eklund and Phillipsie."

The man's mouth dropped open and closed again. "I've been here since nine in the morning. I can prove it."

"You're not under suspicion, sir. But since you did bring it up, can you account for your whereabouts on the night of February the fourth and again on the seventh?"

He nodded so fast she thought his neck might snap. "We got snowed in." He regained some composure. "That was last night. On the fourth, it was movie night at home. I fell asleep before the movie ended. Woke up shivering on the couch."

Emma nodded along and set her business card on the counter. "That sounds reasonable. And thank you for the information. Have you seen an older model station wagon driving around the area?"

He shook his head. "Can't say I have."

"How about anyone suspicious around town or coming in? Maybe somebody showing extra interest in the building, beyond what you'd expect from a customer."

"Nobody like that. Not at all today, except for one lunch customer. A trucker who was driving through on his way out to D.C. The storm closed his usual route, so he took a detour and missed his breakfast. We make a mean breakfast pizza, if you haven't tried one before."

Emma hadn't and wasn't sure she wanted to. Maybe she'd convince Leo to try it first and test the waters.

She pushed her business card forward. "Sheriff Gruntle will be sending a patrol around, just in case. We don't think you're at risk, but—"

"Hey, I get it. Thank you, and tell Sheriff Grunty thanks from me too."

I'd love to, but I don't think he'd like it if I tried that with his name.

"I'll do that, Mister...?"

"Curt Simmons. My wife, Janet, and I run the place. Our kids, Izzy and Jake, help out after school and on weekends."

"Thank you, Mr. Simmons. And please call if you notice anything."

He said he would and tried again to sell Emma on the idea of a breakfast pizza, which she had to admit began to sound better the more she thought about it.

Food can wait. The unsub is still out there.

"Curt, can you tell me if anybody else is open today, downtown or nearby?"

"I think I saw lights over at Rosin's Auto when I came in this morning. They're on the corner, next block over. Might be George is there, but it's probably his boy, Matthew. George's our local plow man. Keeping the streets clear takes up most of his day after a storm like we just had."

Emma thanked him again and left, pulling her gloves on as she made her way down the street, toward Rosin's Auto.

She finally stumbled on a blinking *Open* sign when she reached the garage at the end of the block. It sat back from the sidewalk, behind a narrow parking area. She waved down a young man with a youthful cast to his eyes. He could have been twenty-one but would probably get carded well into his thirties.

"Any business today?"

"Not much, ma'am. Were you needin' service of some kind? My dad's out on the plow, but I can handle an oil change or tires."

Hearing the young man speak, Emma adjusted his age down a year or two and tried for her most charming smile. She flashed her badge, appreciating that he seemed no more inclined to spit on her than he was to be cowed by her federal identification. Neutrality in reaction was rare, but nice. "I'm Special Agent Emma Last." She stuck out a hand and he returned the gesture, giving her a firm shake.

"Matthew Rosin, ma'am. Pleasure to meet you."

"Matthew, my team's looking into the attacks on the diners in the nearby towns. I'm guessing you've heard about them?"

He nodded, frowning. "Hard not to, ma'am. Small towns in these parts are like siblings. You want enough distance to make a visit necessary if you want to see 'em, but you want to know they're safe too."

Emma shook off the brief twinge of jealousy at the mention of siblings and gestured to the pizzeria. "Looks like Leonardo's is the closest thing to a diner in Dellington. Anything you can tell me about it?"

Matthew's face pinched in thought. "Not much. Pizza's decent. Izzy's pretty, and her dad hasn't threatened to shoot me yet. No offense, ma'am." The guy blushed, taking another two years off the age estimate Emma had guessed earlier.

He's maybe seventeen if he's a day. Probably hoping to take Izzy Simmons to prom.

"Know anything about Leonardo's history? It used to be a diner, right?"

"Oh yeah. That place sold when I was in grade school...I think? I don't know. I was, like, six or seven maybe."

"No idea why it sold?"

Matthew shrugged, and Emma read the gesture as honest. "Coulda been anything. My dad might know, but he likes to keep his head down when it comes to gossip, so I doubt it."

"Small towns and siblings, am I right?"

He smiled and nodded. "Yeah, I guess."

"Can I ask if you've seen an older model station wagon in the area? Maybe somebody came in for new tires before the weather kicked up?"

He slid his lips to the side as he shook his head. "Sorry, nobody but an out-of-state truck driver has been through for tires in over a week, and that was before the last big blizzard we had, so late January. I could look up the date for you in our records."

"No need, but thank you." Emma passed over her card before closing out the pleasantries and heading back into the street, colder than before and with little to show for the interview. She should've known the kid would be too young to remember a grill that had closed down a decade before.

Across the street, she strode down the other side of the block in hopes of finding another living face—preferably an older one—but ended up huddling at a covered bus stop. She'd just have to bide her time until Leo came rumbling into view with the Expedition.

Maybe she'd get lucky, and Curt Simmons would drive by with that breakfast pizza he'd offered. At least then she'd have something to show for all the time spent in the cold.

21

Following Frankie Munn through the maze of lumber and back toward his store couldn't have been easier. Not if the man had been wearing a spotlight, leading a pack of wild dogs, and blasting an air horn the whole way. The man wasn't one to be ignored.

"You ever build?" Munn shot a look over his shoulder and couldn't have made his disdain more obvious if he'd rolled his eyes. "Not with those smooth hands o' yours, I guess, huh? Well, you wanna learn, I got some of the best lumber here."

And on. And on. And on he goes. Where he'll stop...nobody knows?

Leo didn't anyway. Ever since he'd found the man in the recesses of the lumberyard, Munn had made a show of leading Leo among the mountains of wood as if he were the pied piper, talking fast about his wares and how much he meant to the community, how he only offered the best product, and how very respected he was.

"We've been the cornerstone of this whole region for decades. Me and my dad before me and his dad before him.

No matter what you've heard, this whole area'd be dead'n gone without us. And my wood's the best in this whole part of the country, I guarantee it."

Of course, any man who felt the need to say all that didn't likely have a breath of honesty left in his lungs. Leo kept mum on that understanding, however.

In the thick air of the store, Munn crossed his beefy arms over his chest and leaned back against the counter with a self-satisfied smirk. "You heard me, Agent Ambrose. You've seen my business and how much pride I *and my community* have in these here premises. I'm more than willing to speak with you, but I ask you this fair and square. Are you really here to make more claims about me burning this business down? Because I've proved in court that no such thing was true. The federal government...your boss...should know that."

Leo rested an elbow on a stack of heavy-duty hardware. Munn's bull-seeing-red approach might've been meant as charisma, but the brashness of it belied any hint of truth. "You've done a great job of rebuilding, I'll give you that."

"And I'm proud of it. That gas leak about tore my life a new one, plain as day. Now, that all you came for? Give me a pat on the back and make sure I'm minding my p's and q's? Or..." the man squinted, planting himself against his counter and glaring, daring Leo to make a real accusation, "there something more you came busting up my afternoon for?"

So much for diplomacy.

"Mr. Munn, I told you. I'm here about the explosions—"

"I didn't do a damn thing—"

"*And*," Leo spoke over him, straightening to his full height, "while I appreciate the tour and the point that you're an upstanding businessman, I'd appreciate it if you tell me where you were in the early morning hours of Sunday, February sixth. *That's* what I'm here for."

Munn's tongue snaked out from beneath his mustache and rubbed at a sore on his lip, but he didn't blink. "You've got a lot of nerve."

Forcing a smile, Leo reminded himself what his yaya had always said about attracting flies with honey. "Sir—"

"Don't 'sir' me, you big-city asshole. You're in my store here, and I can see right through you. Busting in here and asking questions like you own the place."

Leo hadn't exactly busted in anywhere, but be that as it may, this man was beyond listening. And whether they were both grumpy from the cold or not, he did have a job to do.

"That's what the government pays me for, I guess." He tried for a smile, wondering if he'd be relearning his boxing stance in another minute or two.

"Now I just get shit on for fun by the big, bad man? That it?"

A sigh escaped Leo before he could catch it. "No, sir, that's not it. I'm doing you the favor of asking for an alibi here rather than taking you in for questioning, but if you want to know our thinking, I don't mind telling you. It's more that perhaps you were enacting some kind of revenge. On your community, post-acquittal of your case. Which is why I'll need an alibi for the early morning hours of today, as well."

Not that Leo actually believed this man was their unsub. That would've been convenient, sure, but Frankie Munn was all bluster and direct attack, and if he'd have sought out revenge, Leo would wager that the acts would have been far more pointed. More focused.

Not community-oriented.

Because whatever Munn might say, he was out for himself and didn't know the meaning of the word *community*.

Munn's face had gone scarlet while Leo waited, but he finally lifted his lip and sneered. "You want an alibi, fine. I was at home making sweet love to my wife both nights. *All night long.* And she'll tell you the same."

Leo bit down a laugh, which would likely have led to a fist in the solar plexus. The man appeared to be the sort who ate fast food with a few tumblers of whiskey every night of the week, which meant such an alibi suggested he had either a basement full of blue pills or a dime store novelist's imagination.

The man blustered and tightened his arms over his chest, as if daring Leo to contradict him, wanting to be challenged, and while the narrowing of his eyes didn't suggest any truth to the story, Leo suspected the man had indeed been home all night, both nights. Any man who felt this confident in his alibi and defended said alibi this vocally in the presence of law enforcement was either a dolt of epic proportions or a man who needed no excuses.

And Munn might've been a jackass, but he was also a savvy businessman who'd built up his own business twice over.

"Calm down, Mr. Munn, I'm just following procedure." Leo gave the man a minute to follow the turn in the conversation, then pulled out his business card, preparing to hand it over. "Next question, shall we? I have to ask, do you know of anyone in the area who might have a reason to set fire to Randall County businesses, now that we've established that you're a hundred percent sure you yourself are innocent?"

The man's tongue came out again, worrying the lip deeper until Leo thought the sore might actually open up. Maybe that was the man's point, drip-drop blood from a self-inflicted wound and claim abuse.

Probably could have eased off on the passive-aggressive charm there, Leo.

"Sir—"

"You know what? If I'm gonna get blamed for it, maybe I

just will burn the whole damn county down. See what my neighbors and the courts say then. The fuck you say about that, agent boy? You gonna stop me?"

Leo straightened up and allowed his hand to inch toward his gun, a pit of annoyance making the rounds in his stomach. "You should watch your words, Mr. Munn."

"And you should watch your back. Now get out."

For half a second, Leo thought about pressing the matter. About pushing Munn to see if he might break open an inner store of animosity and really let some secrets fly. But realistically, there was no point, not if the man was innocent of these bombings, which Leo fully believed to be the case.

And without a search warrant? Rather than reply, he formed a fist near his gun and then released it, stuffing his fists into the pockets of his coat rather than taking the bait.

No, he'd let it be. Sure, he could flex his authority as well as his muscles if he wanted to arrest Freddie and charge him with threatening a federal agent, but the man was just blowing smoke, which meant that would be a waste of time.

I'd never forgive myself if another business got blown to bits while I was babysitting this idiot in a holding cell.

Of course, he was the federal agent here, mandated to solve crimes and protect the innocent. Munn might want him out of his store, but Leo wasn't going to walk away empty-handed.

"One last question. Have you seen a station wagon in the area? Dark in color."

A snarl curled Freddie's mouth. "No, I have not. Now about that fucking off you were about to do…" He flicked his fingers toward Leo, as if shooing a fly.

Keeping his eyes on Munn, Leo backed out of the business with a wave and a smile so caked with charm that a new shade of red was invented to cover the man's skin in anger.

He'd check the man out a bit deeper, but his insights into others were usually right.

And they better be this time too.

Giving this asshole momentary leniency only to regret it later would be an explosive mistake, literally and figuratively, and was just about enough to blow Leo's better angels off his shoulder.

22

The bumps of a frozen country road made ignoring Sloan not just easy but necessary. Mia's every ounce of attention went to guiding their Expedition around another curve, hugging the tree line in case some other foolhardy vehicle decided to chance the elements. Beside her, Sloan kept her pretty hazel eyes trained out the window.

Those same eyes that her brother had never been able to stop talking about and reminded Mia over and over again of the secret taking up space between them. That all this time, Mia had blamed Sloan for Ned's accident, and now Ned claimed that his death hadn't been an accident at all.

Between the unspoken elephant in the room named Ned Logan and the guilt that had been keeping Mia's heart swollen with grief and anxiety, she wished Sloan had never shown up for this case.

Why the heck did Jacinda pair us up today?

And she'd done it firmly too.

Mia resented the assignment. Dean Donahue had been charged with a felony thirteen years ago after setting fire to two fields owned by a longtime foe. He'd claimed the fires—

both—were accidental, and held firm on that claim even today, according to Sheriff Gruntle and despite the evidence of a gas can and lighter found at the scene of both fields with Donahue's fingerprints on them.

He'd been charged with fourth-degree arson and served a year in prison, during which time his wife left him. His daughter, Luelle, was now a twenty-nine-year-old high school dropout who'd followed in her father's footsteps, having lit up an abandoned church. The girl's excuse circled Mia's memory from reading the report earlier. *"Cause I was bored."*

Dean Donahue's daughter was slightly less successful than him, however. Her fire had burned itself out early, and she'd only been fined a penalty fee for recklessness and trespassing.

On paper, the Donahues didn't necessarily seem bright enough to use the materials Sloan was finding on the sites.

Maybe the SSA was just trying some sort of face-your-problems intervention by asking Mia and Sloan to work this interview together. Her supervisor hadn't shown an ounce of awareness regarding Mia's history with Sloan, but Jacinda was sharper than most, so her playing truce-maker wasn't out of the question.

Sloan pointed at a red mailbox peeking from the trees, just as Gruntle had described it, and Mia edged the SUV into the end of the driveway, thanking her stars it had been shoveled. From what Gruntle had said about the Donahues, this was the last place she and Sloan wanted to be stuck. Mia could only imagine what a couple of arson-happy country dwellers would offer up in the way of hosting efforts.

Better to ask their questions and get out of their suspects' views—assuming they had no cause to arrest them—and do it as fast as humanly possible.

Clearing her throat even as Mia threw the vehicle into

park, Sloan took her time zipping up her coat for the walk up the long driveway they had ahead of them. "I'm sorry you got stuck with me."

Well, shit.

Mia's tongue hit the roof of her mouth in search of syllables but found nothing. And before she could formulate the barest of responses, Sloan was already stepping out of the vehicle with her bag slung over her shoulder.

"Sloan, wait." The other woman halted, one leg out of the vehicle, peering over her shoulder. "I'm just…I didn't mean to make you feel that way. Ned's death is still close, you know?"

When Sloan's lips tightened, pressed together, Mia knew she'd said the wrong thing even before the other woman spoke.

"And you don't think it is for me too?" Sloan huffed hair away from her face. "Let's just get this case over with, all right? Then we can go back to handling our grief in our own way. Alone."

The door slammed behind her on that note, and she took off up the driveway without looking back.

Case first, Mia. Figure out the personal stuff later, since Sloan's giving you the out.

Burying the urge to settle things now—because why had Sloan felt the need to say anything anyway?—Mia huffed a sigh in the privacy of the abandoned Expedition. There was no choice but to get going, though, before Sloan decided to conduct the whole damn interview on her own. She shoved the door open to join her dead brother's ex-girlfriend, who'd already trekked halfway up the long drive toward the Donahues' home.

She'd better get her mind back on the case before they reached the front porch if they were going to make this visit worth anything at all, so she'd use the time in the cold to revisit the reasons they'd come all this way up the mountain. All the better to take her mind off the darkness of the woods lining the driveway, which could be hiding anything from ghosts to bears, for all she knew.

Get your mind back on the case, Mia Logan. Now.

Mia dug her hands into her pockets and followed Sloan, willing her brain to focus on facts and ignore her imagination.

Passing a surprisingly clean pickup at the front of the drive, Mia expanded her stride to catch up with her colleague, whose expensive boots must've had ice cleats strapped to them because she was already at the slate walkway.

"Ready to face our one pair of confirmed arsonists in the county?" Mia stepped up onto the porch, aiming for some lightness in her tone.

"You really think these two are smart enough to make bombs without blowing themselves up?" Sloan gave the house a pointed once-over.

With peeling, maroon paint, some shutters hanging free while others rested on the ground, and an old, rusted swing set creaking in the wind on the edge of the yard, the place was a disaster. If these two individuals were true arsonists, they should've started with their own property and done the county a favor.

Mia grinned her response even as she raised one fist to knock on the old wooden door before them. "Dean and Luelle Donahue, please open up! We're part of an FBI task force investigating the attacks in town. Sheriff Gruntle gave us your names and address."

Just as Mia prepared to knock again, the door swung wide, revealing a bleached-blond Luelle caught in the act of blowing out a wide cloud of cigarette smoke in their direction.

Sloan coughed pointedly, but Mia steeled her lips in a smile. "Luelle Donahue, I'm Special Agent Mia Logan. This is my colleague, Special Agent Sloan Grant. We need a few minutes of your and your father's time."

The woman pulled her cigarette from her lips and reached out to tap ash onto her front porch, likely hoping the detritus would land on the agents' boots. The wind interfered, thankfully. "And why the fuck you want that? We ain't done nothin' wrong."

On that note, the man Mia presumed to be Luelle's father appeared behind her. Same narrow chin and dark-brown eyes, but a head taller and smelling of whiskey instead of smoke. "You heard her, agents. That useless sheriff's got no call to send y'all out here. He's just got his ball sack in a twist that I got more property 'n his family an' that he couldn't never land a date with my Luelle."

With a hiss, Luelle twirled her cigarette like a cartoon diva. "Not in his dreams." She leaned forward and pursed her lips in Sloan's direction next, causing the other woman to stiffen. "But maybe in yours. Didn't know FBI agents came in strawberry blond."

You've gotta be kidding me.

Sloan coughed what might have been a laugh or a curse, but Mia focused over the daughter's shoulder at their main target for the interview. This already hostile encounter had a short shelf life, so they'd better get to it. "Mr. Donahue, we do have cause to be here, I assure you. We've read your record...and your daughter's...and we're here investigating two acts of explosive destruction in Randall County that took place early Sunday morning and, more recently, early this morning."

Her fellow agent gestured in the direction of a blaring commercial for heating coolant, which betrayed an abandoned television or radio. "I'm sure you heard about the events on the news."

As if anyone within a state's distance hasn't heard about them more than once.

Sloan had spoken up a touch too diplomatically for Mia's taste, given the already caustic air around them, but Mia nodded beside her. "We're hoping you could help us out with any information you might have, given your past history."

Dean Donahue stepped up beside his daughter, whose mouth was agape, even though the cigarette somehow remained tucked in the corner of her pink lips.

"You Feds have a lotta nerve. Making excuses when you're just out here...on my damn private property...fishing for alibis."

Luelle took a half step forward, but her dad's arm shot out and barred her from coming closer to the agents, one meaty hand gripping the doorframe even as Mia tensed for whatever might be coming.

"Maybe you should do some more fucking research before knocking on doors!" The man nudged his daughter backward, shifting so that he took up her view of the agents. "Save the taxpayers some gas money."

Sloan inched closer to Mia, preparing for the same fight she herself had begun to suspect might be coming. "Or you could give us what we came for and save us all some time."

Luelle whirled away from the door and stomped back toward the television.

But Dean Donahue's glare only burned darker. "Me and Lu got back about a half hour ago from my mom's funeral. A funeral which was held in Kentucky. We've been gone four days, so yeah, if that's what you're looking for, we got alibis up the wazoo. For both days. Receipts, too, what with those hotels an' grease spots charging an arm and leg for a measly sandwich. All that good enough for the federal government?

Or you want my fucking next born served up on a platter next to my mom's coffin?"

Mia's gut had been sinking with each word spoken. Her reaction was less in response to the man's words and more how he said it. Somewhere beneath the bluster, she heard the pain.

Probably because Sloan stood beside her, she remembered her own anger during Ned's funeral. The casket had been closed. Sloan hung around the back, not up front with the family. At the time, it'd felt insulting to Mia. Sloan could've been part of the family, but she'd rejected Ned.

She shook herself, refusing to examine the memory now that she possessed new information.

Focusing instead on the man in front of her, she felt a stirring of sympathy. Even felons had a right to grieve in peace. No wonder the man in front of them was pissed. Damn Gruntle for not doing some research before sending them out here. "Mr. Donahue, I'm sorry for—"

"For what? Assuming one mistake always means another?" The man spit off to the side of Mia's boots, as if to prove he could be slightly more courteous than his daughter. Sudden and raging, tears sprang from his eyes and reddened his face as they fell, making his words come like bullets shot out from bursts of emotion. "And for your information, no, we ain't heard about any explosions. Serves the county right, but like I said, we're fucking grieving, so unless you have a search warrant, you can go to hell, the both of ya."

"I'm sorry, Mr. Donahue." Sloan's voice was choked, mirroring their interviewee's emotion as it was broadcast out into the bright afternoon light. The man couldn't hide it any more than they could ignore it, and Mia's throat went tight with the awareness of how present the sentiment had become.

Grief had been hanging in the air between her and Sloan

ever since they'd seen each other again, after all, so maybe it was only natural that the tension should blow up in their faces like this.

The door slammed.

Rather than broach the silence, Mia led the way back down the rickety stairs of the porch, down the walkway, and into the snowy front yard. The odor of cigarette smoke hung about her coat and hair but didn't feel nearly as heavy as the weight of emotion slung between her and Sloan. Ned might as well have been lurching along between them, dead or otherwise.

No, she and Sloan might've been avoiding it for a day and a half, but coming out here, they'd just about tripped head over heels into the very emotion they'd worked to avoid discussing.

And Mia couldn't even find the words or the way to tell Sloan that everything she'd thought, everything she'd blamed her for, looked to be a lie.

23

Stationed at the conference table in the police station, Emma cringed at the greasy pizza slice a sheriff's deputy offered her. For once, their team had a truly exceptional place to eat dinner while on the road, given their B and B's track record with the meals they'd been served so far.

No chance was she spoiling her appetite with some chain pizza's to-go pies—though something told her she was going to end up smelling like she'd eaten one anyway.

After what seemed like forever, Jacinda wrapped up the call with D.C. she'd been stuck on, and she collapsed back at the front of their briefing table with a grateful wave at Vance, who'd taken her place at the whiteboard. And Emma had filled everyone in on the day's findings, including her discovery of the pizzeria, which had once been a diner and which was not run by a father-daughter duo.

Yet…

"About the pizzeria I visited today, one more note." Emma paused even though she'd already brought all eyes back to her. Was she putting too much emphasis on the place, just because of the ghost? "It's a family-run business, even though it's not a diner. Until we're sure that a whole family wouldn't attract the unsub's attention—"

"We can't rule it out." Denae nodded, marking something on her iPad. "But don't forget we're in West Virginia's small-town central."

Mia twirled a pen as if to gesture for her to go on.

Sighing, Denae tucked a curl of hair behind her ear as she looked around the table. "Isn't every business in these parts family-run?"

For a moment, everyone went silent, then Emma sensed their group wilting almost as one.

Because Denae was right. In this corner of the world, big-box stores barely existed, and in this economy, that realistically meant that most businesses—diners and restaurants included—were run by families.

But if they didn't have any other father-daughter duos as their unsub's chosen targets, they had very little indeed.

"Time for pressing forward with questions yet?" Leo gazed around the table, and nobody disagreed with him. Denae's last point had brought in a curtain of silence, and now they were down to figuring out what came next. "Do we know anything about the bomb makeup yet? Anything definitive?"

Across from Emma, Sloan nodded. "Yes. Let's go to the evidence room. I have a table set up there."

They followed Sloan like a line of obedient ducklings. Inside the evidence room, Sloan had commandeered a white banquet table. Neatly labeled boxes held pieces of the two bombs. Emma had to admire Sloan's patience. The woman had been meticulous in her work. Tiny fragments were categorized, and that meant Sloan had spent hours hovering over this table with tweezers.

Sloan stood next to the table and started her impromptu briefing. "We just heard back from the lab. The brown powder isn't gunpowder." She held up a small plastic baggie of what looked like dirt to Emma. "It's deteriorated nitrate dust. It's a match for nitrate photography. The material is rare, generally used in film manufacturing before the fifties. I think our unsub is using it for the ignition source."

"Photography film?" Emma didn't quite follow.

"Nitrate film was used for movies and photography in the early half of the twentieth century. It's incredibly unstable. I think our unsub is placing the nitrate powder in light bulbs, near the filament." Sloan pointed to melted bits of glass in one of the boxes. "Then they're plugging the bulb into an outlet near the gas line in the diners. The filament gets hot, blows the nitrate, and creates a burst of flame that ignites the gas. *Kapow*."

Emma shook her head, needing Sloan to back up a step or two. "But where are they getting nitrate powder?"

"And how are they controlling the timing of the explosion?" Leo jumped in. "Wouldn't the nitrate just *kapow* as soon as the light bulb filament got hot enough?"

Mia leaned in. "Wait. How do you plug a light bulb into an outlet? Don't you need a socket?"

"Whoa, whoa, whoa. One question at a time." Sloan's eyes widened, and she held her hands up as if that could fend off the barrage of questions.

"Emma, I don't know where they'd get the powder. Maybe they or someone in their family had old negatives or rolls of film? It's not something you can buy anymore and hasn't been widely produced for over fifty years, so we have to assume our unsub has a store of it on hand. Being a film buff, or involved in archival work, might provide access to a supply of the material."

"So anyone working in Hollywood. Sounds like a long list of people we'd have little to no chance of talking with."

"It's unlikely a celebrity would have access to old film

reels. After a few fires destroyed tons of archived footage, the industry upgraded their storage mechanisms and has been digitizing as much as they can. That's something a film school intern would probably do."

Sloan turned to Leo. "As far as controlling the timing…I think they're using a wireless remote system." She lifted the melted plastic clump she'd tagged from Morty's diner. As she pointed at certain sections, Emma gained a picture of the device.

"It's just a wireless electrical outlet you plug into a regular wall outlet. Then you'd just hit 'on' on the remote. People use it so they can control living room lamps. It's in every major home center and hardware store across the U.S. And before anyone asks, I called Dale Fawns already. He doesn't stock the item, and he confirmed he hasn't had any unfamiliar customers in the past month. That doesn't rule out other nearby stores as a source for some of the materials used, but we should probably expand our search to include larger retailers in outlying cities as well."

Emma thought back to the footage of the second explosion. The station wagon had been dangerously close to the building before it went up. "How far of a remote radius would you have? Don't you have to be in the room?"

"I've been experimenting with a few different brands. There are at least three that'll still work at a thousand feet."

"But how do you plug a light bulb into a wall outlet? It's not like you can screw it in." Mia practically howled.

Emma took that question. "With a work light. It's just a portable frame for a light bulb, so you can use an extension cord and reach awkward places. Usually in garages or cellars."

"They have cages like this." Sloan lifted a warped bit of metal attached to a burnt electrical wire from one of the evidence boxes.

A small thrill rush through Emma. "So we're looking for someone who knows photography or chemistry or both, and might have worked in the film industry. Someone who uses work lights, maybe in a garage or cellar."

"Or maybe they just bought some work lights," Jacinda interrupted, nodding and encouraging Emma to continue.

"We can track manufacturers of work lights and the remote outlets."

"Already on that," Sloan chimed in, "and Dale does stock those. He sold two of them to a father and son who were building an addition to the family home last summer. Hasn't sold one since."

"And we're looking for someone who knows gas lines in diners."

Mia seemed to be following the same line of thought, taking it a step further. "Burning down the businesses was important to our unsub, even in the middle of a blizzard. Both explosions were in Randall County, indicating a local."

"Or a former local." Leo frowned at the evidence table, appearing deadly focused on watching their ideas take shape.

When silence held the table for a minute longer, Jacinda leaned forward and steepled her fingers in front of her, waiting for the rest of them to look her way. "Sheriff Gruntle is sending a state police officer to each of the seven towns within his jurisdiction. Law enforcement will be stationed on all the main streets of the boroughs to keep an eye on local diners as well as any traffic that moves through town overnight. That includes Emma's pizzeria. He's also putting an eye on Frankie Munn, since that encounter was far from reassuring."

Emma thought hard, looking for anything they might have missed, and finally realized Vance hadn't said anything about how he'd spent his day prior to the briefing. "What about you, Vance? You've been quiet."

Vance frowned. "The CCTV footage outside the Gold Moon doesn't show anyone exiting the diner. How do we know it wasn't someone on the inside who snuck out the back? Someone who could have just waited until the time was right to set things off." He drained the last of his coffee. "I get that these people don't want to accept one of their own could be doing this. But what if the bomber knows the families? Couldn't he just be working with them for the insurance scam? Maybe this Munn guy cooked up a plan to split the proceeds, and they're all hiding out at his place?"

Emma jumped on that. "It's a bad camera angle, but we can see the station wagon outside the Gold Moon, and we can see it leaving after the explosion. Our unsub was in the car."

Sighing, Jacinda leaned back in her chair again. "We've searched the entire county for any residents with a station wagon registered in their name, including the charming Mr. Munn, but not one has been found. In theory, that should make the vehicle easier to spot, but nobody's seen it, law enforcement or otherwise. And there's no more CCTV footage to view at this point. We'd have to spread the search out to the entire state of West Virginia for any more immediate leads on that vehicle, which we may well do."

Emma grimaced. "The vehicle could've been stolen, but I guess the original owner could give us some clues."

Leo ran his hands back through his hair, doing nothing to tame it. "Or where it was stolen from."

With another sigh, Jacinda shoved herself to her feet. A sure sign the day was ending. "I know we're all worried that another night means more victims, but at the very least, the downtowns in Randall County are being watched, and we all desperately need sleep after the early morning wake-up call we got today. We'll reconvene in the morning."

While the others shuffled to pack up, Emma stole a quick glance at Mia.

If only she could get past the ghosts. That was the other thing holding her at the conference table, wondering if she could steal her own private moment to talk ghosts with Mia. Every bone in her body ached for the chance to tell her about that hateful dead woman outside Leonardo's Pies, but there were just too many ears around.

Too many sets of eyes to judge her and think her crazy at worst, or sleep-deprived at best.

Maybe later tonight.

Denae let loose a nearly ear-shattering yawn, like her usual yawns, and Emma's giggle turned into her own yawn, if with a bit more dignity than her colleague's.

That settled things, then. Maybe she'd talk to Mia later tonight, or maybe she'd talk to her in the morning. Her bedroom, wolf-haunted or not, called louder than any ghost.

24

Though the lock came off easily, that was nothing compared to the weight of the cellar door. Whether I brushed the snow and ice from the metal or not, the thing was getting heavier every time I had to lift it. Every time I had to bend down, wrap my hand around the metal, and force myself to confront the mess I'd made of things.

The people I'd friggin' kidnapped.

For now, it was all I could do to keep them from freezing.

I'd thought about it, of course. Just leaving them in the root cellar to freeze over and go to sleep in the cold and eventually rot. But I couldn't quite make myself abandon them. Plus, seeing them so miserable took away some of the ache I'd built up after glimpsing their happiness.

And I had no idea what I was working up to do about any of it. For now, things were okay. I hadn't killed anyone or decided on anyone's death, and even if the weight of this door and what I was doing weighed on me, it wasn't pressing me down into nothing.

Not yet.

Things would be okay for me, somehow. I'd figure it all out just like I always had before, explosives or not.

Balancing the latest stack of blankets in my arms, I inched down the stairs and turned on the light. The smell of ammonia greeted me, worse than any gas station bathroom I'd ever visited. If it hadn't been so cold, I'd have brought a hose down and washed them all off.

That'd be another way to kill them off. Faster than a slow, cold-drawn sleep, and cleaner.

All four of my not-yet casualties stared at me, wide-eyed like beaten dogs left on their chains. Silent and accepting too. Like I used to be. When Mom would get her mind made up about something wrong I'd done and get ready to knock me sideways or grind me down into the carpet like a spider, I bet my eyes looked like that too.

Not much of a childhood had happened with that woman around. That awful, hateful woman. Dear old Mom.

But I was not like her. I. Was. Not.

Like these folks here, I'd always been left waiting for the worst to happen. Hell, wasn't that exactly what I was doing now?

Focusing on the task at hand, instead of my heart racing for a solution, I set the new stack of dry, warm blankets down and pulled water bottles from my backpack. I then began making my rounds. First, true to past visits, I ungagged everyone without a word and let them start stretching their lips and necks. Morty Williams looked bad—sunken into himself, his vim and vinegar had deserted him fast after just a day in the cellar—but the others seemed the same.

When it came to the water, Howie and Cassidy were first, accepting the hydration like the good little beaten girl I used to be. I was taking care of them, and I had to ignore how the two of them sat there silent, scared, and squinting up at me like I was the bogeyman. Which I guessed I was, fair or not.

That hurt more than anything.

What I wouldn't have given to tell them I wasn't a scary person, that there was no need to be frightened. That I was just making sure they got what they deserved. Nobody deserved so much happiness, after all. I was living proof of the fact.

"You're useless."

I tried to block out Mom's voice. But as the water dripped down from Howie's freezing lips, over his stubble, I knew it wasn't exactly true that I wasn't scary. I'd become scary. For them.

And I had kidnapped them. Bound them at the wrists and ankles. Cassidy had a bullet hole in her knee for fuck's sake. Tough as it was to remind myself of that fact, I knew it was necessary. And that wasn't all I'd done, was it?

Not to mention blowing up their businesses. Their homes.
Of course they're scared.
Of me.

I draped extra blankets around Howie and Cassidy Freese, tucking them back against the wall before I turned to Laura Williams and her father. The ones who seemed a little dangerous to me still, especially the way the daughter sat against the wall so ramrod straight. Like she was determined not to give in. If Howie and his daughter had been beaten into the ground, these two were defiant by comparison.

Laura, eyes unwavering, hadn't stopped glaring at me since I'd come down the stairs, and she stiffened when I brought the water bottle to her lips. As she drank, I could tell she was thinking about spitting the liquid back at me, but she swallowed it down with a shudder before she spoke, as I'd known she would.

The girl didn't know how to hold her tongue to save her

own life. Not like me. "We're sitting in our own piss on cold cement. You shot Cassidy in the knee. She needs a doctor. Blankets won't fix that."

"You're right." My lips were chapped, but I licked them anyway. A reflex, but it stung me awake again. Made me more aware of what had to happen. "I'm sorry."

At least they'd stopped calling my apologies stupid and pointless, but the urge rose in my throat to keep talking, anyway, to explain why I had to do what I was doing. I was sorry, truly. But I just didn't know how to make it better. Not the cellar, and not the situation as a whole. Not without doing what I knew deep down had to be done.

Beside Laura, her dad had his eyes closed, head rested back against the cement wall. And when I scanned back to the Freeses after covering the Williamses with yet more blankets, I couldn't see much more than pain in either of their gazes. Beaten-down dogs, indeed.

With Cassidy's leg, she was already as good as dead if I just left her be, but I couldn't even kill *her*, gone as she was. And how was I supposed to kill four people when I wasn't sure I could kill one?

Laura grunted behind me, and I knew she was fighting at her wrists again. She'd already made herself bloody with fight, the stupid bitch. And to no avail. I'd watched those YouTube videos on how to break from duct tape as well as the ones that taught me how to make the tape unbreakable by winding it in a figure eight.

My mom used to tape up my dolls and stuffed animals. Threatening me with the same. But she never did it right, so Dad and me could always set my dolls free without too much trouble. We had to do that a lot, the two of us together, when Mom wasn't watching. She was always quick to tape up another doll whenever she saw I'd got the others free.

But the crib—the prison—where Mom kept my dolls, it

was burned in my memories. I was trapped in a prison cell of my past. With nothing but misery for company.

"If you were on fire, I wouldn't spit on you to put you out."

My chest went frozen, as if my mom were here wrapping ropes around me, tightening on my sternum and holding me against my will, and I spun on Morty, a sudden determination not to be trapped filling me up all over again.

Despite Cassidy's bullet wound, Morty Williams was in the worst shape. All his insults had died on his lips by the time I'd come down here a second time with water and blankets. And his daughter wouldn't stop guilt-tripping me for it either. As if I'd intended for all this to happen.

Beneath the blankets, I could barely make out Morty Williams's chest rising and falling. And the way he looked at me with those sad old eyes of his…he might not be willing to give up the fight with his daughter right there beside him, but he'd thought about it.

I bet he's the oldest of these four too. Not long for the world either way.

Laura coughed a curse that would've made a sailor blush, and I narrowed my eyes at her. "Didn't you say you were a nurse? That's some language."

"Fuck you, lady. You and this cellar. You want to judge me?" She let out a deep laugh that, for just a moment, sounded an awful lot like my mom's.

Enough that I couldn't help taking a step backward.

"Ha! You're scared of me? You've really lost it, haven't you?"

Anger, hot and fresh, burned up my throat. "Not like you. You've lost *everything*. I made sure of it. How does that feel?" Leaning in, I stared at her and waited for her to flinch away, but she only narrowed her eyes.

The gall of her. No wonder she'd been the one to drive

me to do what I'd done. No wonder I'd seen her happiness and felt the need to destroy it.

This was her fault as much as mine. But I was stronger than her, and I'd find my way through all of this. I wasn't useless.

Fuck her.

I let that conclusion fuel the little firework in my chest that my own dad had always told me to remember. My hands were cold but warming with the memory of how he'd used to hold them, and how he'd used to lead me around and tell me I was strong, even when Mom had been lurking, waiting for me to slip up.

The gun in my pocket was my dad's. I didn't know why he'd never used it on Mom, but maybe things today would've been different if he had. Maybe...

It slipped out of my coat easily. Like I was meant to be holding it. Behind me, Cassidy let out a little whimper, but the high sound of her fear just focused me more on Morty. And the feel of the gun.

The heavy, cold metal of the gun I knew how to use. I'd used it before, hadn't I?

Oh, how I miss my dad.

I heard him in my head...

"You ever gotta use this on a burglar, you take a deep, deep breath. You take a deep breath, raise your arm, and then you don't think. You don't think at all. You just shoot."

Focused on my dad's words, I lifted the gun, sighting it back and forth between Laura and Morty. Laura still had that glare on her face, daring me to make her suffer. Beside her, her dad groaned, his eyes focused on me. Afraid. Just like I wanted them both to be. He moved in his bonds, though, signaling he knew what was coming.

He knew I had the strength, even if his idiot daughter needed to be taught the lesson.

The bang knocked me backward into the middle of the cellar, shaking an impact up my arm and echoing. The smell of gunpowder, sulfurous and caustic, burned at my nostrils. A scream ripped up out of my throat to echo the bullet, drowning out the screams of the people around me as if they were nothing. Their pain and screams were nothing, compared to mine.

Nothing.

I was deafened by the report of the gun, but the room vibrated with sound, with screams. And I couldn't stop yelling, unintelligible emotion driving itself up and out of my throat in waves.

But no matter how my chest began tightening, things got real as I watched the bloodstain spread across Morty's blanket and over his chest, ringing him in red that glowed wet and bright in the amber light in the cellar. It was on its way to mixing with the frozen piss on the floor.

Probably gonna thaw it out, and that won't be good.

I wanted to turn around and run.

Morty himself was acting the part of a goldfish, mouth gaping and closing and then gaping with his eyes wide and bloodshot. Seeing him struggle, I imagined a groan creaking from his throat, but he was the one person in the room not given over to screams. Either way, I heard nothing but the echo of the gunshot, nearly deaf to all of it.

A calm crept over Morty Williams, as if maybe I'd imagined everything, if not for the blood.

And above his bloody chest, his eyes looked like black holes in the dim light of the cellar, but they were focused only on me.

Beside him, his daughter wailed, "Daddy," and lurched in her bonds.

I'd just killed that girl's daddy.

"Oh my gosh." Falling down to my knees, I watched the

blood spread out toward the wall and start to soak into Laura's blanket too. "I'm sorry. I shouldn't have done that."

Sobs clamped onto my chest, and I rocked on my knees, embracing the cold floor beneath me. Thinking of Dad's gun, I stuffed it back into my pocket. The weapon had done this. Not me. Not just me.

"I'm sorry, I'm sorry, I'm sorry—"

"Daddy! Daddy, please. I need you!" Laura knocked her head against the wall behind her, trembling as she wailed. The whole cellar radiated with her horror and shock, but I could only stare. "Daddy, I need you! You can't die!"

A swallow of air stuck in my throat with my sobs. Laura kept screaming, and behind me, Cassidy cried, and Howie prayed. I ignored all of them.

There was so much blood. So, so much blood.

Who'd done such a terrible thing?

25

With her tears drying into a mask of shock, Cassidy sank back against the wall beside her father.

Anne's odd self-pity and apologies were the icing on this madhouse cake. The woman was kneeling in Morty Williams's blood, pressing her scarf into the poor man's chest as if to soak it all up and staunch the wound.

She'd never even moved the blanket, and Cassidy wondered whether pressure was actually being applied directly to the wound. Laura could scream all she wanted to —and was doing so—but their captor had lost hold of her senses.

"Take him to a hospital, you monster. Now! You're not helping." Laura's throat had gone hoarse, and her next words were unintelligible.

Blood dribbled from Morty's lips, barely visible in the room's low light as Anne seemed to bend all her strength into pressing the poor man into the wall, every ounce of her focused on his wounded chest.

The scene would've been comical were it not so horrendous.

Cassidy's father murmured to her to remain quiet, calm. He must've seen something in her building. To say what, she wasn't sure, but if they hoped to survive, taking advantage of this moment might be their one shot.

Across the room, Morty's eyes popped wider for a moment, then his body went limp against Anne's grip. Beside him, Laura's pleas ascended into a banshee's scream and then bled into heaving sobs that rocked her blankets off her.

"At least release my hands so I can hold him. While he dies. Please." Laura wobbled where she sat, and Cassidy guessed the woman already knew what they all did, that her father was already gone. *"Please."*

Anne settled back on her heels and stared at the man she'd killed, ignoring Laura.

"Oh, honey." Anne leaned forward, kneeling across from the man she'd just murdered with her head down and her voice lowered, apologetic. "I really want to. But I can't."

She sounds like she's crying. Actually crying. But she killed him!

Holy hell, she's lost her mind.

Anne—assuming that was her name—shook her head at Laura. And then she wiped tears from her own face, leaving a trail of blood along her cheek. "Laura, I can't do it. I can't. You'd try to get away if I freed your hands."

For a moment, Cassidy thought Laura would remain quiet, begging, but the raw emotion of grief had begun bleeding into disbelief.

"Of course I would!" Laura shrieked. "You've just killed my father! Who in their right mind wouldn't try to get away from a psychopath?"

Anne straightened where she sat, staring at Laura. One end of her scarf remained in her hands from where she'd tried to stem the flow of blood from Morty Williams. Blood dripped from fabric to floor, joining the spreading pool that had reached her knees and already seeped into Laura's blanket.

The murderous woman was...maybe in shock.

Cassidy's father shifted beside her, the barest shaking of his head drawing Cassidy's eye to him. "That poor girl. At least her father's no longer in pain."

"Anne's lost it, Dad. Completely."

"*Shhh.*" He nodded toward the scene at the other side of the cellar. "Now's not the time to talk, baby girl."

Baby girl. He still calls me "baby girl" like I'm three years old.
But you watch, Dad. We're getting out of this.

Laura screamed again, almost directly into Anne's face, and their captor finally jerked backward, landing on her ass in the middle of the cellar.

Then the woman pulled her knees to her chest and began rocking back and forth where she sat. "I shouldn't have done that. I shouldn't have done that."

Cassidy glanced at her dad, willing him to forgive her if what she was about to do went bad on them. "She's at her weakest."

For a moment, she wasn't sure her whisper had reached her father over their captor's wailing sobs, but finally he nodded, soft eyes meeting hers. He might not agree, but he wouldn't hold what happened against her.

Here goes nothing.

"Anne!" Cassidy called her name once, then again, but got no response. She called more loudly, and then she went for it. "Anne, I know you didn't want to shoot Mr. Williams."

Laura's sobs hit a crescendo, and then she buried her face in her own blanket. Maybe in denial, or maybe trying to give Cassidy room to reach Anne.

"Anne," Cassidy leaned forward, working to ignore the deep throbbing in her knee, "I spent time with you, remember? That whole snowy day? I know you have a kind heart."

A vision of her and her dad's diner exploding nearly caught her voice in her chest, but she pushed forward. She felt almost as crazy as the woman in front of her.

"You're a good person, really. Whatever's happening right now, I can help you through it, okay? If you let Laura and my dad go, I'll help you figure a way out of this."

Anne remained rocking in the middle of the room, showing no sign of having heard Cassidy.

"We have to figure out something soon, Anne." Cassidy took a breath, wondering if this was where things would go bad. "There's not a lot of time. It won't be long before they come."

Anne froze mid-rock, her arms tightening around her knees as she raised her tearstained cheeks to focus in on Cassidy. Her eyes practically glowed with terror even in the darkened cellar, betraying how frayed her nerves and emotions had become. "What do you mean? No one's coming." She released a high-pitched cackle or maybe a sob. "This is all on me! Why would they come? What do you mean?"

Beside her, Cassidy's father choked on his own breath before he cut off the sound, shuddering beside her. She only hoped his heart could take all this.

"Anne," Cassidy softened her tone, trying to hold the other woman's eyes, "you kidnapped us. Four missing people are going to have set the police hunting for you and us. They probably knew Morty and Laura were missing even when you took me and my father. I'm sure they know we're gone by now too."

Anne shook her head, blond hair trembling wildly with her refusal. Flecks of blood stuck to it had dried crimson already where Anne had pushed it back behind her ears. "No. You're wrong. I blew up your diners. Everyone will think you all died in the fires. Nobody's coming."

That can't be right.

Cassidy didn't know much about fires, but she watched crime shows sometimes. Bodies didn't get obliterated in fires. Not normal fires like this woman had set anyway.

"Anne, I'm sorry, but you're wrong." Cassidy took a second more, letting her words sink in as Anne squinted at her, one hand rubbing at a cheek and painting it more scarlet than any blush ever could. "There'd have been remains if we'd died in the fires."

Nausea burned at her gut, thinking of what would've been left of her and her dad if they'd been in that building when it blew, but she forced the sensation back down. Puking up her fear and terror wouldn't do anyone any good right now.

"Bodies don't just disappear, Anne. The police aren't going to find any remains…they *haven't found* any remains… which means they're already searching for us. And for you."

Anne remained still at the center of the room, frowning. "You're wrong. You're flat wrong. I should've left you gagged so you couldn't speak nonsense."

But their captor was also going a little green and pale, lips pinching tight to hold in whatever she was thinking. Whether this murderer admitted it or not, she believed Cassidy.

"I'll help you out of this, Anne." Cassidy leaned forward, ignoring another stab of pain running up her thigh. "I will, I promise."

Anne grimaced, and in another moment, she'd turned her face away from Cassidy's and focused back on Morty's corpse, her body rocking once again. "You're useless. If you were on fire, I wouldn't spit on you to put you out."

The shadow over Anne's face was terrifying. Cassidy held her breath.

But then, as if robotically, Anne rose, turned, and

marched up the cellar stairs without looking back at the chaos she'd left behind.

Cassidy's father let out a deep breath beside her, and then a prayer escaped his lips. Cassidy wanted to join him but couldn't. Tears built of pain and frustration burned her throat and leaked from her eyes again.

Anne was right. She was useless. She'd failed to make a difference. And one way or another, abandoned to the elements or murdered where they sat, they were going to die as a result.

26

Exhaustion notwithstanding, Emma hadn't had an easy time falling asleep. The memory of the wolf in her room had kept her staring into corners and examining shadows. When she'd finally caved to the desire to leave her lamp on through the night, she'd been able to doze off, but only barely.

And then she woke to a wolf howling. The sound seemed to come from everywhere and nowhere, echoing in the room and in her mind just the same.

This waking was gentle, but insistent, and when she sat up in bed to examine her room, she glimpsed no sign of interference from a deadly predator—or anything at all.

But the howling was real.

She let it draw her to the bedroom window, her eyes centering in on the forest behind the old Victorian home turned B and B. The trees were dark, full of a depth that spoke of wildness. As she watched them, the wolf's howl didn't bother her half so much as it had before, and she felt the urge to follow the sound, which had pulled her from slumber.

Some part of her mind whispered the ghost's warning, that she needed to back off—that the Other was coming for her, and she *would* die—but somehow, with the wolf's howling pulling her like a leash, she couldn't make herself care.

Not now. Not with that howling begging her to investigate.

Knowing she was being ridiculous didn't change matters. She tugged on clothing along with her boots, grabbed her phone to use as a flashlight, and tiptoed from her room. Out the back door of the inn, onto the large deck overlooking the woods, she went. Emma stopped at the far edge of the structure, resting her hands on the rail.

The cold air faded from her senses with the awareness of the mysterious forest beyond the rail, dark and wild in the way of a time before humanity, when the natural world had ruled.

I would have been free then. In the wild. Howls like these would have serenaded the night every evening and lulled me to sleep. They would have felt like safety.

Like now.

A hundred feet down, the forest crept up to the foot of the deck and beckoned her to explore. It didn't seem so far away, the more she gazed downward. Shadows shifted, undulating with the howls carrying on the wind, but she wasn't close enough to glimpse their sources.

She needed to be closer.

Looking up at the trees, she leaned into the night and smiled at the darkness. The cold had left her behind now. Leaving awareness of the wild in its wake. Howling shook the tree limbs, and her hair, floating in the breeze, seemed to be drawn by the sound of it, tickling at the edges of her ears, creating pleasant goose bumps along her skin. Tingly.

This is what it means to be free. To be wild and free and part of the natural world.

The howling shook the night, vibrating the deck rail beneath her palms.

The call of the darkness, suddenly so inviting.

What she'd always wanted, if only in her deepest dreams.

Unable to take her eyes away from the forest, she leaned against the deck railing, peering into the blackness. Immune to the cold of the night.

Howling tore through the air, ever more present. More demanding of her. But that was okay. That was just fine. These woods were calling to her, using the howl to do so, and she belonged there.

I'm supposed to go to the howl.

Emma set her hands on the wood barrier before her, gripping hard enough to earn splinters, and she set one foot up on the middle rail. In another moment, she'd pulled herself fully up onto the railing and stood balanced above the deck and the woods, the howl rising all around her and...

"*Emma!*"

Leo's voice blasted through the cry of the wolf like a foghorn as one of his arms caught her around the thighs and his other gripped her arm from behind, pulling her back onto the safety of the deck and dragging her back toward the Victorian. Her body fought him instinctively at first, but then it suddenly occurred to her...

I was about to fucking jump.

Emma went limp against her colleague, allowing Leo to drag her back into the warm safety of the inn—what safety they had, at least—and prop her up against the wall of the lounge that led to the deck.

He left her there only long enough to lock the back door and throw the dead bolt. Then he turned back to her, his eyes as wild as his hair. Cool and calm Leo wasn't his usual self at the moment. "What were you doing? That's a hundred-foot drop-off! Were you trying to get yourself killed?"

She swallowed, staring at him without an answer.

Wearing sweats as if he'd been out for a jog, he appeared white with shock more than cold. His chest heaved as if he'd run a marathon even as his eyes searched over her for understanding. His charisma had disappeared in favor of concern, but Emma had no response to offer. She could barely even think straight.

I was about to jump. Because of that howling I heard. If he hadn't come out onto the deck...

Finally, she could only shake her head, horror sweeping through her blood. "I feel like I'm resurfacing from some deep-sea swim, Leo. I'm sorry. Thank you for being there." She caught her breath, leaning hard against the wall and splaying out her fingers to feel the reality of it. Coldness ached in her blood, knowing what she'd been about to do. "I think...I think I was about to do that."

Leo's eyes had gone a touch wider, as if he hadn't expected her to admit it, but he came closer and gripped her shoulders hard, forcing her to meet his eyes. "Why were you out there?"

Why...? And then, suddenly, there was no other question, and she stood a little straighter. Maybe she did owe him an answer she couldn't give, but what about him?

"Why were you out there?" He blinked at her, at a loss for words beyond that question.

"Leo, what made you come out here? I'll believe whatever you say. Just tell me."

Like a lightning bolt had shot down his spine, Leo released her with a jolt and stepped back, tightening his lips. A visible shiver had gone through him just then, unmistakable, and it made Emma wonder if he'd seen something like what she'd seen the night before.

"I heard…" He trailed off, shook himself, then focused his eyes out the window before continuing. "I heard the howling of a wolf. It woke me up. And I felt like something very bad was going to happen if I didn't go outside."

He stopped there, but Emma could only stare, putting the pieces of the night together as best she could. They were both being woken up by wolves. And her wolf—the Wolf, as she was thinking of him now, the one who'd come to her bedroom and aimed to rip her throat out—had tried to kill her. Maybe not for the first time, in fact.

And, somehow, Leo had known. He'd stopped the Wolf.

When she couldn't.

27

Leo stirred his coffee, wondering how many sugars he'd accidentally poured in. But the brew tasted sweet as sin. He'd twice forgotten he'd already added sugar while standing at the counter, chitchatting about absolutely nothing with his colleagues.

Nothing, because that was about all his brain could accommodate right now.

He'd barely slept a wink after that incident with Emma out on the deck, which had happened around one in the morning.

Since the incident with the wolf and that damn howling.

Instead of finding any rest in dreams, he'd lain awake, anticipating the slightest creak of a floorboard to suggest that she or anyone else on their team was being lured outside. Although, he'd mostly been listening for Emma's door. Things hadn't been right with her lately, and last night proved it.

They'd been like toddlers, it occurred to him now. Each of them refusing to be truthful with the other. Emma had asked him for more when he mentioned the wolf's howl. But he'd held back.

For good reason. She'd think I'm crazy if I told her what I've been experiencing.

He'd have to at some point, though. And it wasn't as if Emma could excuse her own actions last night. Nothing she could say would make him forget the sight of her standing up on that rail, leaning into the wind and the dark like a fucking hood ornament.

Forgetting that sight wouldn't have let him sleep even if she'd been tied to her bed and locked in a room without a window.

Maybe if he was lucky, he'd gotten three or four hours of sleep all night, but he hadn't dozed off again until the sun had begun rising, his alarm blaring far too soon after that. He'd managed to drag himself into a shower and put on a mask of competence to get himself back to the Randall County Police Station and the blasted conference table, but his mind still whirled with what could've happened.

The terror of how things might've gone if Emma had started sleepwalking again without him there to stop her—it overwhelmed him, souring the small bit of breakfast he'd forced down.

That is what she was doing, right? It had to be. Sleepwalking's the only explanation.

Jacinda didn't wait for Leo's subconscious to catch up with his waking brain before clapping for their attention. "As you all have probably guessed by now, nothing blew up while we slept, so at the very least, it's been a peaceful night."

Leo couldn't help raising his gaze to meet Emma's where she sat across the table, but he looked away when she blushed and peered back at her own coffee.

Peaceful, my ass.

"We have reinforcements from the state cops coming in to relieve the officers who were on stakeout duty overnight."

Jacinda tapped at her iPad, then began changing the names of officers assigned to the various stakeout locations on the whiteboard. "This is where we have people now, but all of us know these aren't definite targets, so we need to move on this case before something forces us to *react* rather than *act*. Assuming they're still alive, the kidnapped victims are likely running out of time. We all know the stats, people."

Leo pulled up a map of the area on his iPad as he sipped his sickly sweet coffee and listened to the chatter around him. So much of the map was forested ground, their unsub could be hiding anywhere. Where that left them, he wasn't sure.

As Jacinda wrapped up her notes and told everyone to keep her updated on what leads they were following, Emma leaned sideways to whisper something to Mia. In a few seconds' time, Mia's eyes went wide before she managed to check her expression and flatten it.

But he'd seen it. And now, Mia was already rising to follow Emma out of the conference room, over toward the mostly abandoned hallway that led to interview rooms.

Leo downed his coffee. And, although Denae raised an eyebrow at him, he forced a grin and jiggled the empty cup for her benefit. "Quick refill, and then back at it."

"Okay, Scruffy, you do you, but don't be vibrating with caffeine when it comes time to handcuff someone."

"Like you're one to talk." The joke left his lips lightly, and she chuckled, but he was already up from the table and moving to follow Emma and Mia.

Standing around the corner from the hall, Leo made a show of leaning on the wall and pulling out his phone. Blankly, he stared down at his weather app as he listened in.

"She was outside Dellington's pizza place. Angry as hell, and she let me know it. I think the pizzeria may be significant somehow." Emma paused, and Mia said something quiet enough that Leo couldn't quite make it out, to which Emma grumbled her own unintelligible response.

What the hell? Why wouldn't Emma have told me that when I picked her up after seeing Munn?

The app blurred before Leo's eyes, all his focus on his colleagues and on his memory of the day before. He couldn't recall seeing any angry woman outside the pizza place—or anywhere else in Dellington for that matter—but why would Emma have kept that to herself, only to share it with Mia now? And why not inform the rest of the team?

His gut had been screaming for a while now that Emma knew things she wasn't telling them, but had he really believed those pieces of information were case-related? The sting in his chest told him he hadn't, not truly. She seemed a consummate professional, someone he could trust with cases and to have his back.

But if she was hiding information that could lead to their unsub...

No. She's not.

His gut tightened with resolve. The howling wolf from last night, and wolves in general, might be getting to him, but he could trust Emma. The last three cases had proven that much. There was something else going on here. For now, he'd trust her. But his ability to keep his curiosity in check and his mouth shut was weakening with every case.

Sooner rather than later, she was going to have to answer his questions.

28

I hadn't planned on stopping by the old place. The very idea had sounded too painful, seeing *Leonardo's Pies* emblazoned on the placard that had once read *R&A's Grill*. But then I'd woken up that morning stiff with snot and tears and blood all over and with a burning desire to see the place.

Just once more anyway.

Leonardo's Pies. Cheesy, compared to what this restaurant used to be. Ha.

Dellington's main street hadn't changed much over the last decade, though. The Chinese takeout joint and ice cream parlor had been there for decades, and a new dry cleaner sat at the end of the block where I'd once bought sneakers, but that was about it. The buildings hadn't been updated, and if I hadn't remembered those few businesses that'd been switched out, I could've been striding along on any snowy day from my high school years.

But things had changed, of course. For Dad, and me, and R&A's.

Hell, I wasn't even recognizable compared to my old self.

The old storefront really hadn't changed much though,

making my memories almost feel like reality. Like R&A's was still in operation.

Almost like Dad's still alive.

I'd just have to walk through the door, and he'd be there, behind the grill, flipping patties and dropping fries into the fat.

He'd call out, "Hey, Ruthie!" like he always would, and...

But Dad wasn't alive, and R&A's wasn't here any longer. It had been replaced by a pizza joint. They'd painted the door and brickwork in a pattern of red, green, and white as a nod to Italy. But the building was otherwise mostly unchanged from when me and Dad had run the place. Back then, the decor had been blue and green and white. Mountain-esque.

That had been Dad's idea. He'd wanted the comforts of a home-cooked meal to be served up alongside colors that would remind people why they loved our region. He certainly had.

I thought I'd feel that love at his graveside, with a view of the mountains. And there was nothing. No emotion, no color, just endless white snow. A blanketlike grief.

Truly, Dad's grave had seemed as cold as this very West Virginia February, but maybe I'd be able to sense his warmth inside this building where we'd spent so many happy hours. The endeavor had seemed worth a trip out into the cold, anyway, and now here I was. Away from, well, away from what amounted to all my problems at the moment.

Gazing at the menu taped into the window along with a few newspaper reviews, I read over the accolades and options. I didn't exactly consider myself a pizza aficionado, but the community I called home now had some decent options, and this place looked to be on par with those businesses.

To start, I'd noticed that morning that Leonardo's Pies had a website boasting the best breakfast pizza in West

Virginia, and I'd barely even known breakfast pizzas existed. I figured maybe I'd give one a try, assuming I didn't lose my appetite altogether upon smelling it. Eggs and pizza seemed like a nightmare.

Ridiculous as the fare sounded, though, I couldn't help but be glad about the differences from our old menu. I didn't think I could've handled the place being a burger joint like R&A's. Sometimes when I slept, I still dreamed of our old onion rings and burgers, slathered in seasoning and ketchup. If I'd walked into a sight or a smell like that, I'd have had to walk right back out.

And just like the smells, the inside of the pizzeria couldn't have been more different from what I'd remembered. Even the corner table had been replaced by a big circular booth. Which was a good thing, I told myself.

Instead of seeing my old haunt with West Virginia history in the walls, I took in the maps of Italy, smiling celebrities whom I doubted had ever stepped foot in the place, and memorabilia devoted to West Virginia sports teams.

Inside, I unbuttoned my old sweater immediately. Because my winter coat was spattered with Morty's blood, I'd had to resort to layering myself against the cold, and I'd been freezing for most of the morning. Leonardo's Pies was warm, though, despite the mostly empty dining room.

A few brave souls had made it out for breakfast, but not many. Surprisingly, the smell of bacon and potatoes actually made my mouth water. By the time a cheery little teenage server appeared at the host stand, I'd almost forgotten where I stood.

Almost.

Her name tag read, *Isabella*.

"Welcome to Leonardo's Pies. Party of one?" She grinned at me, showing off blue-and-green braces. *What a choice.*

"Right, just me." I steeled myself for judgment but saw

none. The girl, who couldn't be out of high school, appeared young and perky enough to not know what it meant to eat alone. She only grinned and led me off to a little booth in the corner closest to the front windows.

As I followed her, I wondered if she was working today instead of at school because of a snow day from the storm. That'd happened to me a few times too.

When the server disappeared to get some water, I took my time peering around. Three tables held customers, two already digging into twelve-inch pies that, to be fair, smelled pretty damn delicious. Red-checkered tablecloths set off the kitschy decor, but nothing else remained of R&A's Grill from when Dad and I had owned the place. The colors were different, the decorations new. The place was another world from what I remembered.

But just as warm. *Maybe a bit of my dad's spirit lives here after all.*

When Isabella bounced back, depositing an order of breadsticks on my table, I'd finally perused the menu and decided to bite the bullet. "I'll take the bacon, egg, and cheese pizza for one, hash browns on the side."

She gave me a little curtsy and bounced off, almost making me scoff. Talk about young and innocent.

Laughter drifted my way from the kitchen area behind the counter, and I watched a circle of dough fly upward, garnering a loud giggle. My dad would've loved that this place was still full of happiness. Jolly employees. Great atmosphere. And so fresh.

I broke a breadstick in half and took a bite, enjoying the whimsy of having lunch or dinner fare for breakfast. The stick was all garlic and butter, with just enough seasoning. My tongue practically zinged with the flavor, enough that I considered becoming a food critic instead of a photographer right there on the spot.

Huh. I actually feel pretty good about being here. Better than I have since I arrived in this blasted state.

Heaven help me, I was even beginning to look forward to my bacon, egg, and cheese pizza.

And then I saw them...the one thing I'd hoped desperately not to see.

My perky brunette server, little Isabella, with the god-awful braces was stacking carryout boxes by the kitchen window, and giving a much, much older man a loving pat on the back as he passed.

The garlic of the breadstick turned to ash on my tongue. I'd seen another older server and a delivery boy in the brief time I'd been waiting, but those two? That young server and older man in a chef's apron? They spoke of a connection that went beyond employer and employee.

As the man swept by once again, heading for the older server typing up an order in the register, he almost knocked the girl's carefully stacked boxes over. Instead of getting angry, she laughed and yelled after him, "Watch where you're going, Dad! Seriously."

No. Oh no, no, no, no.

The older server giggled and shrugged off the man as he hugged her from the side, whispering something into her ear. *Her husband.* Smiling her perfectly pink lips, she waved off her daughter. "Izzy, honey, you're just going to have to accept that your father was born a clumsy man."

"Not with pizza dough! Or you!" He cackled good-naturedly, and his daughter groaned in protest as I stiffened, my body going hard and angry from head to toe while I listened.

The woman at the register pointed her loud voice toward the kitchen. "Jake, take over those orders so your poor dad can take his morning coffee break!"

A family. A whole damn family.

My lips tingled, my brain shunting options back and forth in disbelief. A whole family ran this place. And while I'd thought nothing could hurt worse than seeing what I'd once had play out before my eyes, I'd been wrong. I'd never had this.

And witnessing what I'd never once had and barely even dared to dream of was twice as painful.

Unable even to see straight, I dropped the remains of my breadstick and fumbled myself up from the table, ignoring the clatter of my water glass as it fell to the floor and rolled, attracting eyes from every other table. Dimly, I heard Isabella call out to me as I headed for the door, but I didn't turn back. I couldn't.

Coming here had been a mistake, but I wouldn't be the one to suffer for it.

No family deserved this much happiness, not by a long shot, and I'd see to it that this family understood that.

When I got to my car, I turned the radio up high, which my mom would never have allowed, and adjusted the heater as my dad's favorite oldies station blared to life. Some things never changed, like the sound of the Four Seasons and the cold of West Virginia winters and tragedy.

Good ole tragedy.

Frankie Valli started singing "Book of Love," but as I steered down the road, I could only think of my mother. My abusive, and thankfully, very dead mother. She'd never wanted a happy family. She'd instead ruled with an iron fist, terrorizing me and Dad until we couldn't even remember what happiness was.

Tears stung my cheeks, and I swerved around a curve, narrowly missing a red pickup that honked at me. I hoped he loved Leonardo's Pies, and I laughed out loud at the thought.

Dammit, I would've given anything for a happy family

like what that family enjoyed. *Anything.* And that was all Dad had ever wanted too.

If Dad and I hadn't gotten it, nobody else deserved it. I knew that just as far down in my belly as I knew the feeling of a mother's angry fists.

But I'd make things right. I still had some supplies stored in the camper back on Dad's old property. No way would I allow Isabella's picture-perfect little family to carry on right where Dad and I had fought so hard for our dreams.

No. I'd blow their picture all to pieces. That was exactly what I'd do.

29

Collapsing into her chair at the conference table, Emma filled her lungs with sweat-stained air and tried for a minute of mindful breathing. Oren wouldn't have been impressed with the lame attempt, as her mind kept right on spinning.

Speaking to Mia about the Dellington ghost had been a double-edged sword. On one hand, talking about the encounter meant Emma wasn't living with it alone. On the other hand, Mia had looked so worried for her, Emma felt a smidge guilty as she attempted to settle down at her laptop. Her colleague was still coming to terms with the fact that Emma saw ghosts at all, and here Emma was, adding encounters to the fire.

But now there are two of us working on that woman's identity. Can't forget that.

Emma swallowed the guilt along with her quickly cooling coffee and considered the history of that building where Leonardo's Pies sat. The ghost woman she'd seen—Mrs. Middle Finger, as she'd begun thinking of her—had been incredibly angry. Angry enough to hover outside a building and curse the air around it, even though she had the whole of the Other wide open to her.

And if Emma had learned one thing about the dead, it was that the ghosts who clung to a certain spot usually had good reason to do so. Sometimes, it was the scene of their death. Emma had seen circus performers haunting their big top. Or, sometimes, it was their community, like the ghosts in Little Clementine's inn.

If I can figure out what set her off, we might just shed some light on our unsub too. That kind of rage doesn't come easy, so it was connected to something or someone about Leonardo's Pies. But maybe it was connected to something predating that particular business.

When had Mrs. Middle Finger died? How far back? Emma closed her eyes for a moment, mentally shutting out the ghost's anger and focusing on her clothes. Nothing special came to mind, and mom jeans were mom jeans, but they hadn't really been popular until at least the eighties, right? And the woman had a cheap charm bracelet on. Hadn't those had a resurgence in the nineties?

Refocused on the task at hand, Emma turned on her laptop with a working theory that the woman had been killed somewhere between two and three decades ago. Not much earlier, not much later. The building Leonardo's Pies sat in was ancient, but that timeframe narrowed things down considerably.

And it makes that burger joint it survived to become all the more likely a source for her ire, no matter how many restaurants predated it.

Searching the address showed a long history of restaurants that had called the space home, many of them offering American fare like burgers and patty melts. The one immediately predating Leonardo's had been there through most of Emma's estimated timeframe, according to county records.

Emma focused in, pulling up a recent feature article on the history of Dellington's restaurants. Scanning down to Leonardo's Pies, she started reading just under her breath. "Prior to being made into a pizzeria just about a decade ago, the space housed R&A's Diner for eight years. R&A's was a beloved burger joint opened by Allen Alexander, who died tragically in..."

Emma's eyes bugged as her fist slammed into the table beside her laptop.

"Boom!"

Leo skidded to a stop nearby, an *o* of horror springing to his face, making Emma realize her unfortunate phrasing. Before she could apologize, Mia and Sloane appeared from different directions to stare with just as much accusation.

"Uh, sorry. Poor choice of word. But look what I found."

Without any more fanfare she turned her laptop to her colleagues and spoke as they caught up with her. "The pizzeria used to be a diner, and its owner died ten years ago at the age of forty-eight in a *faulty gas line explosion*. Killed while asleep in bed."

Sloan leaned in closer, wrapping her long locks in one hand to keep them out of her and Mia's faces both as she read beyond where Emma had stopped. "The home he shared with his daughter, Ruth Alexander, was destroyed in the fire. Ruth survived only because she was closing up the burger joint that she helped her father run in downtown Dellington."

Emma traded satisfied grins with Mia. "R&A's Grill. Ruth and Allen's Grill."

Leo had already begun searching on his iPad, and he plopped it down on the table in the center of their small group, pointing to a picture of a man and a teenage girl standing in front of a storefront. A large *Opening Day* sign hung behind them. "Lookie here. This is the announcement for the grill's opening. You see what I see?"

"Oh, hell, yes." Emma clicked on the image, enlarging it needlessly. Beside the two restaurateurs sat an old station wagon, midnight blue and gleaming in the sun. The license plate wasn't visible because of the angle, but there was no mistaking the similarity to the video when it came to shape and color.

No way does one small-town diner end up being the center of this many coincidences. We have our perpetrator.

"I'll tell Jacinda. You guys keep digging." Mia pushed herself up from the table, already calling for the SSA.

Sloan moved in the opposite direction. "I'll fill the sheriff in and see if he remembers these two."

Emma pulled out the seat beside her for Leo. "Shall we 'keep digging'?"

With him searching for articles beside her, the information came fast and furious. Emma managed to hunt down Allen's obituary just as Leo homed in on the daughter.

She read fast, offering the highlights. "Allen was preceded in death by his late wife, Karen Alexander, who was also a native of the area and died of a sudden heart attack in 2005, prior to the opening of R&A's Grill.'"

"Daughter moved to Oregon almost immediately after her dad died," Leo hummed to himself, scanning forward, "presumably to start over. That's a long way from West Virginia, but she could have come back since then." He froze.

"What?"

"She's got a bunch of photography credits. Maybe she's a full-time freelance photographer."

Emma's heart sped up. *This is it.* "She'd know how flammable nitrate is. She'd have freedom to travel." She shifted back to the date of the obituary. "This month marks the ten-year anniversary of Allen Alexander's death. I'll bet you a thousand dollars she came back to visit."

"No bet."

Sloan had reappeared behind them as they'd spoken. "So we have someone who knows the damage a gas leak explosion can cause, access to the means to make an explosion like that happen, and someone who might be resentful of successful diner owners. I'll start hunting down Ruth's contacts in Oregon so we can find out where she is for sure."

As she opened her own laptop across from them at the conference table, Emma went back to searching for anything she could find on the Alexander family. And then she came across a photo taken when the whole family had still been alive.

Well, what do you know? I've seen that face close-up and personal.

Glaring at her from inside the family photo, which had been published in honor of Karen Alexander's death, there sat none other than Emma's Dellington ghost—Mrs. Middle Finger herself. The woman wasn't flipping anyone off in this picture, but her image was unmistakable. Same hair color and eye shape, with a mean set to her lips that could be discerned even through a forced smile.

Just holding back from celebrating the identification, Emma began searching records on the mother while her colleagues looked into the daughter. Having died eight years before Allen, the woman had made a habit of being an albatross around his and their daughter's necks.

Her record detailed multiple claims of domestic abuse, all of which had been dropped within hours or days of being filed. Pictures of bruises and even burns littered her file and filled the screen in front of Emma. She bit her tongue in an effort to quiet curses.

Emma popped back to the family photo to check what

she'd seen. There, just above the daughter's wrist...a telltale bruise that could've come from the grip of a hand, hard and punishing.

Her teeth ran against her tongue, ticking at the anger boiling up in her throat. How a mother like hers, a good one, could've been stolen from her, leaving Emma without a single memory. Yet Ruth had had to endure a terrible mother for all those years, scarring her forever. The world really was unconscionable.

She went back to the legal record she'd found, scanning through hospital visits commemorated by way of police record.

How a mother could do any of this to her husband, let alone an innocent daughter...

Back up there, Emma girl. Not so innocent anymore, maybe.

Sloan strode back up to the table and offered a self-satisfied grin. "I just got off the phone with Ruth's next-door neighbor in Oregon, who happens to be house-sitting while Ruth is away. She left to come back to West Virginia last Friday, February third."

"Which means," Leo picked up the thread, gesturing to the dates on the whiteboard, "that she was in the area when both the Williamses and the Freeses went missing."

Emma tilted her screen toward Leo and Sloan. "This is the work of the matriarch of the family. These marks? They're on her husband and daughter. We have an early life of abuse setting up the adult who Ruth eventually became."

"Shit." Leo hissed out a breath. "That would make for one messed-up kid."

As Sloan paced a short distance away, Emma focused back on the computer before them. "All these dropped charges...she either convinced them she'd change every time, or they lost the courage to stand up to her."

Leo tapped the dates he'd been listing out in his notes.

"And when she died, they opened up R&A's Grill almost immediately. It must've been a haven for the father and daughter after all those years of abuse."

Well, that's one way to piss off a dead woman, I guess. She gets dead, and they get happy.

"He bought the place with his widow's life insurance money." Sheriff Gruntle sidled up behind them, frowning at the images remaining on Emma's computer. "I remember my dad and every other lawman in the county knew what a mean bitch Karen Alexander was. You can't be a good sheriff in an area like this without knowing which folks are bad behind closed doors, and my dad was a damn good sheriff. But he couldn't do nothing about that woman when her family wouldn't stand up to her."

Emma flashed back to the scowling woman who'd greeted her outside Leonardo's Pies. "She must've been rolling over in her grave, seeing them flourish all of a sudden, benefiting from her death." Her stomach churned, thinking of the ghost peering in on her own abused daughter and widower, scowling through the front window as the two of them finally found some happiness.

Mia had come around the corner from the break room just in time to hear the end of the conversation, and she held up her phone with a small smirk that appeared an awful lot like triumph to Emma's way of thinking. "Jacinda's calling back Denae and Vance so we can all head out. The property for the house that Allen Alexander lived in is still in the family's name. It was transferred to Ruth's name following Allen's death, and she never sold the estate. The house wasn't rebuilt, but there's four acres of land in her name."

Leo was already typing on his phone. "I'll get us whatever's available via satellite imagery."

Emma shut her laptop without bothering to power the device down, shoving herself to her feet. "You ask me, Ruth got triggered when she came back, and now she's blowing up pictures of happiness that remind her of everything she lost when her father died. The woman was traumatized from her loss, and that pressure's been building all these years, on top of the abuse her mom put her through."

As she slipped on her coat, Mia frowned, speaking as Jacinda entered with her own coat slung over one arm. "Maybe we haven't found any bodies because we've gotten Ruth wrong. She started out a victim, and now she's a totally messed-up adult, but she's not actually a killer. Maybe our kidnappees are still alive."

Though Emma wanted to believe her friend, she wasn't sure she could. Two of their victims had been missing for more than three days. The likelihood of them being found alive was slim, with the odds dropping every hour they remained missing, and the whole team knew it. But Leo shook his head before Emma found the words to offer up a clearer reality.

"I hope you're right, Mia." Leo traded frowns with Sloan, knowing from her flat expression that she didn't feel nearly as optimistic as their colleague. "The problem is, even if Ruth didn't start out as a killer, she might've become one out of necessity. There's a certain recklessness if she's setting off bombs."

Mia licked her lips as Emma gripped her shoulder, coat already buttoned tight. "Either way, we need to find Ruth ASAP. And now we have an address."

Phone in hand, Jacinda came around the corner with her coat already buttoned, the sheriff on her heels. "That station wagon's proof enough for now. I'm working on a warrant and getting a SWAT, EOD, and hostage rescue teams scrambled since we have hostages and explosives potentially in play."

Translation—Jacinda doesn't want us all to go boom.

30

With Mia behind the wheel, Emma leaned sideways in the passenger seat to give Sloan a better view of her iPad and the satellite footage just sent through. They'd nearly reverted to the beginning of the case, team-wise. She and Sloan and Mia rode in one Expedition. Leo, Jacinda, Denae, and Vance piled into the other. Jacinda had radioed to confirm the nearest bomb squad was three counties away and making good time. Everyone should rendezvous at the same time.

Emma only hoped that the symmetry boded well for their case coming to an end.

Even though the snow had started again and snowflakes burst against the glass almost immediately. Irritated, she pressed the windshield wipers button for Mia, who kept her hands on the wheel.

"We have two sheds," Jacinda's voice crackled through the radio, conferencing all of them together, "and a sizable camper, which may or may not still be there since this imagery isn't up to the minute. There's also an old root cellar attached to the ruins of the original family home, and that looks relatively intact from the outside. Or, at least, we have to assume it could be intact. Ruth Alexander could be holing up in any of those locations."

Sloan frowned at the images. "I still don't understand why she'd be driving around an old station wagon instead of her rental."

"More room for bodies." Emma's comment sat in the air, sending both of Sloan's eyebrows skyward. She might have said that a touch too casually. "Sorry. Um, nostalgia?"

Seconds later, Denae's voice sounded through the radio. "Well, either way, we have no sign of the rental car we found in her name or the wagon. Not giving up, though. Both of those sheds are big enough for a vehicle."

Nodding needlessly in acknowledgment, Emma squinted at the satellite imagery. The sheds both sat at the eastern edge of the property, along a drive that wound through a stand of pine trees and emerged before the first shed. Both were simple structures with corrugated siding and steeply pitched roofs. The camper was positioned across from the smaller shed, on the other side of the drive.

Behind the camper was a clear patch of ground stretching approximately twenty or twenty-five yards to the west, where it terminated at the root cellar access and the ruins of the old house. The cellar access looked to be a concrete staircase that descended to a pair of doors. Thankfully the satellite images were taken before the latest snowstorm swept through.

"That cellar is probably where she's hiding. Under cover, secure." She zoomed in until the square entrance was little more than a blur. "I can't even tell if the doors are caved in at all, but the cellar could have survived even if the house blew."

Sloan *hmm*ed under her breath before speaking up for the team. "We're on her home turf, so we should be thinking about her M.O. Nitrate film base becomes unstable as it decomposes and is a massive fire risk. If she has that much on hand, I can only guess about where she acquired it. It's not for sale anywhere these days. As for where it might be, underground storage is probably the safest option."

Though Emma wanted to avoid going anywhere the threat of booby traps existed, that wouldn't help them stop Ruth from hurting anyone else. Or save the people she'd kidnapped, assuming they were still alive.

It's good to want things, Emma girl. Builds character. Now go do your job.

"If she's anywhere on this property, she's either somewhere she feels safe or actively building another bomb."

Sloan tilted her head to the side, pausing. "What if those are the same place?"

"After that storm, and with two father-daughter pairs held hostage...I think Ruth wants to be safe and not hurt anyone else. She's an adult child of abuse and unresolved trauma. I'd say she's either in the cellar or the camper."

"Agreed." Jacinda went quiet for a second, and then more footage came to Emma's iPad. "We'll enter from that gravel road, closer to the sheds. We'll stop in the tree line and walk in. To make it simple, we'll split up teams by SUV. Emma, Mia, and Sloan, you take the small shed and the camper. The rest of us will take the larger shed and then the root cellar. If initial targets are clear, head to the others."

"Sheriff Gruntle, the bomb specialists, HRT, and the state police are on their way," Vance added. "We have plenty of backup, and Ruth is just one person. We'll get her."

Sloan frowned. "Just remember she's one person who may have explosives in her possession that are primed. Our backup is miles away, so we proceed with caution and back off rather than engage if it comes to it."

The statement was so simple, it sat like lead in Emma's

stomach. She could talk a killer down and hold her own when it came to a fight or keeping a steady hand on a gun. Strong nerves and a silver tongue didn't exactly help defuse a bomb, though.

And it wasn't just their lives in danger. Four innocent victims could be in the blast zone as well.

If they're even alive.

Mia swung the wheel right, following the lead SUV onto a rough gravel road that was still slushy with just-melting snow. The wheels crunched as she slowed.

Emma tucked her iPad away. "Hey, don't kill us."

"You're one to talk."

Smirking, Emma examined the property through the windshield, stretching her neck to peer past thick stands of evergreens.

If ever there was a place to build bombs in the woods, this would be it.

A horrible reverb sounded through the radio. The noise scratched at Emma's eardrums, causing her to swerve on the icy road.

"What happened?" Mia's concerned voice joined the cacophony of voices on their radio channel.

Jacinda was talking to someone, but Emma couldn't hear details. The reception was terrible.

Then a distinctive *click* resounded as one party called, "Over and out."

Jacinda's voice broke through the sudden quiet. "The bomb squad and HRT's truck just slid off the road. The weather's apparently ten times worse farther north and headed this way." Emma heard the low-level tension in her boss's voice and understood what was behind it.

The SSA had to make a tough decision. She could call the whole mission off for the moment, let the weather pass by, and regroup with everyone—their team, the SWAT units, and the local LEOs—in place in a few hours. This choice assumed the weather would clear up fast. If, however, the storm lasted as long as the previous one, their hostages would be alone with a very unstable, unpredictable Ruth for hours.

Jacinda's other option was to push forward, using only the team and the local department. The good news with this choice was that they'd beat the storm. Sloan could take point, since she was the explosives expert. Jacinda herself, however, would almost certainly earn a reprimand for the risky maneuver.

But Jacinda, Emma knew from experience, admired a certain level of risk-taking.

As long as everyone immediately involved was in on the decision to take those risks.

"We're going in. We know Ruth has a gun and has materials for explosives, so this is about our lives and the lives of the hostages. We announce as we approach and at every structure. West Virginia law only dictates announcing at a dwelling, but I don't want anyone taking chances. Nobody kicks in any doors. Got it?"

Agreement echoed from around the Expedition, and then their prep time was over.

They'd reached the Alexander family property.

As directed, they pulled the SUVs up on the drive leading into the property. Emma was first out of the vehicle and moved to the nearest pine tree. She peered between the lower branches, examining the camper and cellar access.

Snowdrifts and churned ground surrounded the camper, which sat so Emma had a view of the front end from where she stood. A low-grade buzzing, like a small motor running, came from somewhere on the property. She peered around the camper, expecting a generator, and sure enough, spotted one.

It sat rumbling away beneath a plastic tarp affixed to one side of the camper and staked to the ground. The camper's windows all seemed blacked out or had heavy curtains concealing the interior.

Emma stepped back to join the team as they made their way up the drive.

The smaller shed, the closer of the two, couldn't be seen through the trees, but came into view as they rounded a turn in the drive. Tire tracks through the muddied and refrozen ground led in the general direction of that shed. The camper sat directly across from it, maybe thirty feet away.

"Everyone ready?" Leo's eyes met Emma's until she gave in and nodded. It was clear they both knew he was looking at her for other reasons.

But now was not the time to be thinking about that.

At least there's no howling. Fuck knows how either of us would handle that.

In fact, the whole area was too silent, too still. Emma adjusted her vest beneath her coat once more.

"Sheds first?" Emma whispered.

Mia gave a fast nod. "If there are hostages, they're not likely in the camper, but that generator means she probably is. I'd say get to the hostages first."

Jacinda's focus remained on the root cellar as she tucked her hair into a watch cap that she snugged around her ears. "I want to know what's down there."

Emma stepped up. "The bomb team has a thermal imaging camera. But we can't wait for them to dig themselves out of the ditch. We have four hostages who might be at risk of dying from exposure."

Jacinda took her time in deciding, not meeting any of their eyes. "My team will take the larger shed first. Emma, your team takes the smaller shed. Remember to announce, and no kicking anything."

The teams split off, and Emma led the way, following the tire tracks to the small shed. Jacinda, Leo, and Vance continued around the building, using it for concealment as they made their way to the larger structure to the north. Once they were out of sight, Emma motioned for Mia and Sloan to follow her, but stopped cold in the crusty snow before taking another step.

Ahead of them, wavering in place against the side of the shed by a simple door, was a man whose white-eyed gaze matched the snowy ground surrounding him.

Sloan nearly ran into her but brushed by as she drew closer to the shed door. "Emma, what are you doing?"

Great job acting normal, Emma girl.

Sloan paused at the hinge side of the double doors and began her inspection.

The ghost of Allen Alexander stood beside the weather-beaten shed, as if leaning against the bent and rusty section of corrugated steel that formed a door in the structure's wall. Allen's white eyes roved back and forth over Emma's team. Around the eyes, his skull was charred and bald, just like his blackened, clawed-up hands where they hung by his sides.

"Emma!" Mia hissed from beside the small shed's door. "What is it?"

Stomach turning, Emma worked to look away and answer Mia's soft-voiced concern, but Allen kept her hypnotized. If there was one type of ghost she could never have prepared herself to encounter, this was it. Burnt, bloodied, and only partially present, the man was a walking nightmare.

The white eyes somehow made the image worse, too, as if adding a different layer of reality that Emma couldn't quite chalk up to a special effect from a horror movie.

I am so not prepared for this.

She shot a glance at Mia, whose face went whiter than the melting snow at their feet.

Ghost? she mouthed.

Emma forced a tight nod, her attention already back on the dead man.

He raised a ruined hand to point at the small shed. "I taught Ruthie how to drive in that car. All we had was each other. It's not her fault. Just an accident."

Mia bent closer to Sloan, clearly working to give Emma some cover, and she took advantage of it.

Sidling closer to Allen, taking the even tone he'd spoken with as an invitation, she whispered what was on all their minds. "Allen, where is your daughter? Where are the people she kidnapped?"

He frowned. "My Ruthie's a good girl. Not her fault. Just an accident."

Emma remained focused on Allen, knowing from his presence that her colleagues were about to find nothing more than the getaway vehicle. "But—"

The ghost held up the tattered remnants of a hand and shook his head, cutting off anything she could say, that ephemeral white gaze finally turning away as he vanished.

Fully distracted from the job at hand, Emma caught up to Mia and Sloan, who had just stood and confirmed she saw no signs of a trap around the door.

"I can see through the gap between the door and the shed wall. No wires or anything that looks like it's delivering power out here. The door's not locked either. It's hanging on the hinges."

Vance's voice echoed from deeper into the property as his team prepared to enter the larger shed. Sloan signaled with three raised fingers and mouthed her countdown. "*Three, two, one.*"

"Ruth Alexander, this is the FBI executing a warrant. We are entering this building."

Emma's mind buzzed with the repeated mumblings of Allen Alexander's ghost as she and her team swarmed inside the shed.

"Ruthie's a good girl. It was just an accident."

31

Leo held his position beside Jacinda as Vance and Denae took up theirs on the opposite side of the shed doors. They'd announced and had received no reply yet. Sloan's voice echoed across the eerie stillness as she, Emma, and Mia made their move on the smaller building.

It was doubtful that Ruth would be inside either of the sheds, not with the camper right there on the same property, but they had to be safe.

More likely, Leo hoped they'd find the kidnapping victims, since the space certainly seemed large enough.

If they're in here, let's hope they're alive.

With no windows to peer through, they'd only been able to determine there was no sound or movement inside, but dead bodies made no noise.

I haven't smelled anything yet, but the cold could be keeping decomp at bay.

On a quiet count of three, he lifted and pulled one door open, backing away with it as Jacinda swept in, gun and flashlight aimed, and with Vance right behind her. Leo followed with Denae in the opposite direction.

A newish Honda Civic was parked front and center, West Virginia rental plates attached. "We have her rental," Leo shined his light over it, illuminating an empty interior, "so she's here somewhere."

"Or in that station wagon she used." Denae strode deeper into the shed, playing her flashlight along the wall. "Unless she crammed four people into this thing's trunk."

Leo swallowed down the visual Denae's words created, but Jacinda had already opened the front door and popped the trunk. He glanced inside and shook his head. "Empty here."

Denae's flashlight pooled light over boxes labeled *menus*, *tablecloths*, *kitchenware*, and various other items likely from the family's old diner. Then, against the wall, it played over an old, handwritten sign with bold lettering. *Randall County Wolves Are Gonna GO! FIGHT! WIN! Wolves, HOWL!!!*

Leo froze, even his breath hitched, cutting off the plume of condensation in front of him. He flashed back to the howling from the night before to Emma climbing the railing over the drop-off and to the blank look on her face after he'd pulled her back from the edge.

Vance smacked him on the arm and laughed. "What's with the big eyes, Leo?"

Transfixed, he shuddered, unable to reply. He only tore his gaze away from the sign when Denae spoke up.

"Local high school's mascot is a wolf. We passed it today."

Avoiding Vance's questioning expression, Leo shook off his sudden fright and stepped closer to the boxes and sign. "Guess our perpetrator was a normal teenager once upon a time."

Jacinda raised her flashlight toward the ceiling, looking for any further items of interest, but the place had clearly only been used for basic storage. "Vance, radio Emma's team that we're clear here and moving to the cellar."

Leo remained silent, waiting on Sloan to acknowledge the message, then glanced around their group. "We ready to keep moving?"

The answer was obvious.

Leo took the lead and slipped out the door first. They had a perpetrator and victims to find, and focus was key. He shook off the memories from last night. Waiting for the others to get in position behind him, he led the way in a low-running sprint, following the trees at the northern boundary of the property toward their next destination—the root cellar.

A low-running brick wall broke the clearing between the shed and the home, but the area was otherwise empty. Leo couldn't avoid glancing at the camper. Despite every window being blacked out or curtained, he couldn't help feeling watched.

Seen.

The radio at Vance's belt crackled again, and they all crouched in the snow to listen as Mia's voice rang through.

"Smaller shed's cleared, and good news…we have our station wagon. But no perpetrator, no victims. Finishing here and moving to the camper next."

Vance held the radio to his mouth, thin-lipped. "Received."

Leo settled his hand near his gun, and when Jacinda nodded, he sprinted forward. Whether he imagined the sensation of danger crackling along his spine, there was little to no doubt they'd found the right place. Not after Mia's report.

The cellar, assuming it still held any open space at all after the old home's explosion, would be freezing and dank, not to mention dark. Maybe even overrun with rodents or some toxic remainder of chemicals after the long-ago fire. Definitely not fit for the living.

If he'd had to pick the most likely place on this property for a killer to store away their dead bodies, that root cellar would top the list.

32

The station wagon sat in near perfect condition just where Allen's blackened hand had suggested it would, but the small shed was otherwise empty. No perpetrator, no bodies, no explosives. In fact, there wasn't so much as an old rake or shovel stored inside.

But that didn't mean they had nothing in the way of evidence. Emma stared into the back of the wagon, shining her flashlight along what could only be blood. "That's a lot of red."

Mia stood a few steps back, white-faced. "Head wounds bleed a lot. It doesn't mean she's killed anyone."

Sloan grunted. "Okay, Pollyanna. Just don't lead with your rose-colored glasses when we find Ruth, okay?"

"Shut up, you two." Emma's throat tightened with nerves, and a stab of regret spiked her blood when Mia tensed. "Sorry. I just—"

"No, you're right." Sloan straightened and looked between them. "Now's not the time for trading jabs. We ready?"

"Ready," Mia nodded, "and I'll lead."

Emma swallowed another apology. If she'd centered her colleagues on the danger instead of each other, that was worth some added tension in the air. Hopefully.

"We all saw the duct tape, right?" Mia kept her voice down, leading the way to the camper. "She took them alive."

Emma didn't remind her friend of the bloodstains. And anyway, there'd been less blood than she would've expected of a fatal shot, so that was something. When they got through the line of woods between the camper and the shed, Emma concealed herself behind a tree as the others did the same. Watching and waiting.

The front side of the camper faced them, with the little tarped lean-to over the generator fluttering and snapping in a slight wind that kicked up. Flurries washed across the space between them and the camper.

Curtains were pulled tight across the only potential sight lines into what lay inside, and although tracks led a slushy path between where they stood and the camper's front door, there was no telling how fresh they were. Still…

"If the station wagon's here, and that generator is running, we have to assume Ruth's inside." Emma's whisper barely dented the air, but Mia and Sloan both hummed their agreement. "We follow the tracks. Stick to that path as much as possible, in a line. If she glances out the window and we're already at the camper, I don't want her being able to tell there are footprints that don't belong to her."

"Understood." Emma watched Sloan check her gun for the second time since they'd left the SUVs. "We ready?"

Rather than bothering to answer, Mia ducked from the trees and ran in a crouch toward the camper. Emma followed, unsurprised, and Sloan followed.

When they reached the metal side, Emma motioned Sloan toward the door, mouthing her next instruction. *Cover us.*

The other woman trained her gun on the door, keeping a ready stance, upright and not touching the camper. Stationed there, she nodded at her colleagues.

Emma pointed Mia around the right side of the camper before turning and heading to the left, hunting for any window into the interior that could offer a glimpse of what they'd face. She got nothing but fabric.

When Emma met Mia at the back, they both shook their heads. The windows were all curtained up tight.

"Did you hear the music?" Mia asked.

Emma leaned closer to the back of the camper but got nothing with the generator's rumble and occasional gusting wind making the tarp crack and snap. She did see an extension cord running from the generator though. It vanished under the snow that filled the yard but seemed to head toward the cellar.

Maybe Ruth has a heater down there? That could mean our hostages are still alive.

At the other side of the yard, Jacinda's team advanced toward the cellar steps with Leo in the lead. Emma waved for his attention and aimed a finger at the generator. She drew a line in the air in the direction of the cellar.

He nodded and gave a thumbs-up to indicate *message received*.

Emma returned her attention to Mia, who led her back around the way she'd come and paused near a vent. She could hear Janis Joplin singing about a piece of her heart, just barely.

A sudden, gory image of Allen Alexander's heart falling out of his pieced-together chest sent a reflexive burning up Emma's esophagus, but she put her back to the cold metal of the trailer and forced it down. Now wasn't the time to puke up her imagination all over a colleague's shoes.

"If she's in there, she might've set a trap to take herself out along with all of us."

"Or she could be building her next bomb and jamming out with Janis. She might not even know we're here."

Emma wanted to believe that, but she also wanted to make it home in one piece. "We made it pretty clear we've arrived. I'm not sure who announced louder, Sloan or Vance."

"So we announce at the door and go in."

"But if we smash our way in, she might just blow us all up."

Mia hesitated. "This is Sloan's territory. We should ask her."

Knowing how hard it had to be for Mia to admit that, Emma took a deep breath of the cold air and refocused on her colleague. "That's a good call. You ready?"

Mia offered a small, tense smile that wasn't quite honest enough to display her dimples. But her hands were steady, unlike Emma's gut.

Back in front of the camper, they confirmed the plan with Sloan and placed themselves around the door with Mia on the hinge side and Emma stacked behind Sloan on the opposite side.

Emma blocked out any possible appearance of the family's dead patriarch and met Mia's gaze. Counting to three in her head, Emma mouthed, *Announce.*

Mia nodded and called out. "Ruth Alexander, this is the FBI executing a warrant."

Her words were met with only the weak strains of Janis Joplin, until the music suddenly shut off.

Mia reached for the knob and gently placed her hand around it. She attempted to turn it, and it moved. Without wasting another second, she swung open the door and stepped back with it.

Sloan whipped inside, heading left, with Emma right behind her going right.

Ruth Alexander sat seven feet away on a threadbare couch at the end of the camper. They'd found the perpetrator, but she was holding two items, neither of which gave Emma any sense of comfort.

Emma swallowed hard before finding her voice. "FBI, Ruth. Violent Crimes Unit. It's time to put those down."

A series of light bulbs rested on the coffee table next to a photo album with a tin and what looked to Emma like portable, battery-charged light sockets.

She went portable after all. Did we just miss getting blown up, or have we showed up right on time for the fireworks?

A soldering iron rested nearby in a coiled stand.

Ruth held a duct-taped box in one hand and a remote in the other. Emma couldn't tell for sure, but it looked like the kind used to operate ceiling fans and household lighting. Some of the melted elements on Sloan's table made more sense to her now.

Ruth's frizzy blond hair shook like a messy halo as her eyes went wide and she met Emma's gaze. "Why are you here? You're not supposed to be here."

If I had a dime for every time I've been told that in the recent past.

Emma kept her attention on Ruth's hand that held the small white remote. And if that tin contained nitrate, Ruth wouldn't need a busted gas line to blow them sky-high. "Sloan." She lowered her voice so far she could barely hear it herself as she trained her gun on their bomber.

The other agent's steps shifted behind her, and Sloan appeared in Emma's peripheral vision to her right. Together, they filled the small space of the camper, with a tiny kitchenette counter in front of them opposite the door to a bathroom.

Sloan quietly identified herself, and asked Ruth to put down the box and remote. "I'm guessing it has nitrate in it, right, Ruth? We don't want anything to happen here, no explosions. No fires. If you can put that down, we can go outside and talk."

Mia, with her gun pointed at the floor, inched forward, beside Emma on her left. "Ruth? Is anyone in here with you?"

Though Ruth's mouth stuttered open and shut, her thumb didn't move from the remote.

Emma raised her voice, fighting for the woman's attention. "Ruth, listen to my friend. Is anyone in here with you? Anyone at all?"

Their perpetrator trembled where she sat, eyeing Emma, then Mia. "I'm alone. I'm all alone."

Nodding, Emma held her aim low but was ready to snap her weapon up if she had to. "We still need to confirm that, Ruth. My friends and I are just going to look in the bathroom, okay?"

Still quivering like a leaf, Ruth snapped her head side to side but answered to agree. "I'm alone but go ahead. Go ahead."

Emma moved up to check the bathroom.

It was empty, and she let the other agents know.

"Ruth, this is over." Emma kept her voice even, willing the woman to listen. "It's time for you to put that box down and come with us."

Sloan shifted forward to stand beside Emma again. "That device is probably ready to go, Ruth, is that right?"

The wild-eyed woman nodded but didn't appear to really see any of them.

Emma drew in a sharp breath as Ruth's finger slid back and forth across the remote in her palm.

"Ruth, what my friend said earlier still stands. You can

just put that down and we can talk. Do you want to do that? Just talk?"

As if she'd been prodded by a hot poker, Ruth startled and lifted the box, holding it closer to her chest. Emma backed up to stand by Mia, leaving Sloan closer to their perpetrator and, by default, the bomb and remote she was still holding.

If Ruth pressed the button, there was no telling what would happen, but Emma guessed it wouldn't be good.

And Ruth would have time to depress it, even if they shot her.

That thought in mind, Emma reminded herself that shooting was, today more than ever, an absolute last resort. "Ruth, I need you to put that device and the remote down."

Ruth's hands trembled.

The box threatening all their lives looked innocuous enough. Duct tape covered it on all sides. It looked like a Christmas present prank. No wires jutted out. If anything, Ruth worked in a neat, orderly fashion.

"Let's talk about this, okay? Like my friend said. Just talk." Emma chanced a step forward, and Ruth's jaw clenched.

Ruth waved the remote. "Please. I don't want to blow us all up, but I will. Get back. *Now*."

Sloan met Emma's eyes, and the agent jutted her chin, nudging Emma back a step. With a long exhale, she made a show of leaning back against the kitchen counter, lowering her weapon and holstering it. The sweat on her forehead was the only sign Sloan wasn't as calm as she appeared. "Ruth—"

"It's too late to talk." Tears leaked from Ruth's eyes. "What I've done can't be fixed. I couldn't be fixed. Not after my father died."

Emma licked her lips. That could be the opening she needed. "We saw a picture of your dad and you. You looked close, back when your diner opened. R&A's Grill? The place must've meant a lot to you."

Ruth's eyes went a touch wider, but she nodded. Her hands still trembled but didn't look ready to release the bomb. "Yes."

"I get it. I lost my dad also." Emma lowered her voice. She followed Sloan's example, holstering her weapon, and focused all her attention on Ruth. Maybe if she could make Ruth forget the other agents, she'd give Mia or Sloan an opening. "I know how difficult it is. And I bet it must've been even worse for you, after growing up with such a hateful mother—"

"Shut up!" Ruth brandished the bomb above her head, freezing Emma's heart in her chest. "Never speak of that woman! You hear me? How dare you bring her up when you're talking about my father? When you're in here on my property? My mother is to blame for all this! She ruined everything!"

The anger had dried Ruth's eyes, and now her reddened cheeks looked livid and dangerous against the sneer of her mouth. She was the very image of her mother's ghost, but far more menacing, given the threat she held in her hands.

Sloan cursed beneath her breath, drawing Ruth's glare. Emma took a smooth step forward. Her hands remained aloft, hopefully conveying her willingness to communicate.

Mia stepped forward, passing the bathroom door to stand in front of Emma, with her weapon still drawn. She kept the muzzle pointed straight down at the floor. "Ruth, your mom didn't make you blow up those diners. We all know that. Let's talk reality here, okay?"

A full-body shudder went through Ruth as she bit her lip. In another breath, she brought the bomb down and cradled the device against her chest. "You're right. But it doesn't matter now. I've ruined my life."

Her voice sounded so cold, Emma thought it might have

rivaled the winter outside. There wasn't going to be any reasoning with this woman. Still. "Ruth—"

"No! I've ruined my life good and proper, and if you don't want to ruin your own lives, you should leave immediately. Otherwise..." She rocked the bomb like an infant, stroking the silver tape with a single finger, its nail bitten down to the quick. "Well, you know. You're all going to die along with me."

33

Mia ran her tongue along her teeth, processing Ruth's warning. That bomb in her hand shook like an overworked desk speaker blasting bass, and Mia didn't have any faith that the woman wouldn't set it off by accident.

But apparently, Ruth planned on blowing herself up on purpose, which was a whole different can of worms.

If she'd rather explode into smithereens than turn herself in, we're in real trouble here.

And now I'm farthest from the door.

Taking a deep breath, Mia willed herself to remain calm as she shared a glance with Emma. At least Emma might have a chance at escape if things went wrong—though Mia doubted her friend would save herself if that option meant leaving her and Sloan behind.

Which meant the only choice was getting that bomb out of Ruth's hands. Somehow.

Before Mia could consider what move might make sense, Sloan stepped forward, hands out in front of her and already nearly at the opposite edge of the table from Ruth.

What the hell?

"Ruth, look at me." Sloan crouched to the same level as their bomber. "You can give me the bomb. That's one option. If not, you have a second."

Mia looked at Emma to see if her friend had any idea what Sloan was getting at. But Emma's blue eyes were intense, so bright and hot that one glance could probably ignite the bomb in Ruth's hands. She watched Emma's focus turn from Ruth to Sloan.

"The other agents here will leave." Sloan ignored Mia's startled gasp. "That's the other option. And the two of us will stay here with that bomb, in which case I'll tackle you and maybe set it off. And you and I will join your parents in oblivion. I don't care anymore what happens to me, but these other agents, my friends, are at least going to get out of here. And you're going to let them."

Ruth's eyes went wide, darting between Mia and Emma.

Mia had no words. Shock wrestling terror for center stage, her heart felt as if it were lodged in her throat.

Sloan shifted her focus to Mia, eyes shining in the artificial light of the camper. "You can walk behind me and get to the door, Agent Logan. Please do that now. It's not a request."

Before Mia could respond, Sloan was down on a knee, across the table from Ruth and leaning forward. Toward the damn bomb.

Mia's boots were glued to the floor, her legs like lead. She wouldn't follow Sloan's instructions and leave the woman to blow herself up with their deranged bomber. She wouldn't.

But, at the same time, Mia hadn't any idea of what she should do. None of her Quantico classes discussed talking down a bomber and a seemingly suicidal colleague in one go.

Ruth pushed herself deeper back into the couch, her nose wrinkling in confusion. "You're lying. You wouldn't kill yourself to take me out and keep them safe. But I'll kill all of you. So you need to get out."

Shaking her head, Sloan raised her hands higher, her chest grazing the cheap coffee table between her and their perpetrator. "You're wrong. And I'll tell you why. I don't care about this life anymore. I'm miserable. I lost someone, too, and you know what? It was my fault. How do you like that? I've one-upped you on the tragedy scale, haven't I?"

Ruth jolted where she sat, eyes narrowing, but Sloan didn't appear to be done as she leaned forward even farther, speaking low.

"Your father's death wasn't your fault. We both know that. He died in a freak accident. And your mom was your mom. You couldn't change her. Her behavior was abhorrent, but it wasn't your fault." Sloan paused, eyes only on Ruth. "But my loss? Oh, Ruth, my loss was all my fault. I hurt someone I loved, and he died as a result."

Sloan emitted the saddest laugh Mia had ever heard, and although it was a familiar sound from when Ned was alive, chiming and breathy, it was also a dim echo of what had once been.

In an instant, Mia realized she hadn't heard Sloan truly laugh all week. Hadn't seen the tension leave her body once. And she'd chalked it up to her own presence and their past and to the case, but maybe she'd read things entirely wrong. Maybe this was Sloan now. This more formal, stoic version of the woman her brother had once loved. This more miserable version, to use Sloan's own word.

Ruth's mouth opened and closed as Mia's heart pounded and her whole body ached from Sloan's heartbreak. Despite promising herself she'd remain calm, tears burned her eyes.

Breathing out audibly, Sloan shot a quick look at Mia, and Mia glimpsed the true depth of her sorrow.

"The love of my life," Sloan pitched her voice low, drawing Ruth to lean toward her, "his name was Ned Logan. He loved me like nothing else. But instead of loving him back with no holds barred like I should have, I told him I couldn't marry him."

Sloan's voice shook, but she didn't stop.

"I told him I had met someone. I told him I'd been unfaithful." Sloan took a deep, shuddering breath. Mia had been in enough interrogation rooms that she recognized a person bracing herself to confess. "I could've lied. I could've lied and said yes and married him. But our happily ever after would've been based on a lie. So…I told him the truth and it cost me everything. He drove off…and he died. Because he was crying too hard to see, and that was my fault. I killed him."

Mia couldn't meet her eyes but noticed Emma waver where she stood. Hell, Mia couldn't even see straight at the moment, not with the guilt in Sloan's voice tearing at her stomach and all the damn salty tears stinging her eyes.

"You're not the only person with a sob story, Ruth Alexander." Sloan paused, softening her voice as she continued. "And you're not the only person in this camper who's ready to die."

Mia's jaw dropped, and she shot her gaze at Emma as the first tears leaked from her eyes. Sloan was ready to take one for the team, literally, and they had to stop her.

Emma appeared just as lost for words, though. Meanwhile, Ruth was muttering under her breath, with Sloan repeating that she was willing to die. But it was Ruth's choice to make.

Sloan sounded so genuine. But she couldn't truly blame herself for Ned's death to the extent that she didn't want to live. Could she?

She could. I blamed her. And only her. Dammit.

Mia bit down on her tongue, staring at the bomb cradled against Ruth's chest and Sloan there, kneeling so close to the table. It couldn't end like this, but her mind spun, attempting to understand the words Sloan kept repeating.

It was possible that Sloan was just talking, that this was a spur-of-the-moment play that she thought would serve as a good distraction.

But it was also possible, especially after years of being hated and blamed for Ned's death that, in reality, Sloan Grant was actually suicidal.

And Mia couldn't let Sloan die today, suicidal or otherwise.

Not like this. Not while believing she'd been responsible for Ned's death when Mia herself knew otherwise.

Carefully, swallowing down the burning tears threatening to erupt into sobs, Mia took a step toward the table, eyes trained on Sloan, willing the other agent to listen to her…and believe her. That was the first step. The only step right now.

"Sloan. Sloan, listen to me. Please." Mia inched her boot forward. She was catty-corner to the table now, just six feet from both Sloan and Ruth, who looked more fascinated than threatening for the moment. But one thing at a time. "You are not responsible for Ned's death. It wasn't your fault. Not in any way, shape, or form. I know this, in my head and in my heart. I promise you that. I've been wrong all these years. Do you hear me?"

When the other agent gave no sign of hearing her, Mia could only hope. She directed her gaze at Ruth, willing her voice to remain steady. "Ruth, Ned was my brother. And I blamed Sloan for his death, I did, but things change. I was wrong. Wrong, Ruth. She doesn't deserve to die. Neither do you. There's still time for all of us to make things right."

Sloan's focus remained on Ruth, but her shoulders shook up and down once, and then twice. In denial or with the weight of emotion, Mia wasn't sure.

"If she can forgive me, Ruth…" Sloan broke off, "we can all get out of this, maybe. What do you think? Can we all get out of this together? That's what your father would want, isn't it? I know it's what my Ned would want. Even if it was because of me that he…"

Sloan's voice cracked, and she went silent.

Mia took another step, canting her body toward Ruth even as she kept her eyes on Sloan, hoping the other woman was with her, thinking with an agent's brain as well as a grieving lover's.

"Sloan, what happened was completely out of your control. I'm begging you, please, agent to agent…no, woman to woman, as someone else who loved Ned too…do not do anything rash. That's not what Ned would want."

When Sloan's boots shifted, just barely, Mia took one more tiny step.

"Okay, Mia. Okay. Ruth? Ruth, are you listening? What are you thinking? If I can move forward, you can, too, right?"

Across the table, bomb still in hand, Ruth sat frozen. But her eyes had gone glassy. They appeared mesmerized. She was dazed, lost in the scene playing out before her.

And wholly distracted.

34

Emma's heart ached for Mia, but there was nothing she could say. The plan Mia had made to get them out of this mess was a good one. Ruth was so distracted, they might as well have been putting on a two-woman Broadway show, with her in the front row. Soon, their whole team might just be out of this disaster of a camper. Alive.

And then, smack between Sloan and Mia, Ned appeared.

Thickening the atmosphere around them, training his white eyes on the living, and complicating the ever-loving shit out of an already complicated moment.

Even with his hangdog eyes, translucent head, and bloodied yellow polo shirt, there was still no mistaking him for anyone but Mia's brother. Elfin-faced and dark-haired with pale skin—even before death, he'd been pale—he looked just like her. And, like her, sadness clouded his features, softening him past the tension Emma had gotten used to seeing in his muscles lately. Listening to his sister talk to Sloan, and seeing Sloan, he was every bit as affected as she was.

And sure, Emma had known he'd be back sometime,

yeah, but they also had more pressing matters to deal with at the moment.

If this ghost expected her to tell Mia that he stood nearby witnessing her pleas, he had another thing coming.

Emma crept another slight step forward as Ruth's sight remained fixed on Sloan and Mia's teary-eyed exchange. How much of their conversation was an act, she didn't have a clue. Maybe none of it. Regardless, it was working.

As Sloan's hands inched forward over the table, Emma had to remind herself to breathe.

Mia's voice rose, attracting Ruth's gaze. "Everyone has to forgive themselves sometimes, Ruth. You know that. I know you do. I forgive Sloan, and she's going to have to forgive herself. You believe that's possible, don't you?"

Sloan's hands moved closer to Ruth, who'd let the hand holding the remote rest on top of her thigh.

Emma licked her lips, readying herself to draw her gun if need be. Once Sloan got ahold of that remote, there'd be no time to think. Just to act.

Another inch, and then another, and another. Ruth's eyes remained trained on Sloan's creeping hands while her ears focused on the drama in the words her two colleagues exchanged, until Sloan's hands were there. Right beside the remote.

Once their fingers touched, it was like an electric shock surged through Ruth.

"*No!*"

The move was so slight, almost invisible.

Ruth hit the button.

"Shit." Emma and Sloan surged forward together. Sloan grabbed the bomb. Emma tackled Ruth. The remote skidded toward Mia's feet.

Mia looked at the remote. "There's only a power button."

"Don't hit it again! She might not have actually activated it."

Sloan leaned back with the bomb in hand, Ruth barely realizing what had happened as she lay dazed under Emma's knee.

The woman screamed at them, but she was done having a say over the situation.

"Let me die! Let me die! *Let me die!*" Shaking free from the shock, Ruth yelled pleas that bounced off the camper walls until her words dissolved into guttural sobs as Emma wrangled cuffs onto her wrists.

Sloan stood, taking the bomb to the counter, her face intense and focused as she peeled away the duct tape.

"What did you use, Ruth?" Sloan didn't sound panicked or worried. But a bright-red flush crept up above her collar. She didn't wait for Ruth to answer as she studied the bomb and spoke to herself. "Probably bulbs in a battery-operated socket, right? The bulb filament lights up and heats the nitrate."

Ruth kicked her feet against the floor. In response, the whole camper shook, but one glance from Sloan had Mia pinning her legs down and stilling her.

"But you need to build in some escape time if you're not setting up a remote. So you connected the portables to a timer in here, which you set off with the remote. How long is the time set for? How long do we have before the bulbs light up?"

Ruth's lips formed a thin, bitter line. In that moment, she looked so much like her dead mother. The bruised and abused apple hadn't fallen far from the tree.

"Can you turn it off?" Emma breathed out, waiting.

"Probably. It's probably just a simple circuit, but she soldered it shut. Like an idiot." Sloan glared at the woman on the floor. "The heat from the iron could've set off the nitrate.

It's a miracle you weren't torched before we got here." She gave a small, wry smile to Emma. "This is an amateur job, but it could easily be triggered and set off in the process. I imagine the timer was set for maybe three to five minutes. Enough time to exit a restaurant and make it down the street."

"So we go outside and put it in the middle of an open area and wait for the bomb squad to get their truck out of the snow. Right? Or am I missing something?"

For a moment, Emma almost expected Sloan's easy laugh again, until the look on her face turned dark.

"Get out. Both of you."

Mia perched herself more firmly over Ruth, holding her legs still so they couldn't strike out at the table or floor and set things shaking again. "You first, Sloan. Get clear, then we'll follow with Ruth."

"No, Mia. I need to stabilize it until the three of you get clear. If this goes off before I can get it far enough away, I'd rather that happen without you in the blast radius."

Emma shook her head. "Hell, no. Why not just leave it here and come with us?"

"This camper is full of evidence."

"So take it outside."

"I will, but I can't until the three of you are clear. Get it?" Sloan's face went harder…darker. "Now go!"

35

Leo had gone back to the SUV to collect breaching equipment and returned as Jacinda and the others were discussing their plan for entry to the root cellar. Thanks to Emma, they'd spotted extension cords crossing the yard from the generator, mostly covered by snowfall. The cords ran along the cellar steps and disappeared behind the ice-covered metal doors.

That meant people might be alive down there. The thought of this operation becoming a rescue instead of body retrieval boosted Leo's energy and warmed him against the chill.

He used bolt cutters to snap open the combination padlock holding the cellar doors shut. Denae and Vance yanked open the heavy doors, and Leo moved down the stairs with Jacinda on his heels. Stepping slowly to keep his footing on the frosted steps, he aimed his gun along with his light.

The sunlight wasn't much help in the cold afternoon and only pooled at the base of the steps, barely denting the gloom of the underground storage area.

A stench of urine assailed him as he and Jacinda moved left while Denae and Vance went right. Their flashlight beams picked out shelves in the narrow, low-ceilinged space. Boxes and filthy jars of long-expired preserves covered their surfaces.

A murmur of pain to his left put the entire team on alert. As one they stepped back and held their lights on the very rear of the storage space.

Cassidy Freese peered at him from above the rim of a mound of blankets, her pale father beside her. Two inoperative space heaters sat in the corners nearby.

Maybe Mia had been right that Ruth wasn't a killer at heart, as it was clear she'd attempted to make them comfortable.

"She shot him." Cassidy's voice was a whisper.

Down the wall from Cassidy and Howie Freese, Morty Williams lay on his side, eyes and mouth open. But the man wasn't seeing anything. Even from where he stood, Leo understood Morty'd been dead for hours, with blood dried along his mouth and forming a glue between his head and the cold ground.

His blanket and shirt had been soaked with blood, now long dried. Beside him, Laura sat as still as stone. Her expression was flat, as blank as that of her father's corpse.

The accusation in her eyes was all too clear, though. They'd been too late to save her father.

Too. Damn. Late.

Those words pried at Leo's conscience, hitting his chest like a ton of bricks and mortar. They'd done everything they could to find and save these people, and they'd still been too late.

The rest of his team holstered their weapons and scattered to the victims, but for another instance, Leo stood frozen beneath the defunct overhead light. Held hostage by the part of him that was still a teenage boy, finding out that his grandfather had died while he slept, peacefully unaware. His grandfather had tried to save Leo's dog, and Leo had never gotten the chance to save either of them.

Get it together. Now.

Getting these people to safety—the ones who still breathed—took precedence over all else. They were cold, hungry, and either injured or in shock, and they didn't have time for the damning memories in his head.

Vance and Denae were already hard at work on freeing Laura, having untangled her from her bloody blankets. Tears had begun tracking down her cheeks, shock giving way to some version of understanding that help had finally come. However late it might have been.

Where Jacinda crouched by Howie and Cassidy, Leo hurried to join her, holstering his gun as he did. Howie Freese's bonds looked tight enough to cut off his circulation, but Leo's standby pocketknife made fast work of them regardless. As Jacinda attempted to help Cassidy move, the young woman shrieked in agony.

Leo spun to her side, moving behind Cassidy to support her shoulders, trying to steady her as he sought the source of her pain.

"My knee!" she cried out and rocked back into Leo's grasp.

Jacinda carefully unwrapped the blankets covering Cassidy's legs, revealing a bloodied mess of tissue, angry and swollen with infection.

"She's cold," Leo said, clutching the girl's shoulders, "and it's not from the weather."

Jacinda carefully set the blankets back as Cassidy began shivering against Leo. The SSA stood and moved to the cellar door. "I'm calling in the paramedics. They should be staged a few minutes away. Do what you can for these people until them arrive. Get them out of here and into fresh air."

Howie Freese was able to get to his knees, but barely managed a crawl as he came up beside Leo to help hold his daughter. "We'll get you better, Cass. These folks are here to help. We'll get you out."

She continued to shiver against them both, and Leo called for Vance's help.

"Can we make a stretcher out of those shelves? Or use these blankets?"

Denae moved to help Laura Williams while Vance and Leo built a makeshift litter using the thickest blanket. Howie offered a feeble hand of assistance in shifting his daughter onto the litter but eventually sat back and allowed the agents to work unhindered.

They brought Cassidy up the steps slowly, careful not to bump or jostle her knee as they moved. She'd be lucky if she could keep the leg, given the condition it was in, but Leo forced himself to keep positive, to keep hope alive.

We got here and got them out. That's what matters. Not what we didn't do. Not what we couldn't do.

Up and out of the root cellar, Leo stripped off his coat and bundled it around Cassidy's shoulders. Vance went back for Howie and helped him stumble out a few minutes later, following Denae, who all but carried Laura Williams up from the cellar.

Jacinda had brought their SUV over, and they moved Cassidy into the warmth of the rear compartment, shifting aside their gear to make room for her. Howie demanded he be brought over to her, and Vance helped him make the short trip from the cellar doors.

Cassidy's skin remained clammy and pale, and her eyes were closed. But she was breathing, fitfully.

Leo dug through their trauma bag for anything that

might help. He had a bottle of saline in hand when his focus was stolen by movement near the camper. Emma and Mia were together, frantically hauling Ruth Alexander out the narrow door and into the snowy clearing between the camper and cellar entrance.

The woman wailed and kicked at Mia, sending her sideways into the snow. She got to her feet in time to help Emma fend off more attacks, grappling Ruth's legs and bringing her down.

Jacinda and Vance ran forward to meet them, and collectively, they muscled Ruth across the clearing, depositing her onto the ground between the SUV and the ruins of the old house.

As the agents held her fast, she continued to rage and thrash. Leo wanted to wrap tape over her mouth, anything to silence her so he could focus on helping Cassidy, but he froze as Sloan appeared and flew from the camper.

She sped off to the north, away from the camper and the team with a rectangular object in her hands. She set it down in an open patch of snow about forty feet from the SUV. Then she raced away from it, yelling for everyone to take cover.

Leo didn't have to wonder or guess at its nature as he pulled Howie around the SUV's bumper to place the vehicle between them and the clearing.

Seconds later, a heavy *whoosh* and a ball of flame filled the clearing.

They could have been burned alive.

His breath hitching, Leo fought down the urge to run across the clearing to the camper to check on Sloan. Howie leaned on him—needing his support—though the danger was past. But with his heart beating wilder than it had in years, his mind kept stumbling over what could have been.

What must've gone down in that camper, and how close he'd come to losing them.

Stop. Not right now. Don't finish that damn thought.

Sloan was jogging her way over to the SUV, uninjured. Leo mumbled reassurances to Howie as he returned to washing Cassidy's injury in hopes of staving off an even worse infection. The whine of sirens grew louder while he worked. Several sheriff's sedans rolled onto the property, followed by the SWAT truck carrying the bomb squad and HRT.

Jacinda flagged down the SWAT vehicle, and Vance moved off to direct the sheriff's cruisers. Emma and Mia maintained a hold on the now crumpled and sobbing form of Ruth Alexander. Between her crying and the wailing of sirens, Leo thought his eardrums might burst. He focused on carefully treating Cassidy's leg, making every effort not to further irritate the wound.

Denae came around the back of the SUV, clutching Laura Williams. The younger woman shook and cried until she fell to the ground, Denae going with her to ease her onto her side. Laura quaked, and her sobs turned to howls of anguish.

She'd lost her father, and had been forced to sit beside his corpse, bound and no doubt expecting her own fate to match his at some point.

As Denae comforted Laura, Leo caught her soothing voice, mentioning David Williams's name.

She still has her brother. That's something.

36

An hour later, battered by the heavy snowfall, Emma leaned against the front of the large shed, trying to get out of the worst of it. Off to her far side, eastbound where they'd entered the property, lights from the sheriff's cars flashed through the trees, lending the gray afternoon an eerie glow. Ambulances had already pulled up, with paramedics surrounding the three remaining victims.

For now, she just needed one minute. One fucking minute.

To process.

Her thoughts swam with *might-have-beens* and *what-ifs*, the slushy ground beneath her boots piling up with loose powder seeming more solid than reality at the moment. She and Mia and Sloan could have died. Could have been blown to bits by some deranged woman's handmade IED.

My hands are still shaking. Still.

She brought them up and pushed her hair behind her ears, taking deep breaths. From the moment Allen Alexander had appeared in his pieced-together form, she'd been off her game and struggling for composure. She'd held herself steady and done everything right—she thought—but the whole team surviving the day hadn't been just a matter of skill, awareness, and training.

There'd been luck involved, too, and she hated that. She couldn't control luck. Nobody could.

She scanned the area, especially by the sheriff's cars, seeking any sign of the dead Alexanders. Allen Alexander had never reappeared, but Emma sensed he'd been watching his daughter's takedown.

If he hadn't died when and how he had, would Ruth have been someone else? Someone stable? Emma couldn't imagine that Ruth would've become the broken, unhinged, guilty creature she was, now sitting cuffed in a sheriff's car.

Eyes on the ground, her breath getting steady, just as she was about to push off from the shed, a sudden boot entered her sightline. She stared up and into Leo's eyes as he squared off in front of her, as if to keep her from running.

His face had gone pale, showing lines in his forehead that she wasn't used to, his mouth in a thin, stressed line. He looked stricken, in fact. But it might've just been exhaustion.

"Leo..." She broke off, waiting, but he only licked his lips as if searching for words. Sullen and silent. "Are you okay?"

His eyes remained on hers a beat too long for comfort, the very intimacy of the stare throwing her off guard before he finally shook his head. "I have questions, Emma. And they're questions I've been wanting to ask for a while now."

Emma's mouth dried from nerves as he stepped closer. "Now?"

"You're not putting me off, Emma Last." He leaned forward, way into her space and spoke fast. "It all started with the circus. How did you know to say all those things to Tyler? I saw you speaking to *someone*. Someone who *wasn't even there*. Plus, the way you ran from that trailer in Little Clementine after finding Bud Darl. Yeah, he'd been diced up by an axe murderer, but you don't react like that, not just to gore."

"Leo—"

"Stop. That's not all." He took a breath, and Emma didn't interrupt him. The man had seen too much for her to put him off, and her gut clenched with the awareness of what had to be coming. "How about what happened on the deck last night? Or the wolf?"

Howling echoed in Emma's mind, pressing in along with everything Leo was saying. Accosted by all of it, all at once, Emma leaned back harder against the large shed, defeat coursing through her blood. She wanted so badly to forget what had happened on the deck behind the B and B.

So badly.

"I know about the wolf, and I don't even know how I know. Do you know how frustrating that is?" Leo raised one hand and shoved it back through his overgrown hair, wetting it down with the snow now drifting from the sky and scattering over the both of them. "I feel like I'm losing my shit, and I need you to help me understand all of it. And I know you're not just an FBI agent. You're something…else, something not normal, so don't deny it."

Not normal?

Emma's hands spread against the shed behind her, seeking purchase. She even wished they'd be interrupted, but their team members must've been occupied elsewhere. And she couldn't look away from Leo's stricken gaze anyway.

The expression he offered her was too lost and vulnerable, in search of answers he'd apparently been seeking for a while. Too much a mirror of the way she herself felt, even if she was loath to admit it.

Leo raised one hand, leaning against the shed near her shoulder. His voice leaked out in a careful plea.

"Please, Emma. Now."

He was so close, she could feel the heat of his breath, but this was so not the time. And where to even start, when their colleagues were so close and privacy was impossible? Whatever she told him, the truth wasn't a one-word answer.

"Leo, this isn't—"

"Leo! Emma! Where'd...?" Denae stumbled to a stop, one hand on the corner of the shed as she turned toward them, just a foot away. "What are you two doing? Is everything okay?"

Thank you, Denae. Thank you, thank you, thank you.

Emma pushed herself away from Leo, working not to react to the frustration in his glare, and grabbed Denae's elbow as she turned their colleague back toward the SUVs. "Everything's fine. You just saved me from a lecture about how we should've let the bomb explode in the camper instead of letting Sloan play hero."

37

It had been two days since Leo cornered Emma and demanded answers for her behavior. She'd managed to avoid him in the offices yesterday, while they completed the post-investigation reviews and paperwork. And Jacinda had begrudgingly granted her twenty-four hours of leave for today.

Her phone chimed again with a text that she checked and swiped to the side.

Sorry. I have a psychic to feed and questions of my own that need answers. Take a number, Ambrose, and preferably not mine.

She flipped the last tortilla in the pan, making sure it was browning just right. A little bit of scorch, a little bit of crunch, but not rigid. Tacos were so much work, but they'd set the perfect tone, right?

Everybody loved friggin' tacos.

And psychics weren't everyone, but tacos were safe. Emma scanned the ingredients spread out in bowls along the island. Cheese, lettuce, tomato, freshly made salsa. Plus, her favorite brand of taco sauce sat patiently in the fridge, and the pans beside the tortillas held lime-basted chicken and sizzling peppers mixed with onions.

She'd done her little kitchen proud and could only hope Marigold appreciated it. Because heaven knew Emma needed the woman's help.

When the knock sounded on her door, time was up, and she flipped off the stove switch and hurried to get the night started. She'd been waiting for this all day.

Marigold's nose twitched visibly as soon as the door opened, proving that Emma needn't have worried. Her hair was down, snowflakes resting among the strands, but the understanding in her calm face was just what Emma needed the last few days. She almost hugged her, in fact, but caught herself just in time. If she broke a little, she might break completely after the week she'd had.

The psychic accepted a margarita, but the drinks were all but forgotten when they sat down at the table to eat and nothing but crunching filled the space between them. Emma didn't do much cooking, but tacos were one thing she could pull off, and they didn't disappoint. Tangy, succulent, with perfectly balanced toppings.

Emma's mouth hummed with satisfaction as she let herself focus on the meal. She knew Marigold understood she had problems and that this wasn't just a social visit, but food came first. On that, they agreed, as her psychic seemed to have brought her appetite to the get-together.

By the time the women were sitting back from the table with a second round of margaritas newly poured, nothing but crumbs left before them, Emma could almost pretend the night was normal. Though the conversation wouldn't be.

And her newest friend, the psychic who came from the most domestic town house ever and looked as normal as anyone could, with her long graying hair and oversize sweater, was there to save the day.

Marigold sipped her drink, darting her tongue out to collect some salt. "Don't worry. I promise my crystal ball won't become blurry from tequila. Now, how about you tell me why you sounded like the harbinger of World War Three when we spoke on the phone two nights ago? You look pretty calm now."

Emma forced a smile, her cheeks warming at the reminder of the panicked phone call she'd placed on Wednesday when she'd truly felt at her wit's end. A few days' distance from West Virginia had made something of a difference, but not enough.

One more sip of her margarita swallowed down, Emma began filling Marigold in on the latest developments surrounding the Other. Including her near brush with death by some hypnotic attempt at persuading her to commit suicide, which even talking about made her gut clench. The idea of what she'd almost done.

"The wolf is getting louder." She fisted her hands in her lap, holding composure at bay by her fingernails. "And stronger. I'm scared. And I absolutely hate being scared."

Across from her, the psychic twisted some of her long hair in one hand, pensive and frowning, her margarita emptied around the time Emma had gotten to the deck of the B and B part of the story…just as she stepped up to take a leap of howl-driven faith.

"You have every right to be scared. Anyone in your position would be."

Emma leaned forward. "I want to contact my mother. She's been trying to tell me something with that picture frame falling, just like you said when we met last time. That's got to be it. I'm sure of it."

Marigold's frown deepened, one hand worrying at the edge of her sweater. "Emma, as I said before, the Other is its own realm with its own understanding of time. I agree that your mother may very well be trying to tell you something, but you reaching out to her versus allowing her to contact you in her own time..." Marigold pressed her fingertips to her temple. "That just isn't what I'd recommend."

Taking another sip of her drink, Emma fought down nerves. "I'm already in danger. Things can't get any worse than they were when I was up on that railing. Please, tell me what to do to contact her."

A second passed, and then another, before Marigold nodded. "All right. We'll do this your way. But not tonight. We must be careful."

Emma had no idea what being careful meant in this context. Managing her interactions with the Other wasn't as simple as carrying a gun and announcing herself, that was for sure. Still, if Marigold needed to hear she'd be taking this seriously...

"Yeah, of course. We'll be careful. I promise."

Sighing, the woman closed her eyes and moved her lips, saying something to herself. As if coming to some conclusion, she sat straighter and met Emma's gaze. "Okay, hear everything I'm saying. We'll do this together. Wednesday night," she shook her head as Emma opened her mouth to protest, "and not before. *Not before, Emma.* I've got other clients, and I want you to take some time to think about this. You hear me? Think about what we're doing."

I've thought of nothing else.

"I've thought about it. Truly."

Marigold rose from her seat, wiping her hands on her napkin. "Well, consider this. Maybe if your mom sees you gearing up to contact her, she'll make the first move. Save us the trouble."

Though Emma hated to admit it, that made sense.

Before Emma could push to her feet, Marigold was heading for the door.

"Wait, what do I need to do? Do I need to, uh...get anything? For Wednesday?" Emma stood from the table, fighting every instinct she had to beg Marigold to stop and help her immediately. Not Wednesday, not Tuesday, but tonight.

"No, no special tools are needed." Marigold paused in the entryway. "It's only the mind and true intention that're required. But...but, but, but...understand that opening the door between this world and the Other, even with the purest of intentions and reasoning, can go wrong. It's a two-way portal we're talking about, and an infinite number of lifetimes exist on the other side. Your mother may not be the only one listening."

Marigold eyed her closely, almost like she was forcing the words to sink into Emma's brain.

Emma made herself nod. "I'll keep that in mind. What else do I need to know?"

A narrowing of eyes and pinched look came to Marigold's expression. "You don't. Just think about what I've said, all right? Give your mother this last chance to make the next move. And we'll talk Wednesday. Just think about what you're doing."

Without another word, the woman plucked her coat from its hanger near the door and began slipping her arms into the sleeves.

"That's it?"

"Patience, Emma. I'll see you Wednesday. At my place. After dinner. Let's make it seven o'clock." The woman swung the door open and swirled on a heel halfway through it. "Oh, and thank you for dinner. The tacos were fabulous, truly. I only hope I'll repay you for them in a way that won't backfire. I truly do."

Emma forced another nod, holding her tongue as she

moved to the door, after her new friend ducked out, and locked it up tight.

No way in hell am I waiting for Wednesday. The mind and true intention, huh? If that's all it takes, let's do this.

Emma made herself clean up their dishes and sweep the remaining ingredients into plastic containers first. She'd overestimated their appetites and made more than enough food, but she'd happily enjoy tacos all weekend. Maybe even with Oren. For now, though, that was the last thing on her mind.

With everything cleaned up, Emma seated herself on her new yoga mat and worked to clear her mind.

Focus. Focus. Focus. Just like Oren taught you. Just like Marigold's helped you with. Focus.

Her apartment was too quiet, the clock in her room too loud. And when she focused all the more and got past both distractions, a dog barked outside, and she nearly jumped out of her skin.

"The mind and true intention. The mind and true intention…" Emma muttered, shutting out everything from clocks to dogs to the gathering darkness outside. "Focus, Emma girl. Focus."

Eyes clenched shut and body still, Emma thought her brain might just ooze out of her ears, she was focusing so hard. But whatever she was doing, it wasn't working. Sighing, feeling a curse building in her throat, Emma decided she'd quit for the night. Maybe the margaritas were interfering with her built-in crystal ball.

"Get out of here!" her mother screamed from nowhere.

No, from the Other.

Emma held her eyes closed, searching for further connection. That was her mom, she knew it. She recognized her voice instantly, even though Emma had been tiny the last time she heard it. But none of the beauty or calm she associated with her mother's memory came through. Nothing peaceful or pleasant.

"Emma…go!" Gina Last screamed. "She can see you!"

The End
To be continued...

Thank you for reading.
All of the Emma Last Series books can be found on Amazon.

ACKNOWLEDGMENTS

How does one properly thank everyone involved in taking a dream and making it a reality? Let me try.

In addition to my family, whose unending support provided the foundation for me to find the time and energy to put these thoughts on paper, I want to thank the editors who polished my words and made them shine.

Many thanks to my publisher for risking taking on a newbie and giving me the confidence to become a bona fide author.

More than anyone, I want to thank you, my reader, for clicking on a nobody and sharing your most important asset, your time, with this book. I hope with all my heart I made it worthwhile.

Much love,
Mary

ABOUT THE AUTHOR

Mary Stone lives among the majestic Blue Ridge Mountains of East Tennessee with her two dogs, four cats, a couple of energetic boys, and a very patient husband.

As a young girl, she would go to bed every night, wondering what type of creature might be lurking underneath. It wasn't until she was older that she learned that the creatures she needed to most fear were human.

Today, she creates vivid stories with courageous, strong heroines and dastardly villains. She invites you to enter her world of serial killers, FBI agents but never damsels in distress. Her female characters can handle themselves, going toe-to-toe with any male character, protagonist or antagonist.

Discover more about Mary Stone on her website.
www.authormarystone.com

- facebook.com/authormarystone
- twitter.com/MaryStoneAuthor
- goodreads.com/AuthorMaryStone
- bookbub.com/profile/3378576590
- pinterest.com/MaryStoneAuthor
- instagram.com/marystoneauthor
- tiktok.com/@authormarystone

Printed in Great Britain
by Amazon